Awakening

Convergence Series

Lorel Clayton

LC Books
Sydney

Lorel Clayton/LC Books
156Young Street
Annandale, NSW Australia 2038
www.lorelclayton.com

Publisher's Note: This is a work of fiction. Names, characters, places, and incidents are a product of the author's imagination. Locales and public names are sometimes used for atmospheric purposes. Any resemblance to actual people, living or dead, or to businesses, companies, events, institutions, or locales is completely coincidental.

Book Layout ©2013 BookDesignTemplates.com

Awakening/ Lorel Clayton. -- 1st ed.
ISBN 978-1-7638008-4-7

1   Speed Dating

Walking up to Megan—my supposed friend, more like a frenemy these days—I could feel every muscle in my body tense. Why had I let her talk me into this? Of all the things ... speed dating?

My singlehood had been dragging on long enough to border on legendary status. Megan had somehow convinced me that this little event would change everything. So here I was, not just miserable but also lighter in the wallet, thanks to her. Oh, and did I mention the nerve? She didn't just take my money; she insulted me while doing it. Classic Megan.

"Roxy, sweetie! Come in, have a drink—you'll need it!" she chirped, waving a cocktail in the air like some sinister siren luring me into a trap. Her eyes skimmed over my outfit, and her nose crinkled. "Hmm, girl, I'm just saying, you could have put in a little more effort. I can only help so much."

Yup. Frenemy for sure. I didn't bother defending my dress or pointing out I had worn pumps. Let's just say 'casual' had been my fashion mood lately, so this was a step up for me. My unruly red curls, a sea of freckles, and an athletic frame that was more tomboy than bombshell weren't exactly cover-girl material anyway. But hey, at least I was here, right? Sort of.

Fast-forward three cocktails, and I was suddenly ready to flee—heels be damned. But Megan, standing guard at the door like a nightclub bouncer, was having none of it.

"Ladies, take your seats! The men will be here shortly," she announced with her wicked smile.

I teetered over to my designated table, wobbling in the too-tight heels I'd borrowed from another friend who had, let's say, much daintier feet. Sitting down felt like a victory. Or a trap. Probably both.

Megan clapped her hands loudly, commanding attention. "Alright, listen up! You get five minutes with each guy. Then, you mark your little cards: yes, no, or 'weird vibes,' I don't care. But you will participate!"

Victim number one arrived, and I instantly regretted every life choice that had led me here. He was... well, mole-like. Short, balding, glasses that screamed 'I work in IT,' and a paunch that suggested maybe he worked at it too hard. I tried to tamp down my inner critic. Who was I to judge? I wasn't exactly Miss Universe myself. But still, I felt it. That tingling sensation I always get when I'm about to glimpse something through my ... gift. Or curse, depending on how you look at it.

See, I'm not your average, sarcastic, unlucky-in-love redhead. I have a secret. I can see things in people— things they hide, their true selves, their thoughts. Most call it witchcraft; I call it a nightmare. I've learned the hard way that people are rarely what they seem. But with him? It was simple. All he could think about was my feet. Seriously? I wasn't sure if I should be flattered or horri-fied.

The bell mercifully rang, and I let out a breath I didn't realize I was holding. But my relief was short-lived when my next suitor approached.

God help me, he was the stuff of legends. Towering over the table, he was all broad shoulders, chiseled jaw, and smoldering eyes. If a Viking warrior and a Greek god had a love child, this was him. I could practically feel my body respond—and not in a polite way. I shifted in my seat, praying I could keep it together.

He spoke, his voice low and gravelly, and I didn't catch a word of it. I was too busy imagining all the ways those hands—large, strong, and slightly calloused—could pin me against a wall. Oh God. Get it together, Roxy.

And then I saw it in my mind: The moon, glowing behind him like an ominous beacon. My heart dropped. Of course, he wasn't just any ridiculously hot guy. He was a werewolf. Because, in my world, things like that exist. Naturally.

My mind raced, cataloging everything my third sight picked up about him. Married, kids, a girlfriend—and that wasn't even scratching the surface of his drama. A walking red flag, basically. But damn, did he wear it well.

Before I could say anything stupid, the bell rang again, and he was off. I slumped back in my chair, trying to get a grip on myself.

You might be thinking, what are the odds? Well, in my case, odds are slim to none that I'll meet someone who isn't a supernatural being. I'm a magnet for the weird and otherworldly, drawn to monsters in the same way others are drawn to chocolate or bad reality TV.

Several lackluster dates later, Megan declared it was break time. My feet were killing me, and I was tipsy enough to start regretting everything. Then, my salvation appeared in the form of Jules. My best friend—more like my saving grace—waltzed over, her curves swaying as she moved. She was the complete opposite of me with her jet-black hair, full lips, and eyes that sparkled with mischief. If men wanted sugar and spice, Jules was their ultimate fantasy.

"Roxy, you look like you're two minutes away from death. Come on, let's get you another drink." She linked her arm with mine and pulled me to the bar.

"So," she teased, wiggling her eyebrows, "anyone catch your eye? Or should I say, anyone supernatural catch your eye?"

"Ugh, don't even get me started."

Jules chuckled. "I got three numbers already. Met this giant of a man—dreamy. You would've died."

"I hate to break it to you," I said, wincing at the truth about her new suitor, "but your dreamy giant? Yeah, he's a werewolf. A married one. Sorry, babe."

Jules groaned, rolling her eyes. "Of course he is. Can't a girl catch a break?" She grinned mischievously. "But did you see him? God, that man can maul me any-time."

Ah, romance. This was why I avoided love. It made you stupid—not that I would ever say that out loud to her!

Jules wasn't just my oldest friend—she was my anchor and my safety net when everything else was falling apart. After my mother was taken away, I found refuge in her home, nestled in the warmth of her parents' normalcy. It was the closest I'd ever felt to belonging, even though I never truly felt like I fit.

"Your problem, Roxy, is you act like a nun. You need more confidence—and less discernment," Jules teased, flashing me that familiar grin.

So, I followed her advice, letting liquid courage flow through my veins and blind my judgy thoughts. I was just starting to feel good, light even, when Megan appeared. Oh no, not now. What was she going to say? How was she going to crush me this time?

Megan started her usual tirade, but this time targeting someone who wasn't even there—our friend Emily. Emily, who had promised to come but hadn't shown up. God, I needed her here tonight. I needed extra support, and to be honest, someone telling me not to spend money I didn't have. Jules wouldn't understand, would even give me a loan, and Megan ... she'd never needed anything in her life, not money or friends. She came from a world of silver spoons and silk sheets, where work was just a word in a foreign language. She could steam roll over anything I said, squash all my protests, but still, I couldn't let her tear Emily down.

"Emily's just ... shy," I explained. "She'll show when she's ready."

Jules nodded. "Yeah, I love Emily, but she's got a lot of hang-ups. Afraid of the dark, afraid of men, afraid of her own shadow half the time."

I bit my lip, guilt bubbling up. Why hadn't I stopped by to pick Emily up and help her past all that? Oh, right—I didn't own a car, and there was no bus stop near Emily's place. And these borrowed heels were torture. They made me taller, sure, but walking in them? A death wish.

"How do you wear these things? I feel like I'm about to topple over and break my neck," I said, trying to change the subject.

Jules laughed. "Yeah, but they make your legs look killer. Aren't you glad I loaned them to you?"

Not really. But before I could protest, Megan rang that damn bell again. "Five more minutes, and we're starting back up!" she shouted. The bartender had already cut me off, so no more drinks for me.

"I need one of those flasks people carry," I muttered to Jules.

"Girl, you're drinking too much."

"Yeah, yeah, just help me to my table."

The night dragged on, Megan's bell ringing like some kind of death knell. We called ourselves the Four Musketeers, but sometimes it felt more like three Musketeers and one evil overlord. We'd stuck together since middle school, since my mother disappeared from my life, and without them, I'm not sure I'd have made it through those dark days.

I was lost in my thoughts when another one sat down in front of me. "Hey. It's Matt."

He was the thinnest man I'd ever seen, and the smell—oh God, it was a stench. But beneath the awkward exterior, I saw something in him. He seemed so alone, so vulnerable, it tugged at my heart. But I wasn't the girl to lead him on, not when I felt nothing more than pity.

"Matt," I started gently, "I don't think we have that spark, you know? But I do have this friend... her name's Emily."

His eyes widened. "Don't you remember me? We went to school together."

Damn, what do you say to that? I blinked. "I'm sorry... I guess I was in a dark place back then."

He shrugged. "It's okay. I'm pretty unremarkable."

Unremarkable? I didn't think so. Maybe he just needed a little help, someone to pull him out of his shell. But as I contemplated how to fix Matt's lonely heart, I noticed Bob. He was hovering nearby, his eyes glued to Jules.

"Bob," I whispered, "just go talk to her."

But he didn't even glance my way. Jules was the center of his universe, and he didn't have the courage to orbit any closer.

Then Megan rang the bell one last time. "Final round, ladies. Hope you've all found the love of your life!" she called, her voice dripping with smug satisfaction.

I was about to give up on the night when the air shifted, like the energy in the room had shifted. And then he walked in.

The most beautiful man I had ever seen slid into the seat across from me. He radiated power, his alabaster skin glowing under the soft lights, and his eyes—oh God, those eyes—pierced straight through me. Everything else faded into the background as he spoke, his voice deep and rich with a European lilt.

"Aamon," he said, and my heart skipped a beat.

Jules whispered from behind me. "What kind of name is Aamon?"

"It's an old family name," he replied, his gaze never leaving mine.

And just like that, Megan ruined everything, her usual smugness in full force. "Sorry, but you're not signed up for this. Maybe next week."

Aamon rose gracefully, his presence commanding the room. "Perhaps we will meet again, Roxy." He paused, noting my name tag. Until then, good evening."

He turned and walked away, and every eye in the room followed him, men and women alike. The air felt electric, as though he'd left something behind—a charge, a tension.

When the moment passed and the blood rushed back to my head, I sat there, dazed. Something about Aamon was... otherworldly. He was beautiful, yes, but there was danger in him, a darkness that I couldn't shake. Had he done something to me? To all of us?

Megan's voice broke through my fog. "He's way too much for you," she said, smirking.

I clenched my fists under the table. Count to ten. Don't say anything. She's not worth it.

The night was a disaster. I didn't meet anyone, didn't solve any problems. But Aamon ... I couldn't get him out of my mind. Something about him had awakened a part of me I didn't know existed—a part that yearned for more than just ordinary discomfort. A part that craved danger.

2   The Crossroads

The night wrapped around me like a velvet cloak, heavy with silence and the whispers of possibilities. My escape was long overdue. Nothing this evening had turned out the way I'd hoped. The warm buzz of alcohol was still sprouding through my veins, at least. I'd had enough to justify the money spent on a night that was fast slipping into obscurity, much like the rest of them.

The world blurred around me, my steps unsteady but light, like I was floating between reality and dream. Then the night shifted. It suddenly had a kind of magic to it— one of those rare moments when the mundane transforms, and the air hums with untold secrets. Above me, the stars shimmered, hanging like a thousand tiny diamonds across the dark expanse, each one a silent witness to my reckless wanderings. I was untethered, adrift in the quiet town where the streets were empty but for the occasional car humming by, their headlights sweeping like ghosts through the darkness.

My breath turned to mist in the crisp air, cool against my flushed skin. Everything felt surreal, like I was caught between the euphoria of tipsiness and the serenity of a perfect night. The streetlights cast long, dancing shadows, and for a fleeting moment, I entertained the thought of spinning under them, arms wide, shouting at the stars. Freedom, sweet and sharp, pulsed in my chest.

As I slid into the backseat of the Uber I'd wisely called earlier, a shiver that had nothing to do with the cold traced its way down my spine. The driver glanced back at me, his eyes lingering just a second too long, his smile not quite reaching the surface. It wasn't a polite kind of smile—the type that dissolved into the rearview mirror. No, this was something else, something darker, something that made my skin prickle with unease.

I fumbled with my phone, the bright screen an anchor to reality, a shield against the weight of his gaze. I pretended to be engrossed, my fingers typing nonsense, but the tension wrapped around me, tightening like a vine. He didn't get the hint. His eyes kept flicking up to the mirror, catching mine for just a moment before sliding away, like a hunter testing the boundaries of his prey.

Small talk, harmless enough at first, quickly shifted. Compliments about my looks, his words dripping with implication, followed by questions that felt like they pierced through my armor. I tried to laugh, to keep the mood light, but it was thin, brittle, and I could feel his intent, creeping closer with every word. The walls of the car seemed to close in, the air thick with something unspoken but felt.

I glanced at the app. Five minutes left. Too long. Far too long. As soon as the app flashed "6 minutes," I felt a cold weight in my gut. Something was wrong. My destination was nowhere near that far away.

"What's going on here? You're not taking me where I booked," I said, my voice sharp with suspicion. "What are you doing?"

The driver met my eyes in the rearview mirror, his lips curling into a slow, unsettling smirk. "I'm taking you exactly where you told me, sweetheart," he drawled, his tone dripping with condescension. "The app says to take you to the Crossroads, and that's where I'm headed. Unless..."

He paused, his gaze flicking up to the mirror again, eyes dark with suggestion. "Unless you want to make a little detour. My place isn't far. I could get you another drink. Maybe we could ... see what happens."

Panic bubbled up inside me, clashing with the alcohol blurring my thoughts. My pulse quickened as I tried to steady myself. Why am I scared? I'm a badass witch. But reality hit me hard—magic wasn't a cure-all. Not with humans. There was a cost, a hefty one: the threefold law. Whatever spell I cast on a mundane would come back to bite me three times worse. And right now? That risk didn't seem so bad.

"Turn this car around and take me back. Now," I ordered, my voice firm despite the way my heart pounded in my chest.

The tires screeched as he slammed on the brakes. He spun around in his seat, eyes flashing with rage. "Nothing but a tease. Get out of my car."

His behavior wasn't normal. Surely, he knew I'd report him? But he seemed out of control. His anger was more than just words. It was dangerous, tangible. If I stayed, something terrible would happen—either to me or, definitely, to him.

I shoved open the door and stumbled out, feeling the cool night air hit my face as he peeled off.

Classy. But at least I was out. I stood there, watching the taillights disappear into the distance, and tried to catch my breath. Safe, right? Totally safe. Out in the middle of nowhere. At night. Alone. Drunk.

The woods loomed around me, the silence broken only by the distant rustling of leaves. I took a deep breath and counted to ten, the ritual grounding me. I couldn't afford to lose control. Not here. Not now.

I pulled out my phone, the screen glowing in the darkness. No signal. Dead zone. Of course. I was stranded at the Crossroads—a place of mystery and danger. Always in-between. Always somewhere people avoided. My only option? Walk.

Stupid alcohol. I cursed under my breath, feet aching.

The Crossroads had a way of messing with everything—technology, magic, even the air itself felt ... off. Something was out there. I could feel it. Watching. Following.

Distant lights grew closer, flickering through the trees. My stomach sank as the noise reached my ears—the loud growling of engines. Bikers. And not just any bikers. No, these had an edge. A dangerous energy I'd sensed before. Werewolves.

The engines stopped. There were loud voices, shouts. I should have headed the other way, but something drew me. Someone was in danger, and I had a weird code—one I'd sworn after my mother left. I'd never leave anyone to the monsters.

I could see them now, surrounding someone, fists flying. My heart pounded, but I wasn't about to stand by.

Gathering my will, I marched towards the chaos, power buzzing beneath my skin. "Hey! What the hell do you think you're doing? Let them go!"

"This ain't none of your business, bitch," the bald, tattooed brute sneered, his eyes full of malice. His words slithered over my skin like something poisonous.

"Is it a guy thing to constantly call women 'bitches,' or did y'all take a class for that?" I shot back, forcing my voice to stay steady, though my heart hammered in my chest. His grin widened, twisted with something dark and vile.

"Smart mouth, huh? I can think of something better you could do with it." His eyes raked over me like I was prey.

"Shut up, Milton," one of the other men barked. "We've got a job to do. If we don't get it done, we're not getting paid."

Thank God it wasn't a full moon. Werewolves could usually shift a few days before or after, but none of them seemed ready to transform, because none of them were alphas. Alphas could turn any time. This situation would've been a whole lot worse otherwise.

The third man, silent until now, spoke up, his voice low and dripping with intent. "Maybe I'll keep her company while you boys dig the hole for the body."

They're going to bury him alive? I realized. My breath hitched with horror. The body of the man they were talking about lay crumpled at their feet, face hidden beneath a hood. Whoever it was, he was barely clinging to life—but he wasn't dead yet. I had to act fast.

I reached inside myself, deeper than I ever had before, feeling for the magic in the earth. The Crossroads pulsed beneath me, not canceling out my power like I'd feared, but amplifying it. Stronger than I'd ever felt before.

"She's up to something," one of the men shivered. "I can feel it. She's small, so she'll fit in that hole just fine."

The words hung in the air like a death sentence.

"Not just yet," another sneered, his gaze crawling over me. "I want a taste first."

My stomach turned. They weren't just going to kill me. They were going to make me suffer.

Not happening.

The Crossroads hummed beneath my feet, whispering secrets through the ancient forest. The wind stirred as if listening to my plea. I could feel the deep roots of the trees, gnarled and powerful, buried beneath us like sleeping giants. Their rage simmered, and I reached out to them, asking for their help.

The ground trembled. Roots exploded from the earth, lashing around two of the men like angry snakes, pulling them down, tightening with every second. Their faces contorted with shock and fear, the realization hitting them too late that they had underestimated me.

"You bitch!" one of them screamed, his body convulsing as the roots pulled him deeper into the ground.

But then, before I could catch my breath, the third man grabbed me from behind. His arm wrapped around my throat, pulling me off the ground, crushing the air out of my lungs.

"You let go of my pals, or I'll snap your neck right here," he growled, his voice dark and full of evil promise.

My vision blurred, and I could feel my control slipping. The men I held with the roots were still screaming, their bodies twisting under the earth's relentless grip. My head pounded as the man's arm tightened around my throat.

And then, the man on the ground stirred. He ripped the hood from his head, revealing a face that was pale, bloodless ... and terrifyingly beautiful. His eyes, blood-shot and desperate, locked onto mine.

A vampire.

Before I could even process it, the vampire launched himself at the man holding me, sinking his fangs into his neck with a savage growl. The grip around my throat loosened, and I fell to the ground, gasping for air as blood sprayed across my skin. The vampire fed hungrily; his eyes wild with bloodlust.

"Stop!" I whispered, my voice hoarse. "You don't have to be this. You helped me ... let me help you."

He hesitated, blood dripping from his lips, his body shaking as he struggled against the hunger tearing through him. His chest heaved, and with a sob, he collapsed, cradling his head in his hands.

"What am I?" he cried, his voice raw with despair. "Who am I?"

"I don't know," I whispered, pushing myself to my feet. "You've forgotten. It's what happens to fledglings. But you can remember your humanity. I'll help you."

I didn't tell him that the vampires I'd sensed before usually hadn't recovered their self-control until after they were responsible for a lot of spilled blood, often deaths. I stopped those I knew were guilty, but this vampire had been a human moments ago, on the cusp of turning, and it was only the blood he'd spilled saving me that had fully turned him now. I felt like I should help him. I owed him that much.

The other two men were buried up to their necks now, their curses muffled by the dirt. I released them, the tree roots slowly obeying as if questioning my wisdom. The bikers were terrified, so I expected them to remember this lesson well.

"Never cross me again," I warned, my voice cold as ice.

The vampire's eyes met mine, still filled with hunger but also something else—something vulnerable. His beauty, even smeared with blood, was undeniable. A part of me, one I wasn't ready to acknowledge, felt drawn to him.

"I should go," I said, though my legs refused to move. Instead, I found myself standing still, caught between danger and something darker, more enticing. "Or … we can help each other," I added softly. "Help me walk."

I knew why I couldn't move. Wielding so much magic wasn't usual for me. My body was in shock. I felt I'd topple over any second.

"Please."

His eyes flashed with regret. "I can't … I'll feed on you. I won't be able to stop."

"You still have a choice," I said, my heart pounding. "We both do. Either help me or end me. I'm in your hands."

For a moment, he just stared at me, torn. Then, with a resigned sigh, he lifted me into his arms as though I weighed nothing. His touch was gentle, careful, despite the power lurking beneath his skin.

He carried me to one of the motorcycles. I slumped against him, exhaustion pulling at me. "Can you ride one of these?"

"No," he said, a hint of amusement in his voice. "But it can't be that hard."

I handed him my phone, my vision blurring. "Follow the map," I whispered. "The sun's coming … and I think I'm going to pass out."

We sped into the night, the wind howling around us, and I let the darkness take me, trusting that when I woke, he would still be by my side.

3 A Vampire in the Basement

I drifted awake, the world slowly coming back into focus. I was on a motorcycle facing a gorgeous man while sitting in his lap, my head nestled against his chest, the warmth of him wrapping around me like a blanket. How did I end up here? Memories of the night trickled back: The Crossroads, werewolves, and then him saving me and me saving him.

I tilted my head to look up, and there he was, a dark angel with a face streaked in blood. Yet, even like this, he was devastatingly handsome. Why did he have such an effect on me when I didn't even know him? It had to be the alcohol, or my complete inability to function around men.

He gazed down at me, his lips curving into a slight, bemused smile. "So, you live at a video store? They still exist?"

I sighed, trying to push myself up. "Yeah, as crazy as that sounds. This is my day job. I live below the shop. Pretty sure I'm drunker than I've ever been, but not drunk enough to forget that."

He made a move to pick me up, but I stopped him. "No, I'll walk."

"Are you sure?" he asked, his voice low, concerned.

"Damn it, I said I was sure." I wobbled when I climbed off but stayed standing. A normal girl should go to the hospital and get checked out, but I was covered in blood that didn't belong to me and drained from wielding magic. Too many questions. Besides, I was a witch and could heal myself.

As we walked towards the shop front, I couldn't help but notice how sad and rundown the place looked. The once-bustling strip mall was deserted, most everything shut down and forgotten. A relief, really—no one around to see me stumbling inside with a blood-splattered man, looking like we were caught in the aftermath of some twisted, fetish party.

"Now, where is my key?" I mumbled, fumbling through my tiny purse. I finally managed to unlock the door, stumbling into the dimly lit store, reaching for the light switch.

When I turned around, he was still standing outside.

"Well, are you just going to stand out there?" I said, slightly annoyed.

"I ... can't. Something's holding me back," he said, his brow furrowed.

It clicked. Vampires—of course. They couldn't enter without an invitation, even if it was technically a public place. Maybe it was because I lived here, too.

I gave a dramatic little bow, rolling my eyes at the absurdity of it all. "Fine, I invite you in. Come in before the sun rises and turns you to ash."

Beneath the flickering neon sign, the video store felt like stepping into another time. The windows were covered with faded posters of movies no one rented anymore, and the shelves were crammed with dusty DVDs and VHS tapes. The smell of stale popcorn lingered in the air, mingling with the scent of something else— nostalgia, maybe. Hidden at the back, almost like a secret, was a narrow staircase that spiraled down into the shadows.

The steps creaked as we descended, leading to my tiny basement apartment. It was dark, cramped, but cozy, with mismatched furniture, a stack of half-read books, and an old turntable that had seen better days. It was a little hideaway from the world, a place you could get lost in by accident.

I glanced at him, taking in his disheveled, blood-streaked appearance. He looked as lost as I felt. And if I looked as bad as he did, we were quite a sight.

"Go take a shower," I said, pointing towards the bathroom. "I'll find something for you to wear. There's no way you're staying down here looking like that."

"Yes, ma'am," he said with a faint smile, and the way he said it made my stomach flutter. What was I? His mother? Yes, ma'am. Who said something like that? But somehow, it worked on me.

I sat on the edge of my bed, listening to the sound of the shower running. What was I supposed to give him to wear? I rummaged through my drawers and pulled out the largest pair of sweatpants I owned, along with an old, oversized T-shirt I'd bought online—something from The Vampire Diaries. Don't judge me. That show was way better than people gave it credit for.

I went over to the bathroom and opened the door just a crack, enough to toss the clothes inside. Steam billowed out and ... damn it, I looked.

He stood under the spray, his back to me, water cascading over his sculpted muscles, sliding down the curve of his tight, perfect ass. I caught a glimpse of his ... well, everything. Not aroused, but still very, very visible.

I was such a bad girl. Close your eyes, close the door, I told myself. But I stole one more look.

"Here are the clothes," I said, my voice a little breathless as I threw them in. I retreated to the bed, trying to regain my composure. "I'm just going to talk loudly. Can you hear me?"

"Yes," he replied, his voice echoing over the sound of the water. "I can hear everything. It's ... kind of unnerving."

"Yeah, well, probably a vampire thing. I don't know. But we'll figure it out. My friend, Emily, is kind of obsessed with vampires. She might know more than we do. I'll text her. But first, you need to get in here before the sun comes up and you black out like I did. Pretty sure that's bad news."

When he stepped out, hair wet and wearing the clothes I'd given him, I almost lost my breath. The sweatpants clung to him, revealing just how fit he was, and the T-shirt—well, it stretched across his chest in a way that was almost unfair. He was gorgeous, and yet, the look in his eyes was one of fear. He had no idea what to do, and he was relying on me, a stranger. But there was also something else, something darker. A hunger. Not just for blood, but ... for me.

Stop it, Roxy. You just met him. But the way he looked at me ... I could feel it, like electricity.

"Sit down in that chair," I said, gesturing to the old armchair by the mirror. "We need to talk. And no, don't sit on the bed. You're not getting that close to me. What do you remember before the bikers?"

He hesitated, then began to speak. "I was walking down the street. Someone called out in pain, so I went to check it out. Next thing I knew, someone pushed me up against a wall, covered my mouth so I couldn't scream, and whispered, 'Your life has been empty. You've done nothing but bring darkness. Now, you will serve me. You'll do one good thing, and it will be what I want. You will serve me.'

"I tried to fight back, but he was so strong," he continued, his voice trembling. "I couldn't see his face, but he was taller than me. He forced me against the wall and ... bit my neck."

"Do you remember anything else?" I asked softly.

"It's ... embarrassing," he admitted, a flush creeping up his neck. "But I think being bitten and turned by a vampire is already as bad as it gets. I ... I was scared, but also ... aroused? I was so hard when he fed on me, and that's not my thing."

Oh, wow. That was unexpectedly hot. I did not know I had a thing for being bit or watching two men. But apparently I did.

He looked at me, his eyes heavy-lidded. "I'm feeling strange, like ... really tired."

"Yeah, I figured. The sun's coming up. You're probably going to pass out until sunset. Take the bed. I have to go upstairs and start work soon."

"What about you?" he asked, concern creeping into his voice as he indicated my scrapes and bruises. I'd washed up in the kitchen sink, but a bit of the blood was mine.

"I'll manage," I said. "I have my ways."

As he walked past me, the room felt smaller, more intimate. When his hand brushed my shoulder, it gave me goosebumps. I shouldn't have looked at him in the shower. I shouldn't have been turned on by his story. I needed to get out of there before I did something I couldn't take back.

"Stay down here. Don't come up for anything," I ordered, trying to sound firm. "I'll come to you. And if you wake up, don't make any noise."

He caught my arm, his eyes dark and searching. "What do I call you?"

"Roxy," I said. "And you?"

He hesitated, then said, "Logan."

"How do you remember your name?"

"I don't know. One more mystery for us to figure out. Like why you saved me. Why did you do that?" he asked.

"I have one rule—never leave someone to the monsters. And you're still someone, right?"

"I hope so."

"Then that's why," I said. Nothing to do with how gorgeous he was or how he made my insides do somersaults.

I turned to head up the stairs, but I could feel his eyes following me. And his thoughts? They weren't just about feeding. He was checking me out, and he definitely liked what he saw.

"Roxy, stop getting into people's heads," I muttered to myself as I ascended the stairs, my heart pounding. But I couldn't help the smile tugging at my lips. Logan was going to be trouble, and I wasn't sure I could resist.

When I got upstairs, I saw the sun was rising. Not long before the boss showed up. She came early every morning with pastries and coffee. I think it was more important to her to have a friend than to run a place that made money.

Time to do something about my injuries. I pulled out my worn yoga mat, the foam flaking off, where I frequently sat and watched the sunrise through the big windows overlooking the mall's parking lot. Not the most beautiful view, but still a connection to nature.

I reached deep into what I called the core of who I am and grounded myself with the Earth, asking it if it would heal me, if it could remove some of my pain. I didn't hear voices; it didn't sound like anything spoke back to me. But I could feel the cut on my head closing, and some of the blurriness leaving my vision. I must have hit my head when the biker dropped me.

I took a breath and just sat there for a while, taking in the sunrise. It was such a calming thing for me, a place I could go to reset my day and start anew. Then my stomach started to hurt violently—I'd drunk too much. No magical cure for the hangover. The Earth must have thought I needed to learn a lesson.

My version of a hangover is a splitting headache, and it feels like worms coursing through my whole body, especially in my guts. As always, I question, Why did I drink? Why do I do this to myself? Oh, who am I kidding, I'm probably going to do it again tonight.

I tell myself it's the way I drown out the thoughts I pick up from people's heads, the things I see that I don't want to see. But honestly, I just enjoy that tipsy feeling, the feeling of being able to do what I wouldn't do without having a drink. Enough self-examination. It is not my strength. My strength is just getting on with it.

I stood up while trying not to throw up. Then I turned the sign and opened the doors for the masses that would come. Hah. We were lucky to get a couple of customers a day, usually old people or the owner showing up to make sure I was working.

So, I acted like I was dusting. I hadn't truly cleaned this place the whole time I'd worked here, and I'd started when I was about twelve and too young for an official work permit.

Shortly after what felt like an eternity of the most boring job you could possibly imagine, two people came in.

Busy for me. One was returning a laser disc—yes we had those too—and another asked, "How do I find the Starbucks?" Must be someone passing through.

"We haven't had a Starbucks in town for years. If we ever had one. Sorry."

Shortly after they left, my boss, Madge Wilson, came through the door. I steeled myself for whatever this morning's speech would be.

"Oh dear, you look terrible," she began, taking a big breath to fuel the outpouring of words to come. "Did you get any sleep last night? Oh, I'm sorry, I forgot. You were going to that dating thing, right? Maybe you didn't get any sleep for a good reason. Give me the details." As she handed me the box of donuts, something clunked downstairs. "I knew it!," she said. "Do you have a man down there? Or a girl? I'm not judging."

She went right on before I could answer: "Let me tell you a little something about love. It's not always grand gestures and sweeping you off your feet. Sometimes, it's in the quiet moments, the ones you hardly notice at first. The way his eyes soften when he looks at you, or how he remembers the smallest details—like how you take your tea or that book you mentioned in passing.

"Don't rush. The world will try to convince you that love is a race, that if you don't find it now, you'll be left behind. But the best kind of love is patient. It waits until you're ready, until you've learned to love yourself enough to know what you're worth. And, darling, you're worth the moon and stars.

"If he makes you feel like you're competing, then he's not the one. The right man will see you as a partner, not a prize. He'll see your flaws, your fears, and your dreams, and he'll want to stand beside you through it all. Love isn't perfect; it's messy, unpredictable, and sometimes it hurts. But when it's real, it's worth every tear, every laugh, every late-night talk that turns into dawn.

"Remember this: it's not just about finding someone who sets your heart racing, but someone who makes you feel safe. Someone who brings you peace when the world is storming around you. A love like that doesn't come around every day, so when you find it, hold on tight, but don't be afraid to let it grow at its own pace.

"And if you have to chase him, then let him go. The right man won't make you chase. He'll meet you halfway, hand outstretched, ready to walk with you, step by step, through whatever comes. So, take your time, sweetheart. The best love stories aren't rushed—they're written slowly, with care, and they bloom when the time is just right.

"And that's my advice. But I never took my own advice. I basically just went after the darkest, most mysterious man I could find in the room. Don't get me wrong; it was amazing when I was younger, but now? Oh, I wish I had done what I said to do. I have some good memories, though, don't get me started. So, are you going to tell me what you have downstairs, or are you going to keep me guessing?"

I blinked. My turn? Finally?

"Sorry to disappoint you, Madge. Nothing really happened, nothing torrid. Just met someone, we got in a bad situation, we helped each other get out of it, and we drank too much and just went to sleep. Nothing really happened. OK, he is really hot though."

She stayed for about thirty or forty minutes longer than usual, just talking about different things. I think she was really lonely, and it was good for me to have someone to talk to. Before she left, she said, "You could close the shop early today if you wanted to go wake that boy up. Oh, I'll quit pestering you. I'll see you tomorrow, dear. I love you."

"I love you too. Now get out of here and see if you can snag one of those old men by the park you've been pining for."

"Old men by the park? Sweetheart, I'm not going to go for that. Too much baggage. I'm going to find me one of those 20- or 30-year-old men. They don't know that I'm manipulating them!" She giggled and left through the swinging door, making the bell jingle.

A few excruciatingly boring hours later, the bell rang on the door again, and I saw Emily come in.

"I saw your text," she said. "I was going to call you back and also explain why I didn't show last night, but you haven't been answering your phone again. Besides ... I have to tell you something, Roxy."

I reached in my pocket and checked my phone—flat, dead battery. It was low when I sent the text hours ago. Should have plugged it in. It could never keep a charge. "Yeah, figures. What did I miss?"

"Jules just got hold of me. Someone called her because, you know, that's where you lived when you were younger. And, well ... I don't know how to tell you this, but ... your mother's passed away."

"What? My mom?"

I hadn't heard from my mother in years, and I was surprised how hard it hit me.

I never went to visit her when she was in the institution. She had been locked away for self-harm. I always thought she was just crazy, but the older I got, the more I wondered if she could see inside people like I did. Maybe it had driven her mad? And when I realized that's what it could be—then I couldn't bring myself to visit her. I worried she'd see into me, see my secrets and know I feared becoming like her. How would that have made her feel?

Now, I'd never be able to talk to her. I'd never be able to ask her who she was or tell her sorry I had never built up the courage to be her daughter.

"My sympathies, Roxy. I know you weren't close, but still ..." Emily trailed off weakly. "Apparently, it happened a week ago. The funeral service called Jules when they finally realized that you were her daughter. Someone else arranged everything. I don't know who, but there were plans in place for her funeral. I know this is weird, but it's tonight. There was some sort of request to have it in the evening."

"That is weird," I mumbled, feeling foggy headed again.

A nighttime funeral made me think of vampires and their restrictions. I now had one downstairs. One that werewolves had wanted to bury at the Crossroads. My instincts told me something strange was going on, but my curiosity couldn't get past the dull blanket of regret that had settled over me at news of my mom's death. I felt numb.

"I'll go with you. You won't be alone. Are you OK?"

"Truthfully, no. I never got to know her."

There was a long silence where Emily just let me process. She knew me well enough to let me be for a moment.

Finally, she said, "Why did you want me to come over? Your text said you wanted to show me something?"

"I'll just come out with it, I guess. I have a vampire downstairs."

"You have a what? You do realize that's a terrible idea, right? I've only known one vampire, and she pretty much screwed my world over. I was basically just her blood bag for about a year, and she messed with my head ... and my heart. She kind of made my sexuality a little confusing for me. So why in the name of all things holy do you have a vampire in your basement?"

"It's not like that. He's a fledgling. There's nothing … he hasn't messed with my head. I'm trying to help him. Do you remember anything that will help?"

Emily's gaze softened, but there was a hint of hesitation. "I'll tell you everything I know, but my last encounter with Vicky left a fog over my memories, blurring the lines between truth and illusion. That's the thing about vampires—they can twist your mind, make you doubt your own reality. I'm pretty sure that's how everything got so messed up for me, especially when it came to men. Vicky planted a fear deep inside me, and no matter how hard I tried, I couldn't seem to shake it.

"And the sickest part? I missed her. I missed that dark, dangerous creature who had fed on me and left my life in ruins…. I'm sorry. Here I am again, drowning in my own twisted feelings, while you're grieving the loss of your mother. Let's rewind. I'll tell you what I know, but … I need to see the vampire, okay?"

I nodded. "Alright. I wanted to check on him anyway, but I didn't want to go down there alone."

When we got to my room, the sight of him made my heart skip a beat. That's why I hadn't wanted to come alone. He was lying there on the bed, shirtless, his skin smooth and flawless, like he was carved out of marble. The shirt he had been wearing earlier must have been too tight, and now it lay discarded on the floor.

Emily's breath hitched too. "Wow, you sure know how to pick them. Look at him. He is sculpted. But I bet you don't know much about him yet, do you?" She glanced at me, her eyes twinkling with a mix of curiosity and mischief. "You already know that when they're turned, they lose their memories. They might hold onto a few things, but not much."

We sat there for a while, staring at him as he slept, his chest rising and falling so peacefully. It felt ... wrong, and yet I couldn't look away. Emily began to talk, her words flowing easily as she recounted everything she knew, but my attention kept drifting back to him, the way the light played across his body. My mind wandered, and I thought about what it would be like to reach out, to let my fingers trace along his skin. God, what was wrong with me?

"Can they make you feel things even when they're sleeping?" I asked Emily, breaking the silence.

"I don't think so," she replied, trying to sound casual. "I mean, yeah, he's sexy, but I'm not feeling anything supernatural. Are you?"

I gave a little laugh, shaking my head. "Oh, no, of course not." Then I sobered, glancing at her with a softness that made my chest ache. "Thank you for agreeing to come with me tonight to the funeral. I appreciate it."

She nodded. "No problem. I'll be there. Unlike speed dating last night. So sorry I bailed on that one."

"Forgiven. I got myself into a hot mess without you there—but it's a mess I haven't regretted yet."

Emily's gaze shifted to the vampire on the bed. "What are you going to do with him?"

"I don't know," I admitted, my voice barely a whisper. "There's probably no good choice when it comes to dealing with him."

Emily stepped closer, wrapping her arms around me in a warm, reassuring hug. "It's okay. Whatever you decide, I'm here for you. If you need anything, anything at all, just call me. Okay?" She pulled back, giving me a playful smile that still had a touch of sadness. "You're the sweetest, most beautiful person I know, and you deserve to feel safe. I'll see you later."

She slipped out of the room, leaving me alone with the vampire, my mind a tangled mess of fear, desire, and confusion

4 Life and Death

I had barely scrubbed clean after last night, my skin still tingling with a strange mix of excitement and anxiety. I needed a shower, desperately. After closing the store, I wandered through the aisles of Goodwill, searching for a suit that might fit Logan—and a funeral dress for me. I hoped I'd guessed his size right. Clothes in the dryer, I would have enough time to slip into the shower before Logan woke up.

I had decided he was coming with me. If the weird evening funeral was arranged by a vampire, it might be the same one who had turned him. And if they had organized all this for my mother, what else might they know about her? It was a place where both of us might find answers.

A sigh escaped my lips as I leaned against the bathroom sink, catching a glimpse of my reflection. What on earth was I thinking? Bringing home a man, let alone a vampire, into my tiny apartment? Was this what I'd signed up for when I decided to start living again? In just twenty-four hours, everything had spun wildly out of control. Yet ... I couldn't deny the thrill that pulsed through me. For once, I felt alive, more than I ever had before. Not that I'd done anything outrageous. Nothing to cross the line. But something was different, electrifying, and it scared me as much as it exhilarated me.

My friends weren't wrong—I lived like a nun, clutching onto a life that felt safe but sterile. It had been so long since I'd been with anyone. The last time, I was just a teenager, awkwardly fumbling my way through everything. But now ... now there was Logan, lying there, barely a few feet away. Stop it, I told myself. Stop staring at him while he sleeps. I was starting to creep myself out.

With a frustrated groan, I undressed and stepped into the shower, letting the hot water pour over me. Maybe a cold shower would have been more sensible, but who was I kidding? I wasn't looking for sensible. I wanted the heat, the rush, the feeling of my heart pounding against my chest. I stood beneath the steaming cascade, the hot water enveloping me like a comforting shroud. My crimson hair clung to wet skin, trailing down my back in rivulets. I closed my eyes, biting my lip, my hands gliding over the curves of my body, savoring the warmth, the solitude, and the momentary escape. But beneath my touch was an ache, a craving that pulsed just beneath the surface—a desire that went beyond what I could provide for myself, a hunger that refused to be satisfied.

I was lost in my thoughts, more like fantasies, which featured smooth, pale skin, washboard abs ... barely noticing the subtle shift in the air. The steam thickened, swirling around me like an ethereal hand, beckoning me closer. I gasped, startled, when I felt the cool, ghostly brush of lips against my neck, a whisper of a kiss that sent a jolt through me. Heart pounding, I peered into the misted glass of the shower door. And there he was—Logan. His presence was dark and magnetic, his grey eyes glowing with a predatory intensity, a slow, wicked smile playing on his lips.

"How long have you been watching?" I breathed, my voice trembling, a sign of the tremor cascading across my body.

"Long enough," he murmured, his voice low and smooth, like velvet sliding over my skin. "I couldn't stay away any longer."

Before I could respond, Logan stepped into the shower, the heat of the water mingling with the chill of his skin as he moved closer. His hands slid around my waist, pulling me against his chest, the contrast of his cool touch against my heated skin making me shiver. I could feel the firmness of his body against me, every inch of him pressing into me, as his lips grazed the delicate curve of my neck, lingering just at my pulse, teasing, promising.

"You're trembling," he whispered, his fangs barely grazing my skin, hinting at the pleasure and danger he brought with him.

"Because of you," I confessed, my voice barely more than a breath.

His hands moved down my stomach, achingly slow, making my body arch into him, my need for him growing with every teasing caress. When his fingers found me, I gasped, and he smirked against my neck, his lips brushing my ear as he nibbled, his cool breath mingling with the hot steam.

My hands braced against the shower wall, my mind spinning as my body surrendered to his touch. Logan's lips trailed lower, kissing along my collarbone, his tongue flicking against damp skin, leaving a trail of heat in its wake. The sensation was electric, sharp and sweet, and it sent ripples of pleasure through me, building, intensifying, until my heart was pounding, breath coming in shallow, desperate gasps.

I whimpered as I felt the sharp, thrilling press of his fangs, a blend of fear and exhilaration that had me trembling. Logan's hand cupped my chin, gently turning my head, exposing my throat to him, and I offered myself to the darkness and desire he represented.

"Do you trust me?" he asked, his voice a low, seductive purr, hypnotic and irresistible.

"No, but don't you stop," I breathed, eyes fluttering shut, surrendering to him, to the moment.

He bit down, the sensation sharp and sudden, and at the same moment, he entered me, slow and deliberate, every movement a calculated promise of pleasure. I gasped, a cry escaping my lips as the dual sensations intertwined, each one amplifying the other. Logan's mouth latched onto me, drinking deeply, his lips pulling, each pull sending a wave of ecstasy coursing through me, reaching into the deepest parts of me, igniting a fire that burned hotter than the shower around us.

His hands gripped my ass and hips, pulling me closer, his need matching my own, urgent and insatiable. As the pleasure built, my nails dug into the slick tiles, my body arching against him, my head falling back onto his shoulder. The line between pain and pleasure blurred, each bite, each thrust, a step closer to the edge. When I finally shattered, my body tensing and releasing in a euphoric wave, I felt as though I was unraveling, lost in him, in us, in the dark, consuming pleasure as he drank deeply, our bodies moving together in a perfect, primal rhythm.

When the waves of sensation finally subsided, Logan pulled back, his lips stained crimson, his eyes glowing with a dark, triumphant hunger. He captured my mouth with his, letting me taste the metallic tang of my own blood, the intimacy of it making me gasp. I clung to him as the water continued to pour over us, washing away everything but the memory of what we had shared—a connection raw, intense, and unforgettable.

I turned in the shower, letting the water cascade down my skin as I faced him. I tilted my head up, meeting his gaze. There was a flicker of something in his eyes, something searching, almost lost. I felt a pang of guilt, but not for what we'd done. No, that had been pure and raw, a connection unlike any I'd ever known. The guilt was because he had no memories, no anchor. He was adrift, and I wondered if I had taken advantage of that. Used him? Probably. But he had used me, too, hadn't he? It wasn't just me who craved that connection. The real question was, what now? Who were we, now that the rush of it all had settled?

He reached out, brushing a thumb gently along my jaw, and asked, "Did I hurt you when I bit you? If you had some of my blood, it would heal the bite."

A part of me was tempted, drawn to the idea of tasting him again, letting that strange intimacy between us deepen. But I could heal myself. I shook my head.

So we stayed there, hands and bodies moving slowly under the warm spray, washing away the remnants of the night. It was intimate in a different way, tender and soft, like an unspoken promise. The way his hands lingered, the way our eyes met—it felt almost more intimate than the sex had been.

The water was starting to cool, snapping me back to reality. "Go get dressed," I murmured, nudging him gently. "I want to wash my hair."

I watched as he hesitated for a moment, his eyes lingering on me, before he turned and left. God, he was beautiful. And God, we were beautiful together.

But there it was again—the question that hung between us, unresolved. What were we supposed to do now?

I lathered shampoo into my hair, letting the repetitive motion calm my thoughts. When I finally stepped out, steam curling around me, I found him waiting, leaning against the bathroom doorframe. There was a slight frown creasing his brow, a question forming on his lips.

"You should come with me," I said, catching him off guard. "To my mother's funeral."

His eyes softened. "Your mother's funeral? You hadn't said anything."

"I just found out today." I tried to sound nonchalant, but there was an ache under the words, a heaviness. "I don't think you should be left alone—and there's a chance that whoever made you could be there. I don't think it's a coincidence that some weird Uber driver drops me at the Crossroads just after you've been turned, and the next day I find out some mysterious stranger has organized a night funeral for my mother. We might learn what happened to you and why. It must be hard with all the ... new vampire things. Any more memories?" I asked, my voice low, almost hopeful.

"No," he said, his eyes darkening, "but I have this terrible sense that I wasn't a very good person before. I think I did horrible things."

I stepped closer, the towel slipping from my shoulder. "We all do terrible things," I said softly. "Things we can't take back, things we wish we'd never done. But right now, in this moment, you can decide who you want to be. Believe me, I mean it. Twenty-four hours ago, I was stuck, just drifting through life, and now ... everything has changed. I've decided I'm going to act. You can do that, too. You can choose who you want to be."

I realized then that I was still standing there, half-naked, delivering this heartfelt speech, and he ... well, he wasn't exactly hanging on my every word. He was devouring me with his eyes, his gaze searing, making me shiver despite the warmth in the room.

"Can vampires sense the emotions and feelings of others?" I asked, trying to pull the conversation back to something rational, something that didn't make my pulse race.

"Yes," he said, his voice husky. "It's ... intense. I wasn't sure if I was feeling what we were about to do in the shower, or if it was you. I think we're sensing each other, and it's making everything so much more ... vivid."

I had to smile at that. My fantasies, now laced with real memories of his body against mine, had an extra layer of color to them too.

"I want you, Logan. God, how I want you again, right now ... but we're going to be late. It hurts my heart to say this—get dressed." I handed him the Goodwill suit.

The dark suit was a bit baggy, but it fit him. My dress was plain and black, all it needed to be. We looked good standing next to each other in the full length mirror on my bathroom door.

"Not like the movies. I can see your reflection," I said, teasing.

"I'm glad. It would have been scary never seeing myself again," he said, frightened, imagining it might have been otherwise. He wasn't having as much fun with this as I was.

If I were one of those romantic heroines, I would have grabbed his hand and led him straight to the sleek, stolen motorcycle we'd taken the night before. "Get on," I'd say, all daring and wild.

But me? I was still terrified of that thing. So, I said, "Let's do what all cool vampires and badass heroines do: let's take the bus."

We sat close on that bus, our hips touching, shoulders brushing. Neither of us said a word, and yet, I'd never felt so understood, so completely at peace. I think we did that for each other—he could feel what I felt, and I could feel what he felt. It was like we were connected on a level I hadn't even known existed, and everything just ... flowed.

The night was cool, a whisper of autumn threading through the air as the bus rattled down the road, passing the old cemetery that sprawled like a dark, forgotten city. Twisted iron gates creaked in the breeze, and weathered headstones peeked out from the shadows, giving the place an eerie, preternatural vibe. I could see Logan's reflection in the bus window, his sharp, stormy eyes watching me like I was the only familiar thing in a foreign land.

"This is our stop," I said softly. "Just ... let me handle this, okay?"

As we stepped off the bus, Emily came up to us, her expression a mix of concern and caution, her gaze darting from me to Logan. "You okay?"

"Better than okay," I replied, trying not to blush, but there was no missing the way Emily was sizing Logan up like he was a puzzle missing too many pieces. "Emily, this is Logan."

Emily's lips pressed into a thin line, and she hesitated before speaking. "Don't take this the wrong way, but ... don't trust him. He's a monster."

Logan's jaw tightened, but his voice was calm, almost tender. "You're probably right," he said. "But I don't mean Roxanne any harm. I don't think I could. There's something inside me ... something that pulls me to protect her. I don't understand it. It's ... confusing."

Emily looked at him skeptically.

"Can you two not kill each other for a moment while I go talk to the priest?" I said.

I headed off but soon noticed Logan's steady presence beside me. "I feel safer with you." He smiled.

The cobblestone path wound its way through the old cemetery, leading us to an odd structure—a church that looked part Gothic cathedral, part crumbling barn. I'd never been this deep into the cemetery before, and it felt like stepping into another world, one where the air was thick with secrets.

Inside, dim candlelight burnished dark, rich wooden pews, and stained glass windows threw eerie, jewel-toned patterns onto the floor. The first window by the dais showed a hunting scene—wolves circling, as if guarding or threatening, a strange twist on a familiar story. But there, standing by the altar, his back to me, was a tall man, broad-shouldered, with a cascade of blond hair. My pulse quickened. It was impossible, but I recognized him.

The werewolf from my date night.

I went up to him, and he turned, a slow, deliberate movement, and a crooked smile spread across his lips. "Well, well. Surprised to see me?"

"You've got to be kidding me," I muttered. "You're not seriously a priest, are you?"

His laugh was low and throaty. "Sort of. The old priest passed, and I ... stepped in. But let's be real—this is a bit of a sham, and we both know it. I'm tired of playing nice, Roxy. That's your name, right? You didn't speak much at date night—just stared—which is understandable, as I'm pretty awe inspiring. My name's. Rick. And there are things you need to know, things that could change everything. About your mother's death, for one."

"What do you know about my mother?"

"She didn't just pass away. She was murdered. And I know who did it. But I need something from you first."

I was shaking, rage and confusion roiling inside me. "Tell me now."

Rick stepped closer, his eyes dark and intense. "Not yet. You need to do something for me. We've got a ghoul problem in the old cemetery—a real nasty one. It's feeding off the dead, and it's only a matter of time before it gets bold. You help me get rid of it, and I'll tell you everything you want to know."

"Ghouls?" I scoffed, trying to hide how my stomach twisted with fear. "You can't be serious."

"Oh, I'm dead serious," Rick replied, his voice dropping lower, almost a growl. "The boys went in, and they barely made it out. Werewolves heal all wounds except those inflicted by undead. Rock, paper, scissors type of thing. You're the only one who might stand a chance against it. Do this, and I'll give you the truth about your mother."

I glanced over my shoulder to where Logan and Emily had settled into a pew a few rows back, giving me space for my 'sensitive' conversation with the priest, only it was not what I had expected. Megan and Jules came in as I watched, shooting me sympathetic expressions before taking a seat just behind Emily, who was the odd one out of the group. I felt like I was an odd one out too, or maybe I was the gum that stuck all the weird bits together? Jules noticed Logan watching me and shot me a string of questions with her eyebrows alone, but I ignored her.

My mind was racing. I could still walk away, pretend none of this was happening. But the way Rick looked at me, like he had all the answers and could see right through to the heart of me that wanted them and would do anything to get them ... it stirred something dangerous and reckless.

"Fine," I said, my voice steady even as my heart pounded. "I'll deal with your ghouls. But you better keep your end of the deal."

Rick's smile was slow and knowing. "Oh, I always keep my promises, Roxy. You'll see."

I sat next to Logan, and I heard Megan inhale with surprise. She hissed a question. Jules murmured a dumbfounded reply, and then both of them whispered at Emily who tried to explain quietly without mentioning vampires. I heard something about 'soft-hearted' and 'homeless drifter'.

Not everyone knew vampires were real. Or were-wolves or anything else. I read minds, so I knew more than most. And Emily had been victimized, so she knew more than she wanted. She'd only ever told me about Vicky because I'd seen the pain in her thoughts and persuaded her to open up.

I could tell my friends wanted to pummel me with questions, not satisfied with Emily's answers, but this was a funeral, so they kept themselves in check and gave me my privacy. I was grateful for that.

The ceremony that followed was strange, a mix of somber rituals and eerie, new-age chants. Rick moved through it all with a commanding presence, his eyes finding mine across the room. When it was finally over, he handed me a simple, dark urn. My mother's ashes.

"Let's talk outside," he said, his voice soft, almost gentle. "We have a lot to discuss."

As we stepped out into the cold night air, the weight of the urn in my hands, I could feel the truth hovering just out of reach, waiting for me to reach out and grasp it. And I was ready.

"What makes you think I can do this?" I asked.

Rick looked at me and said, "Let's not play games. You know what I am, and I know what you are. I know you put my boys in the hospital last night. They were the rough ones of the pack too. Not my favorites, never following orders ... utter assholes really—but as pack leader I don't have a choice. I have to take care of them, all of them. That means I need you. You're a lot more powerful than you look."

A smirk played on my lips. "You have no idea what I can do." The words felt bold, daring, but they were laced with an undeniable truth. I didn't have a clue what I was capable of—yet. But I felt something powerful, waiting, desiring to be set free.

I could see it, just a flicker in his eyes, a hint of fear. Rick feared me, even if he didn't want to admit it. I could feel his anxiety shifting, morphing, as his gaze drifted lower, checking me out like I was something he could possess.

Seriously? Was that all he could think about? I should have been annoyed, but, God help me, it got to me. Anytime someone had a surge of desire, a craving so intense, I could feel it. Like a wave crashing into me, drowning me in their longing. And he was no exception.

"Emily," I called out, trying to keep my voice steady. "Can you take—well, my mother—back to my place?" I did not want to hold the urn; it was slightly creeping me out, and I had business here.

Emily's brows knitted together, her concern as clear as day. "Are you sure, Roxy? Do you want me to take you home too?"

"I can take you home—and your new friend," Jules volunteered, her desperate curiosity about Logan clear.

"I have a bigger car," Megan said. She had never offered me a ride in her Mercedes before, probably afraid

I'd dirty it with poverty, but the fact she had mentioned it meant she was dying of curiosity too.

"Thank you all, but I want to spend some time talking with my mother's priest. You understand?"

They nodded like a bunch of chickens in the yard bobbing for grains. "Oh, of course," Jules said. "I understand."

"Suit yourself." Megan stood disdainfully, as if I'd passed up a ride in a limousine.

They left together, casting a few more glances at Logan and me before exiting the church.

When Emily came up to take the urn, I met her eyes, my smile fading just a little. "You're worried I'm about to dive headfirst into trouble, aren't you?"

She didn't deny it. "You're gonna get involved in something dangerous because of that vampire, aren't you?"

A bitter laugh slipped out before I could stop it. "I think that ship has already sailed. Danger's practically my middle name at this point."

But as I said it, something stirred inside me. It felt right, like stepping into my own skin for the first time. I wasn't running anymore, wasn't hiding. I was alive, and it felt damn good. For once, I wasn't letting life pass me by—I was grabbing it by the horns, pulling it close, and kissing it on the mouth. There was this wild, electric connection humming through me, something raw and real, like the pulse of the earth. Maybe this was who I was meant to be all along.

If I could just get through tonight, make it out on the other side, who knew what might come next? Maybe there was more to my future than I'd ever dared to dream. Maybe, when I was ready to let it all in, it would be even better than I'd imagined.

5 Unleashed

The moon hung heavy and full, casting an eerie glow over the abandoned graveyard as I descended the worn stone steps into the crypt. Rick had warned me about the ghouls, but I hadn't expected this—the thick scent of decay, the oppressive quiet that smothered every sound. I clenched my fists, nails biting into my palms, drawing blood.

From the shadows, the ghouls emerged—twisted, skeletal figures, their eyes glowing with a malevolent hunger in sunken gray faces. They hissed and snarled, yellowed claws scraping against the stone as they circled me. But I was ready. With a flick of my wrist, roots burst from the earth, tangling around the creatures' legs, trapping them. I whispered an incantation, my voice low and commanding, and a surge of energy pulsed through me, twisting and constricting the ghouls, snapping their limbs like brittle twigs.

"Behind you!" came a familiar, deep voice. Logan. He moved like a shadow, dark hair tousled, eyes gleaming crimson in the crypt's dim light. In an instant, he was at my side, his fangs bared, tearing into a ghoul with a swift, almost graceful brutality. Together, we were a storm of nature and death, my magic and Logan's raw power blending seamlessly, a dangerous dance of light and darkness.

In the chaos, I hurled a blast of energy that ricocheted off the crypt wall, striking Logan in the chest. His eyes widened with shock before he crumpled to the ground, motionless. Panic surged through me, but I didn't have time to think. The ghouls were still coming, and I had to make a choice: save Logan now or finish the fight.

With a roar of fury, I unleashed everything I had, sending vines snaking around the ghouls' throats, pulling them down, crushing them. I fought like a woman possessed, my heart hammering as I dispatched the last of the creatures. Then I dropped to my knees beside Logan, hands trembling as I pressed them to his chest. "Come on, Logan, stay with me," I whispered, my voice break-ing.

Just as his eyes fluttered open, a chill swept through the crypt. The air grew impossibly cold, and a dark, op-pressive presence washed over us. My breath caught in my throat as a figure materialized from the shadows, its form flickering like smoke.

I could get into its mind as much as it was getting into mine. I could sense who it was. It was not another ghoul-ish creature, but the ghost of a witch called Harper. Not a ghost—a wraith. Far more dangerous. Once a witch, she refused to fully die and was now a hollow, spectral thing, her eyes burning with ancient, desperate rage.

"Free me," Harper whispered, her voice slithering into my mind, promising power, release, salvation. And for a moment, I believed her. With trembling hands, I began to weave a spell to release the wraith from her eternal pris-on.

But as soon as the last word left my lips, Harper lunged, her essence flowing toward me, trying to force its way into my body, my soul. I gasped, struggling against the dark tendrils wrapping around me, tighten-ing, suffocating.

She wanted to possess me. Take me over. Steal my body.

Then, a flash of movement. A new figure stepped into the crypt—a man with a presence that commanded the shadows, his eyes a deep, dangerous black. With my senses heightened by the fight, my ability to see into people's minds was heightened too.

Aamon. I had sensed him since the night before, always at the edge of my vision, lurking in the woods at the Crossroads, just outside the church at the cemetery. But now he was here, exposing himself, his lips curling into a wicked, knowing smile.

He moved with lethal grace, closing the distance between us, his voice smooth as he said, "You really should be more careful, little witch." In a blur, he was at my side, his hands steady on my arms, pushing back against the wraith's power. Together, we fought Harper, magic and shadows swirling around us, the crypt shaking with the force of our struggle.

The air crackled with tension, heat rising between me and Aamon as we moved in sync, our bodies almost touching. I could feel his breath on my neck, his fingers brushing my skin, leaving me torn between fear and an aching, dangerous attraction. Aamon's dark eyes met mine, and for a moment, the world around us seemed to vanish, leaving just the two of us, bound by the darkness we both wielded.

Harper was relentless. The wraith screeched, fighting to stay. With one final surge of power, we drove her back. She shrieked, dissipating into a cloud of smoke, retreating deeper into the shadows of the crypt. But it wouldn't contain her now. When I had been under her spell, listened to her plea to be released, I had foolishly undone something chaining her here. Now, she was free to haunt the world above.

My heart was still pounding as I turned to Aamon, but he stepped back, the heat between us dissolving like mist.

"Who are you?" I asked.

Aamon's lips curved into a smile that was both charming and menacing. "Someone you'll be seeing a lot more of." His gaze lingered on me a moment, before he melted into the darkness.

I blinked, and he was gone, as if he had never been there. I whirled around, desperate to make sense of what had just happened, but the crypt was silent, empty except for Logan, who was slowly stirring, his eyes still dazed. Relief flooded through me. I knelt beside him, cradling his head in my lap.

As I looked down at him, I realized how close I had come to losing him, and the fear that had gripped my heart was replaced with something warmer, deeper. "I'm here," I whispered, stroking his hair. "The wraith, Harper, is gone, but I'm not going anywhere."

Still, as I glanced back at the shadows where Aamon had stood, a frisson ran through me. He was gone—but something told me he hadn't gone far. And I wasn't sure whether I should be relieved or terrified.

As we made our way out of the crypt, the silence between us was thick, the darkened path back to the church stretching like an unspoken question. Logan finally broke it, his voice low, almost cautious: "How did you know that creature's name?"

I hesitated, my pulse quickening. Did I dare tell him the truth? That I could do more than just feel emotions—I could actually hear thoughts? It was a part of me I'd kept hidden for so long, afraid of what people might do if they knew. But lying now would only build walls between us, and God knows I'd had enough of those.

"Well," I began, my heart beating louder with each word, "ever since I was a little girl, I've been able to hear people's thoughts. What they were really thinking, not just what they were saying. I learned how to lead them to reveal more than they intended, to coax the truth out without them even realizing. Sounds like a neat party trick, huh?" I tried to laugh it off, but it came out weak. "Except it's not. It's exhausting. And it makes being close to someone ... almost impossible."

I glanced over at him, trying to read his expression. Would he understand, or would he see me as some kind of freak? "When I hit my teens, things got worse. I didn't just hear thoughts—I felt everything. If someone was sad, I was sad. If they were angry, I was angry. And if they were attracted to me..." I trailed off, my cheeks flushing. "Well, let's just say it was impossible not to feel it, to be drawn in by it. I didn't have a choice. So, I learned to keep my distance, to hide. Until last night."

I paused, my breath catching at the memory of our night together. "Being with you, it ... it made me feel free.

Like I didn't have to hide anymore. But this isn't about you," I said, my voice firmer now as I stepped closer, closing the gap between us. "This is me, Logan. I'm the one with all this ... mess."

Before he could say anything, I grabbed his shoulders and pulled him toward me, my lips crashing into his. The kiss was raw, intense, and I felt his hands start to wander, as if trying to memorize every curve, every inch of me. My fingers trailed down his chest, feeling the steady, solid rhythm of his heart beneath, while his body pressed against mine, hard and undeniable. For a moment, it felt like we might just lose ourselves, right there in the graveyard, surrounded by shadows and secrets.

But then I felt it—a presence. Watching. Waiting. My skin prickled, and I knew exactly who it was. Aamon. What was his game, lurking in the dark? The thought of him, a vampire with eyes that seemed to see right through me, made me feel unbalanced. And, strangely, it made my blood run hotter, a forbidden thrill curling in my stomach.

I broke the kiss, stepping back, my breathing ragged. Guilt gnawed at me, knowing I was thinking of Aamon while Logan's lips were still warm on mine. Worse, I could sense Aamon's eyes on us, and somehow, I knew he was enjoying it. That twisted, thrilling energy was seeping into me, making it harder to think straight.

Logan helped me drown out the chaos in my head. So, I kissed him again, softer this time, and whispered against his lips, "We need to go. Now, okay?"

I felt his disappointment, a flicker of confusion and hurt, but he nodded, his lips brushing mine in a lingering kiss. "Let's go, then," he said, and I could hear the unspoken promise in his voice, that this wasn't the end and we would more thoroughly 'celebrate' our survival soon.

As we walked away, I could still feel Aamon's presence, like a shadow that wouldn't fade. What did he want? And why, despite everything, did a part of me want to find out?

6 Deception and Pizza

Back at the church, I paused on the threshold. "Logan, please stay out here. I need to talk with Rick alone." I could feel Logan's distrust radiating off him. Was it because Rick was a werewolf, or was he just worried I might lose interest in him? Men and their possessiveness—it was infuriating.

"I'll be right here if you need me. Just give a shout," Logan said.

Stepping inside the chapel, I didn't see Rick, just a couple of his henchmen lighting incense. It was a bit too heavy-handed for a church, but I had a hunch they were trying to mask the scent of something less holy, like marijuana.

"Roxy," one of his packmates said, noticing me. "Rick's at his place in the back. Are you okay? You look like you've been through the wringer."

I recognized the voice. Little Timmy. Except, Little Timmy wasn't so 'little' anymore. He'd bulked up since high school, back when he'd earned the nickname that no longer applied.

"Timmy? I had no idea you were still around. Weren't you off somewhere on a football scholarship?"

"Yeah, but I didn't have the brains for college. I mostly fooled around—drugs, parties, women. Sure, I could say I blew out my knee, but the truth is, I was a mess. When they finally kicked me off the team, there went my shot at a degree. I was only a few credits shy of graduating in Sociology, but it wasn't meant to be. So, I came back and joined the pack. Rick really helped me pull myself together. You and him ... I know it's rocky because you're both alphas. He's an alpha wolf and you're an alpha witch—natural enemies. But he's got a soft side."

"If you say so."

"How's Megan doing?"

"Megan?" Few people liked my overbearing frenemy. "Did you two have a thing?"

"Not exactly. I liked her, but she's got this ... edge. Maybe we could've been something, but she scares the hell out of me, and I never pushed it."

Megan with someone like Timmy? It was hard to picture. That girl would probably chew up and spit out anyone who got too close, even if he was a werewolf.

"You know, she's got this routine now, speed dating nights on weekends. You should take a shot, tell her how you feel. She acts tough, but even tough girls get lonely."

"Good to know. Thanks, Roxy. It was nice catching up, but don't keep Rick waiting. He's not the patient type."

Timmy was a rarity—a nice guy no matter what life threw at him. He didn't check me out once, and I was wearing that too tight Goodwill dress, which was saying something.

I walked the narrow, cobblestone path between the church and a detached garage, leading to a small, quaint cottage. It looked like something out of a fairy tale, with ivy crawling up the walls and a handful of lazy cats lounging around. The door was ajar, but I still knocked.

"Rick, I'm here."

I heard his voice from inside. "Come on in. I'm cooking."

Cooking? That was unexpected. For a moment, I hesitated before stepping into the wolf's den. The aroma hit me, and I had to admit, it smelled incredible.

"You cook? I never would've guessed. It's definitely not my forte."

"Yeah, I'm full of surprises—read, cook, watch documentaries. This is my space where I can be myself. The pack wouldn't understand half of it. Come in, grab a seat at the bar. I'll finish up, and then we'll talk."

I watched him knead the dough, realizing he was making pizza from scratch. Who even does that anymore? Everything I ate came straight from Domino's.

"So, you're still alive?" Rick's voice dripped with sarcasm.

"Don't test me. I ran into something nastier than you—a wraith."

The look on his face told me he already knew about the wraith.

"Yeah, figured as much. This house used to belong to the witch you met. It was here long before the church, part of an old coven. So, you want answers, huh? There's a vampire. I didn't get his name."

"I already know Aamon's involved. I guessed that much. I just don't understand why. So, tell me, what good are you, Rick?"

He smirked, a glint of mischief in his eyes. "Oh, I have plenty to offer."

I rolled my eyes. "That's not going to happen."

"Let's be real—sex isn't about trust. It's about having a damn good time."

"Rick, focus. What do you know about the vampire? About the wraith?"

"Alright, alright. I owe you that much. I don't know everything, but I do know that bloodsucking fiend has been spending a lot to dig up dirt on you. Didn't say why, but there's some curse. He thinks you can break it."

Great. Just great. "So, there's a curse. I'm still not getting how this helps me."

"That's where I come in. This house belonged to that witch turned wraith, Harper. She didn't have a last name that I know of, but she led a powerful coven. She had grimoires, knowledge on the curse. I read one of her diaries, which might just have what you need. You read Latin, right?"

"You read Latin, Rick? Seriously?"

"I'm like an onion—layer after layer."

"More like you make people cry."

He laughed. "You know, I think you have a thing for me."

"Stop. What's in the diary that can help me?"

"Harper wrote about grimoires she needed to hide. Didn't say where, but if I had to guess, they're somewhere near the old quarry. The coven had ties to three places—this church, a field that's now a strip mall, and the quarry."

"How does a witch turn into a wraith?" I asked.

"Obsession. Usually, it starts with trying to live forever. But if you push it too far, you lose your body and end up as a wraith. You can possess others, but it's temporary. I'm not sure how she managed to stay as a wraith for so long. Must've been powerful."

Rick leaned closer. "You're quite the scholar yourself, sweetheart. Maybe we're not so different. Stay for the pizza, and after, who knows? We could see if we … click."

"You're almost laughable. But I'm tempted. I could use a break from Logan. Things are … intense."

"Vampires and their mind games, you can't trust them. Me? I'm straightforward. Best love you'll ever have, no strings attached."

I wanted to call him sleazy, but another part of me thought, 'God, he's hot.' It only took 48 hours to turn me from a nun into a flirt.

And damn, that first batch of pizza smelled amazing. Watching Rick bend over to pull it out of the oven wasn't bad, either.

"Rick, I've been here too long. Logan's going to freak, and you haven't been as useful as I'd hoped."

"Jealous type, is he? I didn't know you had the vampire figured out. But I pay my debts. That Harley you swiped from my boys? It's yours. They couldn't keep it, so they didn't deserve it." He handed me the signed registration. "It's yours."

"What am I supposed to do with a motorcycle? Those things scare me."

"Roxy, that bike suits you. I feel it. And don't you want to try new things?"

He saw through me. No magic, no tricks, just saw me. There was more to Rick than I'd given him credit for.

"I need Harper's diary and a few things from your kitchen—salt, flour, herbs. That okay?"

"You said you couldn't cook."

"I can't. But I can do a spell."

The bus ride back to my place was uneventful. And after I cleared out the little storage room, it was time to start the ritual.

My fingers traced the edge of a plastic compass, crimson-painted nails catching the candlelight as it flickered in the dim, smoky room. The space beneath the video store was cloaked in shadows, heavy with the scent of incense, and threaded with a hint of musk—Logan's scent, spicy and dark, like a promise. I stood over a makeshift altar, a bundle of sage in one hand, the compass in the other, murmuring incantations that hummed with power.

Logan's gaze never wavered; his gray, seductive eyes fixed on me. "You look ... mesmerizing when you work your magic," he said, his voice a velvet purr, laced with that familiar, teasing edge.

A smirk tugged at my lips. I didn't look up, trying to keep my focus, but I glanced at him through my lashes. "Trying to distract me, vampire? Careful, or this compass might lead us straight into a ditch."

He stepped closer, the cool brush of his breath grazing my neck. "Maybe that's the plan. Just you, me, and nowhere."

I bit back a real smile, determined not to let him see how effortlessly he got under my skin. "I'm not losing the location of the grimoires because you want to play games," I said, voice still sharp but softer, like a warning wrapped in silk.

With a final, whispered word, the compass glowed, its needle springing to life. I exhaled, feeling the enchantment lock into place.

"There. Done," I said, turning to face Logan, catching the glint of his smile—a smile that was half invitation, half challenge.

He leaned in, close enough that I could see the gleam of his fangs, hear the promise in his voice. "Good. Now that the magic's handled, how about we handle ... something else?"

My heart skipped, but I kept my cool, even as the air between us tightened. "You're impossible," I said, stepping back, though not entirely out of reach. "Let's save the flirting for after we find what we need."

"Fine," Logan replied, his grin widening into something almost predatory. "But I'll hold you to that."

We climbed the narrow stairs, passed through the dark video store, into the street and the cool embrace of the night. The parking lot was quiet, just a few flickering streetlamps casting pools of light. My new Harley gleamed under the soft glow, sleek and powerful, a gift from Rick that I was still getting used to. I ran a hand over the leather seat, the sensation grounding me, making the bike feel like an extension of myself.

Sliding on my helmet, I caught Logan's reflection, leaning against the wall with that infuriatingly charming smile. "You're not putting on a helmet?" I asked, raising an eyebrow.

"Immortal, remember?" he said with a chuckle, sauntering over. "Besides, where's the fun in that?"

I rolled my eyes, but there was a smile there, too. "Fine. But if you fall off, I'm not stopping to pick up your pieces."

"Deal," Logan said, climbing on behind me, his arms snaking around my waist, pulling me close. The sensation was electric, his cool breath whispering against my ear. "You sure you're up for this, witch?"

"Only one way to find out," I replied, revving the engine. The Harley rumbled beneath me, a beast ready to be unleashed, and I took a steadying breath. The fear was there, coiled in the back of my mind, but I was learning to push it down, like everything else. I could handle this.

With a twist of the throttle, we tore out of the parking lot, the wind tugging at my hair beneath the helmet. Logan's hands tightened slightly around me, and I could feel his smile, could almost hear it. The road stretched ahead, dark and winding, leading to the quarry where the grimoires—and whatever else awaited us—would be found.

7 Riddle Me

The wind whipped around me as I gripped the handle-bars of the motorcycle, pulse matching the engine's hum. Logan's cool, steady presence behind me felt like an anchor—solid, reassuring, but also a reminder of the danger we faced. The motorcycle thrummed between my legs, a raw, thrilling power that belonged to me now. I was in control, and I loved it.

We tore through the night, the enchanted compass I had crafted glowing faintly from where I had fastened it to my wrist, guiding us away from the abandoned quarry and up a treacherous, winding path. The further we climbed, the thicker the magic in the air became, crack-ling with the promise of trouble. My eyes narrowed as I spotted a faint shimmer—a magical snare, practically glowing against the dark underbrush. It was so obvious I almost laughed.

"Well, that's cute," I said as I pulled to a stop, glanc-ing over my shoulder at Logan, his eyes fixed ahead, scanning for threats. "It's a trap. Specifically designed for the undead. Someone doesn't want your kind getting too close."

Logan's jaw clenched, a flicker of frustration in his eyes. "Can you disarm it?"

"Of course I can," I replied with a smirk. "But not without a little show."

I slid off the bike, boots crunching on the gravel as I moved towards the trap. As I knelt to work, I couldn't help but feel the familiar prickle of eyes on me. Aamon. I could sense him, lingering somewhere in the distance, watching. "Goddamn bastard," I muttered under my breath. "Still stalking me."

The snare was trickier than it looked. It took every ounce of my focus to unravel the intricate spell without setting it off. Sweat beaded at my temple, but my hands were steady as I carefully dismantled the trap, piece by piece. I could feel Logan's gaze burning into my back, a mix of admiration and concern. When I finally stood, brushing off my hands, I flashed him a triumphant grin. "See? Easy."

We rode on, deeper into the woods, until the dense trees gave way to a stunning, moonlit glade. The air was sweet with the scent of night-blooming jasmine, flowers glowing like tiny stars scattered across the grass. For a moment, I forgot about traps and grimoires and even Aamon's shadowy presence. All I could see was Logan, his face softened in the silver light, his eyes fixed on me as if I were the only thing that mattered.

"Roxy," he said quietly, and I could hear the unspoken worry in his voice. "Are you sure you're okay? That trap wasn't as simple as you claimed. We don't have to keep going if—"

"—I can handle it," I interrupted, voice firm but gentle. I wanted to reassure him, but there was no room for doubt now. I turned away, senses scanning the glade. Something was hidden here; I could feel it, a ripple in the magic that wasn't quite right. It took a moment to spot the subtle distortion, and another to dismantle the illusion, revealing a stone staircase spiraling down into the earth.

With a deep breath, we descended, Logan close behind me. The air grew cooler, and the darkness seemed to press in around us, but I felt a strange sense of calm. I had faced worse than this, and I wasn't alone.

We encountered more traps, each more insidious than the last, but I was relentless. By the time we reached the bottom, Logan's eyes were full of something I hadn't seen before— respect, maybe even awe. "You're

incredible," he said softly. "But this is getting dangerous."

"And yet, here you are, still following me," I teased,
but my smile was genuine. I liked the danger.

We came to a massive door, its surface crawling
with dark, twisted runes. I could feel the malevolence
pulsing from it, like a heartbeat. It was alive, and it was
waiting. I knew, with that witchy sense of mine, that I had
to speak to it, to earn its trust—or force it to let us
through. And that would not be easy.

"Hello?" I began.

The door responded with a riddle, its voice echoing
through the cavern like a dark whisper:

It has no light of its own but can make the night
bright as day and compel beasts and seas to obey its
wild commands.

I hesitated for just a second, mind working furiously
before the answer clicked into place. Simple. When I
spoke, the words felt like a release, a sudden burst of
clarity that shattered the tension. "The moon, of
course."

There was a soft click, and the door creaked open,
revealing a dark passage beyond. I turned to Logan, triumphant.

"Let's see what is waiting for us."

The hallway was dark, shadows flickering along the
walls as we moved closer to the heart of the place. It felt

like stepping into another world, one where the air was thick with ancient mysteries and unspoken warnings.

We reached a library, and at the center of the room, a sarcophagus loomed, its presence chilling the air around it. My breath caught as I took a step closer, every nerve tingling. The wraith was here. It was tethered to this crypt more strongly than the one at the cemetery. Something about this place, this moment, pulled the two locations together. And Harper was at the heart of it.

A scream shattered the silence, the wraith's voice echoing in my head: "You brought one of them here. A vampire. Foolish, girl." The words were sharp, laced with venom. I barely had a chance to react before the wraith lunged at me, its cold, dark energy suffocating, like icy hands wrapping around my throat. "I must end it, Roxy. End your life to save them all."

I fought back, summoning every bit of nature magic I had, but it was like trying to punch smoke. The wraith wasn't just powerful; it was untouchable.

"There's something in the crypt," I gasped, turning to Logan, my heart pounding. "The sarcophagus. I need to get in there, but it's too heavy."

Without hesitation, Logan stepped forward, his muscles straining as he tore the lid off the tomb. Inside, an amulet glowed—a twisted, intricate thing, with veins of magic running deep into the earth. It was beautiful, but I knew it was wrong. Dangerous.

I shattered it with a single, decisive spell I instinctively wove, and the wraith's scream turned into a guttural growl.

"You fool! You don't understand. Breaking my tethers won't rid you of me; it will only make me stronger. We'll meet again, Roxy." And then, just like that, it was gone, leaving the air cold and empty.

I took a deep breath, my gaze drifting to the shelves that stretched endlessly around us, packed with books. "It would take forever to figure out which grimoires are important," I muttered.

"Not with the compass you made," Logan said, his voice low and soothing. "It'll lead us to what mattered most to Harper."

The compass needle moved, pointing to a small, unassuming book on the bottom shelf. I pulled it out, my fingers tracing the cover. "Well, at least it's not in Latin. Old English, I think. I can probably figure it out." I settled down, flipping through the pages, trying to make sense of the faded script.

As I read, Logan came up behind me, his hands slowly massaging the tension out of my shoulders. His touch was gentle, but I could feel the strength in it, the way he held back.

"Don't get me sidetracked," I said, a hint of a smile tugging at my lips. "This is important."

"Okay," he murmured, his lips brushing my ear. "But you're intoxicating."

Time passed in a blur, my eyes skimming over the words until they started to form a story. "It's some sort of history," I said, my voice barely above a whisper. "A long time ago, supernatural creatures roamed freely, without any rules or limits. The witches—who were powerful back then—decided that humanity wouldn't survive unless they were restrained. So, they performed a ritual to create checks and balances. You know, like werewolves only changing at the full moon, or vampires being cursed to the night. It was magnificent, but it cost them everything. Most of them died, leaving only a few weak ones behind."

I paused, letting that sink in. "The spells were designed never to be broken. No witch was supposed to be powerful enough to undo them. But there's this hint ... about a witch who was neither truly alive nor dead. It's almost poetic." I ran my fingers over the spells, feeling the power humming beneath the words. "There are other powerful spells here, Logan. I think ... I think I can break the bond between you and your master. I can set you free from Aamon."

I was sure Aamon had created Logan for some dark purpose, which was why he was always watching us. Let's see how he reacted when I changed the rules of his game.

Logan's eyes softened, a flicker of hope lighting them up. "Yes," he said, his voice steady. "If you think you can."

"I think everything I need is here. Yes, I can do it."

The room felt electric as I set up for the spell, my heart pounding with anticipation. "Now for the fun part," I said, trying to keep my voice light even though my hands were shaking. "I need to trigger what I've set up. Come here and kiss me."

His lips met mine, soft at first, then growing more urgent, more desperate, as the magic began to weave around us. It was like nothing I'd ever felt—hot and cold, wild and controlled, all at once. The power swirled between us, confusing the ties that bound him, blurring the lines. At the peak of it all, I whispered, "Break this one's bond to the vampire Aamon. Manifest to be what I have designed."

We collapsed, drained. We lay there a while, breathless and tangled, the room still humming with residual energy. Like the energy had gone nowhere. I still felt some tether between Logan and his maker. We'd unleashed so much power ... but it hadn't worked. I botched the spell somehow, I knew it. "I don't know if I freed you," I said, my voice barely above a whisper. "But it was sure freeing for me." I had never wielded a spell like that before, and it had been better than sex.

Logan's eyes were heavy, his smile almost sad. "I don't know if I feel any different," he said. "But I can sense the sun rising. I'm sorry, Roxy. I think I'm going to fade out."

I held him close, not wanting to let go, but knowing I had no choice. I watched as his body stiffened, then relaxed, his eyes drifting shut.

"Sleep till sunset," I whispered, brushing a stray lock of hair from his face. And then he was gone, leaving me alone in the silence of the library, surrounded by the echoes of a battle I wasn't sure we'd won.

8 Broken Bonds

I felt as if my soul had been stripped bare, exhaustion weaving itself into the very fabric of my being. Two nights without sleep had left me weary, a heaviness settling over me like a shroud as I lay next to Logan on the ground beside the sarcophagus. But even in my fatigue, a strange warmth pulsed through my veins, whispering promises of something I could not yet name.

The earth beneath me felt alive, a thrumming heartbeat echoing deep within. It called to me, wrapping me in an unshakeable pull.

And then, from that abyss of darkness, Harper's voice broke through the silence like a sharp blade, cold and unforgiving. "So, you foolish girl, you fell in love with a monster. Logan will destroy you like he destroyed me."

My heart raced, a sense of dread slowly rising within me. "What are you talking about? Logan ... he loves me," I breathed, desperation lacing my words, hoping for a thread of truth in the chaos.

"Love? How naive," Harper scoffed, her voice smooth like silk yet laced with venom. "Don't you know it yet? Vampires lie. They can weave webs of deceit that fog your memory, cloud your mind, twist your very heart. He once said he loved me, which was my undoing, and it looks like he's going to be yours, too."

"No. I refuse to believe that. We saved each other. Logan can't be lying to me?"

Harper's laugh was sharp, cutting through my resolve. "That monster beside you convinced me to become a vampire, a rare choice for a witch like us. Few can cross that threshold, but those who do? They can break the curse. Now that you've done what he wanted and set me free, he will kill you, girl—turn you into a vampire in some sneaky way to make you think you're willingly joining him. Once you do that, you'll help him break the curse and unleash a nightmare upon this world."

"You're wrong. Aamon is the head vampire; it's not Logan. He's newly made, not ancient enough to have turned you into a vampire. He's good," I argued, desperation flooding my veins, even as a gnawing doubt clawed at my heart.

"I don't care who you think he is," Harper retorted, bitterness dripping from her words. "Not all these creatures wear the same mask, but there is always a mask. If you don't believe me, leave this crypt before that thing wakes up. Find out where your mother's body is, for you can be certain they did not burn it. I suspect it is still walking around, another monster like this one. Discover who truly killed her. Wake up, girl, before you destroy everyone."

"How can I trust anything you say? You were just trying to kill me moments ago."

"You know nothing about magic, do you? You are self-taught, stumbling about through intuition, learning fragments of spells and ideas from whatever books you've been able to find and translate. I come from a great line, so listen to me. I am tethered to this wraith form by three anchors, and whenever those anchors are threatened, I lose all control. All I can think about is stopping who is destroying the anchors. Kill them, drain their soul. Anything. Just stop them. I lose all rationality. You've broken two of my anchors."

"Even if I believe you, what can I do? How do I find my mother?" My voice came out a whisper, fragile as glass.

"It's obvious," Harper replied, the impatience in her tone palpable. "If you don't know, ask another undead. They can find each other; they can sense each other."

"Are you talking about Aamon?" The name slipped from my lips, igniting a flicker of hope, mingled with fear.

"Wake up, child. You may think you're safe, but the shadows are always watching, always waiting," She warned, her voice fading into the echo of the crypt.

With each word, I felt the solidness of my reality disintegrate. My heart was torn between love and betrayal. The weight of my uncertainty hung heavy in the air, threatening to crush me as I clung to the idea of Logan's love, knowing it might all be a lie.

Could he have clouded my mind? Could everything I felt so certain I knew be wrong? Was Logan no fledgling but a master vampire? One old enough to have turned Harper and led her astray centuries ago?

Only one thing was clear: I had to find the truth—before it was too late.

9 The Fire Inside

The early dawn mist curled around me like a shroud, cool and damp, carrying the scent of earth and lingering night. Harper's words echoed in my mind, relentless and sharp. Logan was using me.

I wanted to deny it, to shove the thought away into a dark corner where it couldn't hurt me, but I couldn't. The idea gnawed at me, unyielding. If Logan had clouded my mind, then what was real? What was a lie? Each step felt heavy as I climbed up from the library, the weight of my doubts dragging me down, and as I reached the surface, I sucked in a deep breath, craving clarity.

The field stretched out before me, the mist softening the edges of the landscape. But it wasn't serene. It was a battlefield. Rick, standing tall, his stance commanding, had his wolves encircling Aamon. The vampire looked a hair's breadth away from disintegrating in the pale, weak morning light. Smoke curled off him in wisps, but his eyes, though weary, still held a flicker of defiance.

"Roxy, stay back. I'm trying to help you," Rick called out, his voice breaking through the haze. His eyes, bright as full moon light, locked on mine. "This vampire's been tracking you, and I'll take care of him. If we corner him until daylight, we have the advantage."

I felt the electricity of my magic thrumming beneath my skin, crackling, urging me to act, but my mind was still a whirlwind of confusion. Rick was trying to protect me, but what if there was more to the story? What if Aamon wasn't the enemy I had imagined he was? The thought slithered in, uncomfortable, but persistent. My hand trembled as I raised it, and I shouted, "Stop!"

The wolves halted, muscles tensed, eyes flicking between me and their prey. The air hummed with my spell, freezing them in place. Rick's jaw clenched, his hands balled into fists, and for a heartbeat, I thought he might defy me.

"What the hell, Roxy?" he barked, his voice dripping with frustration. "Are you crazy? Let us finish this. Vampires are monsters. I'm trying to save you ... and maybe make a little cash off this bloodsucker when we end him. A vamp this old is bound to have grateful enemies."

Of course. Rick would never pass up a payday, and greed wrapped him in dark, dangerous intentions.

I stepped closer, feeling the power pulsing within me, cold and sharp, almost seductive in its force.

"I don't know what's true anymore," I said, my voice steady but quiet, a whisper carried by the wind. "But if Logan's been tampering with our minds, I need to find out. I need to know what's real. Let me check. I can't do it on myself, but I can help you remember."

Rick's eyes narrowed, his wolfish instincts coiling beneath the surface, and for a moment, we stood locked in a silent standoff. "You're playing with fire, witch," he warned, his voice low, almost a growl.

"Maybe," I said, feeling the surge of magic curling around my fingers. "But it's my fire to play with."

He hesitated, his expression twisting with a mix of concern and frustration. Then, with a reluctant nod, he stepped back. The wolves quickly moved to cover Aamon with a canvas tarp, shielding him from the sunlight, and snapped chains around him, thick metal links that would hold a rhino. Rick was prepared.

"Put him in the van," he ordered, eyes flicking to me, still wary but giving me the opening I needed.

I reached out with my magic, letting it slip between Rick's thoughts like a silken thread, feeling the familiar chill as our minds connected. The current of power that flowed was an intoxicating rush. But there was something else—dark, oily, like a cloud smothering his thoughts. Someone had been there, twisting things, planting seeds of distrust and confusion. I pulled back, my breath hitching as I severed the connection, and Rick's eyes widened, a spark of realization flaring in them.

"Damn it," he muttered, his hands running through his hair, as if trying to shake off the revelation. "Aamon wasn't the one who paid us to go to the Crossroads. It was that Logan kid you brought to the church. He wanted me to kill Aamon and get rid of any loose ends."

The world seemed to tilt, and I had to catch my breath. Logan. His name hit me like a punch, my heart clenching. Every tender moment, every whispered promise felt tainted, like a beautiful lie unraveling at the seams.

"I need to talk to Aamon," I said, my voice stronger, steadier than I felt inside. "I need him to find my mother. Vampires can track each other, and he might know where she is."

Rick's expression softened, and he took a step closer, his gaze searching mine. "Roxy, let me come with you," he said, his voice gentle, protective. "Something's going on, and I don't like it. I can't just stand by."

I looked at him, really looked at him, and for a moment, I saw past the sarcasm and bravado to the man who stood before me. In his mind, he truly only wanted to help. "Okay, Rick," I said, a hint of a smile tugging at my lips. "But we need to be smart. We can't do much until sunset. Where can we keep Aamon until then?"

Rick's lips twitched into a small, grim smile, a hint of mischief in his eyes. "There's an old shed down by the quarry. It's hidden, out of the sun. We'll take him there."

As we loaded Aamon into the van, the air felt charged, a dark tension crackling around us, like the calm before a storm. I could feel it, a sense of impending change, like everything was teetering on the edge, ready to tip over. Whatever was coming, it was going to alter everything I thought I knew. And deep down, I wasn't sure if I was ready for it, but I knew I didn't have a choice.

The shed at the quarry was suffocating, the air thick with dust, and the windows blackened to block out any trace of daylight. I could barely breathe in there, but I knew he was awake. Aamon. The vampire had somehow slipped out of his daytime slumber. My skin prickled as I stepped deeper inside, the creaking of the old wooden floorboards echoing through the silence. I wasn't sure what I'd find, but I had to see him.

I stepped forward, my heart pounding, trying to mask the shock in my voice. "How are you not asleep, vampire? As far as I know, your kind is catatonic during the day."

Aamon's lips curled into a smile, shattering the illusion of harmlessness. He shifted, the dim light from the opened door catching in his eyes, making them gleam like polished obsidian.

"Thank you for saving me," he said, his voice low and smooth, sliding over me like velvet. "I was following you. The sun was rising faster than I expected, and I planned to go underground, wait until nightfall. But then those damn wolves showed up, stopping me from helping you with Harper."

I folded my arms, trying to play it cool, but my stomach twisted. The way he said "saving me" sounded almost ... tender, like it held more meaning than he let on.

"You still haven't answered me. Why are you awake?" My voice was steady, but I could feel my pulse racing, betraying my calm facade.

Aamon leaned closer, his gaze never leaving mine. "Young vampires need to sleep during the day," he explained, his voice almost hypnotic, each word sinking deep under my skin. "They grow out of it, but it takes time. I'm old, Roxy. Very old. I don't need to sleep. I can go on for days before it catches up to me."

I remembered Harper's warning, her words echoing in my head. "She said vampires can track others if they're close enough. Is that how you found me?"

He nodded, his eyes darkening like storm clouds rolling in. "Yes. I wasn't tracking you, though. I was following Logan. I've been tracking him for a long time. He's been trying to break the curse, hunting for a witch powerful enough. When I followed him, he led me to you. At first, I thought it was a mistake. You didn't seem like someone who could break the curse. But then ... something changed. You changed. You shifted your perception at the Crossroads, and it amplified your power. You always had strength, but a choice can change everything. It can change futures, even the world. And I think you're one of those people."

His words pulled me in, drawing me toward him, closer than I knew was safe. There was a raw intensity in his gaze, something that made me want to look away but kept me rooted to the spot. Was he trying to manipulate me? "Are you trying to control me, Aamon? With ... desire?"

Aamon's smile faded, replaced by a look that was almost vulnerable. He stepped back, a small, sad smile tugging at his lips.

"No, Roxy. I'm not trying to control you, but I know I can't make you believe that. The truth is ... I desire you. I have since I started following you, long before the other night when we 'met'. I know it sounds ... unsettling. Even to mo. But when Logan led me to you, it was like waking up after a long, cold sleep. Sometimes, when you live as long as I have, you start to shut yourself off from everything. But you ... you were so alive. You couldn't see it before, probably can't see it now, but it's there. I see a fire in you. It sparked something in me, something I haven't felt in centuries."

I was torn. Caught up in his words, in the way his eyes held mine, like he could see everything I was trying to hide. I wanted to reach out, to touch him, but I had already been fooled once. Vampires messed with your mind. Is this real? I thought, a flicker of doubt gnawing at me. Or is he just messing with my head?

"I still don't know if I can trust you," I said, my voice barely above a whisper. I could see the muscles in his jaw tighten, but he didn't look away.

Aamon's expression softened, his tone gentle, like he was trying not to scare me off. "Trust isn't built in a day, Roxy. It takes time. I'll do whatever it takes for you to see that I mean no harm. What do you need from me?"

I hesitated. "I need to find my mother. Harper said she wasn't dead—that she'd been turned by a vampire. It's probably Logan who did it. It's probably some trap, another manipulation, but I have to help her. I can't just walk away without trying. Will you help me find her? Maybe ... that could be a start."

Aamon slowly stood, the tarp sliding off his shoulders, revealing the lean, predatory strength beneath. His presence filled the small space, making it feel even more claustrophobic. With a casual flick, he snapped the shackles the wolves had used to hold him, as if they were nothing.

"I can't help you until nightfall," he said, his voice dark, steady. "But I will."

I turned and left the shed, trying not to look like I was fleeing, but I was running from something. Rick was loitering outside, like he had all the time in the world.

"Can you keep an eye on Aamon until I get back?" I asked. "There's more to this than we know, and he isn't telling me everything. But right now, I can only deal with what I have. I need time. I'll be back by tonight."

"Sure thing, Roxy. Grabbing some shut eye?"

"Something like that."

"I'd ask if I could join—okay I am asking … is there any chance?"

I raised an eyebrow in answer.

"No? Fine. I understand. You look like you haven't slept in days. See you later."

I rode my motorcycle, the wind whipping through my hair, cutting through the chaos inside me. It was one of the few things that still felt real, that made me feel free. But it wasn't enough to clear my mind. When I finally reached my place, the apartment below the old video store, I let it all fall apart. The tears came, hot and blinding, as I faced the ugly truth—I'd been fooled. Used. Everything with Logan had been a lie.

I stumbled into the shower, still fully clothed, and let the hot water pour over me, the heat burning away the numbness until I could finally breathe.

"Quit being weak, Roxy," I whispered, voice cracking. "No matter what's happening, your life is still yours." I stripped off my wet clothes, let the water soothe my bruises. I could feel the bite on my neck where Logan had claimed me. I healed it, wiped it away, like it had never been there.

Afterward, I dressed and called Rick. "Hey, change of plan. Can you bring Aamon to my place? I want to start from here. I don't want to be anywhere near Logan when he wakes up. Be careful, okay? Aamon is stronger than you think."

"Yeah, Roxy, sure," he replied, his voice dropping into a sleazy tone. "And maybe you can give me a tour when I get there."

Even through the heartbreak, the anger, and the fear, I couldn't help but smile. Rick being Rick was a small comfort, a reminder that even when everything was falling apart, something could still make me laugh. I ended the call before he heard me giggle.

It was full morning, and Madge would help open the store soon; she always showed up early for our morning chats. I needed her calm, motherly presence more than ever.

Sitting cross-legged on my worn yoga mat, I tried to find some inner peace. The shop's big window gave me a view of the grimy parking lot, not exactly picturesque, but it was home. I closed my eyes, breathing deeply, grounding myself, imagining roots extending from me into the earth, solid and unbreakable. But it was hard to focus with Logan's betrayal still gnawing at my heart. The pain was raw, jagged, like a shard of glass lodged in my chest. I forced myself to breathe through it, repeating, You're stronger than this.

A flash of silver caught my eye, pulling me out of my meditation. I opened my eyes just in time to see Madge's sleek Tesla pulling into the lot. How she managed to afford that car was still a mystery to me, but if anyone could, it was her. She moved with effortless elegance and poise, even at her age. Dressed in a chic, emerald-green coat that matched her sharp eyes, she looked like she'd stepped out of a classic film. Madge wasn't just my boss; she was the closest thing I had to a mother.

"Roxy, darling," she said as she stepped inside, her voice warm and smooth, like honey as she opened a large box of 'breakfast'. "You can't let me eat these doughnuts by myself, you know." Her lips curved into a teasing smile then faltered. "Are you okay?"

I hesitated, but the moment our eyes met, the words started spilling out. I told her everything, about Logan and how he'd played me like a fool. I tried to keep my voice steady, but I could hear the tremor, could feel the betrayal seeping into every word. Madge listened quietly, nodding, her eyes softening. She didn't interrupt, just let me vent until I was practically gasping for breath.

"Oh, Roxy," she murmured, placing a hand on my shoulder. "Putting yourself out there is always a risk. You can't love without opening yourself to the possibility of getting hurt. But that doesn't mean you stop trying. You're strong, like me. Even when it feels like you're losing yourself, you can always find your way back."

She plopped down next to me, squeezing into my little meditation space, and handed me a doughnut from the box. "Scoot over," she said, nudging me playfully. We sat there, sharing pastries, watching the lot like it was some grand vista instead of a concrete wasteland.

"It's not exactly the Paris view I've heard so much about," I said, my voice shaky as I tried to laugh off the tears.

Madge smiled, her eyes twinkling. "I've been to Paris, and believe me, it's lovely. But I'd rather be here with you, dear."

The moment was interrupted by the distant roar of engines, shattering the quiet. A line of motorcycles cruised into view, followed by a beat-up black van that I recognized instantly. Rick.

His head poked out of the window, grinning in that cocky way of his. "Ladies, got a special delivery for Roxy," he called out, his voice carrying over the rumble of the bikes.

Madge raised an eyebrow, her lips curling into a smirk. "Seems like you've got quite the fan club," she teased. "You're a beautiful young woman, Roxy. Maybe it's time to just have a little fun. Stop giving your heart away so easily; it's okay to keep a piece of it for yourself."

I was about to argue when Rick hopped out of the van. With his rugged, blonde Viking looks, he was hard to ignore, and he knew it. He sauntered over, hands casually tucked in his pockets, and my cheeks flushed when I noticed Madge giving him an appraising look too.

"So, Roxy," he said, flashing that cheeky grin, "who's your hot younger sister? You might not want to go out with me, but maybe she will."

Madge laughed, a low, warm sound that seemed to make the morning a little brighter. "This one's trouble. But maybe that's just what you need—a little trouble without any strings attached." She polished off her doughnut, then winked at me. "Take care of yourself, darling. You don't need to keep the shop open if you're not up for it. Time heals everything, even if it's the biggest cliché."

As she walked away, Rick's eyes followed her, lingering a bit longer than they probably should have. "She's not my usual taste in women. But … I'd be into it."

I rolled my eyes, and I couldn't help but smile. "Rick, you're into anything that moves."

He turned back to me, smirking. "Only when it's as pretty as you, Roxy." Then he called over to the bikers, "Alright, boys, bring it out."

I blinked, squinting against the morning light as I saw them heave something heavy out of the back of the van. My heart skipped a beat when I realized what it was. "Rick ... is that a coffin?"

"Yeah," he said, completely nonchalant, like this was a normal part of his day. "You wanted Aamon, right? I work at the cemetery, Roxy. Coffins are kind of my thing."

I let out a groan. "Fine. Just bring him in, and make sure it's downstairs. No sunlight, you know that."

Rick's grin turned wicked as he stepped closer, leaning in just a little too close. "Are you finally going to give me that tour of your place, then?" His voice was low, teasing, but there was an edge to it that made my pulse race.

"Rick, just do what I said, and stick around after. We need to talk," I said, trying to sound firm but failing miserably. He was too close, his scent—cologne mixed with the faint smell of motor oil—clouding my thoughts. He gave me a look that made my stomach do a slow, lazy flip, like he knew exactly how flustered I was.

"You know, Roxy," he said, voice dropping to a whisper, "you talk too much. There are other ways to pass the time."

I swallowed, praying my cheeks weren't as red as my hair. For a moment, the world shrunk down to just the two of us, the space between us electric, like something was about to snap. I could barely breathe, caught between wanting to kiss him and shoving him away. But I knew one thing for sure—whatever happened next, that I was not ready for it. It was not going to happen. Things were too raw with me.

I took a deep breath, trying to hold my world together even though it was falling apart, piece by piece. "Rick, I don't know if you realize it, but last night everything I thought I knew got ripped to shreds. Logan ... he was manipulating my mind. Everything I felt for him, everything I thought was real, it was all a lie. And now, I'm left feeling like I don't even know what's real anymore. I get that flirting is just ... your thing, but this really isn't the best time. Besides, I know you're married."

Rick's gaze softened, his usual cocky grin replaced by a look of sympathy. "Roxy, I'd never push you into anything. You have to believe that. I live in a different world, one where ... well, sex is just always there, simmering under the surface. Being an alpha werewolf, it's not just in my head. It's in my blood. There's this constant pull—fight or make love. It's either one or the other, and it's always there, pushing, demanding. You might not understand, but as an alpha, I need to be with the alpha female. That's just how it's always been. Two alphas together, leading the pack. And for me, that's Drew."

He hesitated, as if he was searching for the right words. "I know how I come off—like I'm always looking for my next adventure. But Drew and I ... we're complicated. There's fire between us, yeah, but not love. We got married when she got pregnant, for the kids' sake, to show them what a family could look like. We agreed on it. It's not perfect, but it's what we thought was best. I know it sounds messed up, and maybe it is, but I'm not betraying anyone by flirting with you. Saying all this out loud, telling you this makes me realize how messed up my life is."

He laughed, but there was no humor in it, just a bitter edge. "Drew is a powerful wolf, beautiful," he added. "She's got more fire than I do, and that's saying something. When she's in heat, well, it's mind blowing. And the pack ... the pack needs their alphas to be together."

I tilted my head, studying him. "It's not really any of my business, but ... where is she? If you need her so much? I remember Drew in high school. She just seemed like a goth girl who was really into mushrooms."

He smiled, the corner of his lips quirking up. "She hasn't changed much. She's off near Seattle, on an island. Some pack asked for help with a mushroom farm, and they were willing to pay a lot for her expertise. She's been there for a while now, so it's just me and the kids. Sometimes I think those mushrooms have made her a little ... off. But you, Roxy, you've got a way of pulling things out of people. I've told you more about myself just now than I have to anyone since my dad died."

I blinked, not sure what to say. "I don't know, Rick. Maybe it's good to hear someone else's problems so I don't have to drown in my own. But staying with her just for the kids ... that can't be good for you, or for them. Not that I'm judging. I'm no expert on pack dynamics, or ...

whatever this is between you and me. But I need to ask you something, and I didn't think I'd ever say this: Will you stay today? I can't be alone with Aamon downstairs. If he starts messing with my head, making me do things I don't even realize.... I need someone to tell me, someone I can trust. And if you're not in the room, you'll still be able to tell, right? Werewolves have good hearing."

Rick's eyes darkened, but there was a warmth there, too. "Yeah, we hear things pretty well. But it's our sense of smell that's sharper. And yes, I'll stay. It's what an alpha does—protects the pack, the village. My dad taught me to be a good alpha, and that's what I try to be. I don't want to make you uncomfortable, and I'm sorry about whatever Logan did to you. But I can't promise I won't be hitting on you again in ten minutes. That's just who I am."

"Damn it, Rick," I muttered, torn between frustration and something warmer, something I didn't want to name. "If this were any other time, I'd admit I feel something for you. But it's not love. It's maybe lust. And right now, I'm way too messed up to even think about that."

Rick's grin was slow, wicked, full of a promise I wasn't sure I wanted to keep. "Don't worry, Roxy. You don't have to do anything. I'll do all the imagining for both of us."

10 Classic Movie Vampire Stuff

I spent most of the day with Rick. I don't think he went ten minutes without flirting with me in some way, tossing out cheeky comments and sly winks that kept me from sinking too deeply into my thoughts. I was grateful to him for sticking around and helping take my mind off Logan. It was strange, really. Rick had more depth to him than I would have imagined. Beneath the teasing grins and cocky demeanor, there was a softer, protective side. He wasn't as shallow as he seemed.

"So, yeah, DVDs, huh? Do people still rent these?" Rick said to me, raising an eyebrow as he twirled a movie case between his fingers. "Well, we've been here all day, and has anybody come in? No. Just a UPS guy looking for directions."

I chuckled, shaking my head. "That's a busy day around here," I replied, a hint of sarcasm in my tone. But then I got serious, my smile fading as I looked at him. "Thank you for today. Seriously. You've been a good distraction. But night's coming soon, and I'm going to have to go downstairs and talk to Aamon. We'll see what he can do to help."

Rick's expression changed, the playful glint in his eyes replaced with concern. "I'll be up here, Roxy. Just yell, and I'll be down there as fast as I can."

I hesitated, feeling a sudden warmth at his words. For all his jokes and bravado, there was something solid about Rick. Like he was someone I could lean on when everything else felt like it was crumbling. I gave him a small smile, trying not to let my nerves show. "I know. Thanks."

With a deep breath, I headed down to my little apartment below the shop. My heart thudded louder with each step, a mix of dread and anticipation coiling in my chest.

"Aamon, no funny business, I'm coming down," I called out, my voice echoing in the dimly lit stairwell.

When I reached the bottom, I looked around, but he wasn't there. Where the hell did he get to?

Then I noticed a darkness in the corner of the room, a shadow that seemed thicker than the others. Slowly, Aamon emerged from it, leaning against the wall like a desirable dream, his eyes glowing faintly in the low light.

"I wasn't eavesdropping, but I could hear everything upstairs throughout the day," Aamon said, his voice smooth and calm, a little too calm. "Rick seems like he could be a true friend, despite his shortcomings as a wolf and a lecher."

I rolled my eyes, trying to shake off the unease that his sudden appearance gave me. "Don't change the subject. I'm here to talk about you. I've had all day to think about it, and I'm wondering why, if you're so powerful, you haven't stopped Logan. You told me that trust is a delicate thing. Show me I can trust you. Why haven't you done anything about him?"

Aamon's eyes darkened, his smile fading as he pushed off the wall and took a step closer, the air around him seeming to grow colder.

"There are many things you may not know about … my kind," he said, his tone low, almost a whisper. "I'll try to enlighten you. While Logan is quite a bit older than you, he is a fledgling compared to me. Yet, he shows a great deal of power—the ability to fog minds, and a cunning I would not have expected from someone so young. I suspect there is an elder vampire behind him, and if I were to stop Logan, I would still have to deal with whoever is supporting him. That's why I'm following Logan. To find his master, the one who is helping him plan all this, and lending him power beyond what he should have."

He stepped even closer, until I could see the fine lines around his eyes, the way his lips barely moved as he spoke. "From my research, Logan has been here before. I believe he was the one who trapped Harper as a wraith, trying to break the curse even back then. I'm not sure why it didn't work, but I think Harper played a big part in stopping him. I gleaned most of this through the minds of others after the event. But much of it is second-hand."

I shivered and wrapped my arms around myself, trying to ward off the cold. "You've noticed I've been bitten by Logan, haven't you?"

Aamon nodded slowly. "Yes, and now he can sense where you are, and sometimes ... control you. I assume you haven't partaken of his blood? If you had, you could find him and, to some extent, control him in return. But I'm glad you haven't. There's no true bond between you two, and that's a good thing. I feel your anguish, and I am sorry. My kind can be ... cruel."

I swallowed hard, trying to push down the rising fear. "You said you'd help me find my mother."

"Night has fallen, and I can sense a few vampires in my range," Aamon replied, his eyes flicking towards the window. "I know you doubt me. What can I say to reassure you that I am not clouding your mind? All I can do is show you through my actions. I will seek out your mother, and the fastest way I can do that is if I change form. Don't be frightened. I cannot harm anyone when I change."

I watched as he stood there, his form blurring at the edges. He began to fade, turning into smoke, like an apparition—a misty, dark cloud that clung to the ground, swirling around my feet before creeping up the stairs like a ghostly fog. It was mesmerizing, in a haunting sort of way, and I couldn't help but feel a pang of fear as I followed it up to the shop.

When Rick opened the door to let the fog leave, he glanced at me, his eyes wide. "Did you know they could do that? That's movie vampire stuff, right?"

I managed a weak smile, even though my heart was pounding. "I don't know what I'm doing, Rick. I'm just bumbling my way through all of this."

Rick took a step closer, his hand brushing against mine. "Hey, you're doing your best. That's all anyone can ask for. And besides..." He gave me a lopsided grin. "I'm here to make sure you don't bumble off a cliff or anything."

I looked up at him, and for a moment, I wanted to say something, to tell him how scared I was, how much I felt like I was losing control. But the words stuck in my throat, and all I could do was nod.

"He said he'll be back shortly," I added, trying to sound confident, even though I felt anything but.

Rick's phone buzzed, slicing through the tense silence. He glanced at the screen, his jaw tightening as he read the message. He looked up at me, his eyes hooded with concern. "Damn it, Roxy. Logan knows what's going on. Apparently, he ambushed a few of the pack and dragged Timmy off. He's okay, in the hospital. He doesn't remember much, just that he was mind-raped by Logan, so Logan knows what's happening. I think maybe we should get out of here before he shows up."

The room suddenly felt smaller, the air heavy with the weight of what he was saying. I could almost feel Logan's presence, lurking in the shadows, just waiting to pounce. My heart raced, but I forced myself to stay calm, to focus. Rick was right—we needed to move, but I had to be honest with him.

I hesitated, swallowing hard. "Rick, there's something I have to tell you," I began, my voice softer, almost tentative. "Logan can probably find me no matter where I am. He's had my blood."

Rick's expression twisted, a mix of shock and disgust flickering across his face. "Ick. You know, I'm into some kinky stuff, Roxy, but sharing blood? Oh, that's beyond me." He tried to make light of it, but I could see the unease in his eyes.

I managed a weak smile, trying to shake off the cold dread creeping up my spine. "Well, I thought it was beyond me too, Rick. But ... it was mind-blowing." The words slipped out before I could stop them, a strange mix of confession and deflection.

Rick's lips curled into a smirk, his eyes twinkling with amusement. "If you don't want me to keep coming on to you, you've gotta stop telling me sex stories. It's not helping," he teased, though his voice was softer, almost comforting, before he reminded me: "We have to go. Now."

"Okay." We were in way over our heads.

We hurried toward the door, the urgency driving us forward, but before we could make it out, a deep, smooth voice echoed through the room, stopping us dead in our tracks. "No need. I'm back and can protect you from Logan. I've found where your mother is being held. She's on a farm."

I spun around, my heart leaping into my throat. Aamon stood in the doorway, his dark eyes fixed on me, the usual cool confidence replaced with a hint of something more—worry, maybe? My stomach twisted at the sight of him, a mix of relief and dread washing over me. He had come back, like he promised, but that didn't mean we were safe. Not yet.

"A farm?" I repeated, trying to keep the skepticism out of my voice. "Like ... an actual farm?"

"Yes," Aamon replied, his tone serious. "There's some sort of glamour around it. I didn't get too close, but

I believe there's Fae involved." His gaze locked on mine, and I could feel his presence; it was almost intoxicating.

Rick raised an eyebrow, glancing between Aamon and me. "Fae? So, we're talking magic, right? The kind that makes people disappear?"

"Exactly," Aamon said, his eyes never leaving mine. "It's not just a farm, Roxy. It's a trap. Logan knows you'll come for her, and he's counting on it."

The room fell silent, the weight of his words settling over us like a suffocating cloud. I could feel Rick's eyes on me, waiting for me to say something, to make a decision. But all I could think about was Logan—his eyes, the way he had looked at me, like he could see right through me. Like he owned me.

"We have to go," I said finally, my voice barely more than a whisper. "We have to get her out of there."

Aamon stepped closer, his hand reaching out to brush against mine, a small, reassuring gesture that gave me goosebumps. "We will," he murmured, his voice low, a promise. "But you need to be careful. Logan won't play fair."

"I know," I said, meeting his gaze, trying to draw strength from the intensity I saw there. "But I'm not afraid of him. He should be afraid of me."

Rick let out a low whistle, breaking the tension. "Well, damn. If that's not the sexiest thing I've heard all day, I don't know what is. I like strong women, Roxy. But seriously, let's get out of here before things get even weirder."

I couldn't help but smile at that, even as my heart hammered in my chest. "Agreed. Let's go."

We turned and headed for the door, ready to face whatever waited for us.

11 Surrender

The night was heavy with the smell of damp earth and a tantalizing hint of magic that wrapped around me, Rick, and Aamon as we crept toward the old farmhouse. The moon's pale light sliced through the mist, casting ghostly shadows that stretched and twisted over the gnarled trees, their branches like skeletal hands clawing at the dark sky. With every step that brought me closer, my pulse drummed with a dangerous mix of fear and determination. Somewhere inside, my mother was trapped, and I'd be damned if I let anything stand in my way.

The air was suffocating, as if the very land was holding its breath, waiting for something to snap. My crimson hair hung in damp, wild strands around my face and stuck to my skin. I cast a quick glance at Rick, drawing strength from his solid, reassuring presence. His broad shoulders moved with a predator's grace, blue eyes sharp and alert. With his long, blond hair pulled back, a neatly trimmed beard, and muscles straining against his shirt, he looked every bit the barbarian warrior. But it wasn't just his look; it was the way he moved—like he was ready to pounce at any moment. I felt a strange comfort in that, knowing he'd tear through anything that threatened me.

To my other side, a little too close for comfort, was Aamon. His dark eyes glinted with an intensity that made my stomach twist. He moved like a shadow—silent, graceful, and dangerous. I'd only known him for a short time, yet there was an undeniable pull between us, an electric tension that made my skin tingle. But I couldn't let myself fall for it. Not after Logan. Not again. That path led to heartache, to vulnerability I couldn't afford, especially tonight.

Aamon's lips curled into a teasing smile, as if he could sense my thoughts. "You're quiet tonight, witch. Nervous?" His voice was smooth, a dark whisper that seemed to wrap around me, heating my cheeks despite the chill in the air. It was infuriating how easily he could unsettle me, how he seemed to take pleasure in it.

"Focused," I snapped, trying to ignore the way his voice slid under my skin, tangling with my thoughts. "This isn't a social visit."

Rick let out a low growl, his eyes narrowing at Aamon. "Enough, bloodsucker. We're here to save her mom, not flirt." The tension between the two was palpable, their energies clashing, making the air hum with it. They'd clashed from the moment they met, and tonight was no exception. Whatever their issue, I didn't have time to play referee.

Aamon's smile widened, but his gaze shifted to the farmhouse, his expression turning serious. "Something's wrong. I can feel it." His voice lost its playful edge, replaced by a grim certainty.

I nodded, my senses tingling. The glamour surrounding the farmhouse was thick, layered like cobwebs, giving it the appearance of a rundown, abandoned building. But I knew better. Closing my eyes, I let my magic flow, peeling back the layers of deceit, each more intricate than the last, until the truth was laid bare.

The farmhouse shimmered, revealing its true form—dark and decaying, with twisted vines snaking up the walls like serpents. The windows were black voids, swallowing the moonlight. And beyond it, the standing stones pulsed faintly at the far end of the property, glowing with dark energy, arranged in a circle that felt like a snare waiting to snap shut.

The air shimmered, almost crackling. I turned and saw them—dark fairies, slipping from the shadows, moving with an eerie grace. Among them, a figure stepped forward, and I felt a chill. She was different, standing out even among the wicked, beautiful chaos of the fairies. Short, voluptuous, with a gothic edge that bordered on intimidating, she wore a black dress that clung to her form, adorned with silver chains that glinted under the moonlight. Her raven-black hair cascaded around her shoulders, framing a face that was both breathtaking and cruel. Dark, sharp eyes assessed me, and a slow, taunting smile spread across her lips.

I used my sight to reach into her mind and discover her name was Sable. The name felt wrong, like a curse that I wasn't meant to speak aloud. She was their leader—powerful, commanding, and dangerous. Every movement she made radiated a dark authority, and as her eyes met mine, I saw a glint of something predatory, like a cat toying with its prey.

"I suppose you're the one making all this noise," Sable said, her voice smooth and laced with a cold amusement. "Logan didn't mention how ... persistent you'd be." Her words were sharp, each syllable carrying a hint of mockery, and I could feel the threat behind them.

I clenched my fists, magic crackling at my fingertips, but she didn't flinch. She only tilted her head, as if daring me to make a move. "Logan hired you," I said, my voice steadier than I felt. "To hold my mother."

Sable's smile widened, but there was no warmth in it. "Oh, yes. But our agreement has ... limits. You see, Logan thought he could meddle with the Convergence, but he doesn't understand that it belongs to us. If he insists on playing with powers beyond his understanding, we'll have no part in helping him."

The Convergence. My mind raced, trying to piece together what she was saying. There was an alignment of magic that Logan was manipulating, and they planned to use it themselves. I didn't know what their endgame was, but I could sense Fae magic pulsing in the air, heavy and oppressive. It was like a web they had spun around us, a trap waiting to be sprung.

"If I'd shown up a moment later, you would've been gone," I said, trying to keep her talking, trying to buy time. "Why are you telling me this?"

"Because, little witch," Sable said, her voice dripping with disdain, "you're a danger to King Tristan's plans. He's very powerful and someone you do not want to upset—just in case you are ignorant of Fae politics, as I am certain a know-nothing like you is. Logan's antics threaten us, and we won't allow it. The spell on the supernaturals must remain intact. It keeps everything ... orderly. It ensures that when the time comes, the Convergence will be ours to use. Logan manipulated us, getting us to put your mother inside the standing stones, but you need to walk away. You won't have the ability to get past the traps. That's my 'friendly' warning. But if you die in the process, it suits me too."

I could feel the weight of her words, the danger embedded within them. If Logan's plan threatened their own, they would do whatever it took to stop him—including turning on him. But that didn't mean they were on my side. Not by a long shot.

"Consider this your one and only warning, Roxy," Sable said, taking a step closer, her eyes glinting with a cruel amusement. "We won't allow the spell on the supernaturals to be broken. And if you think you can disrupt the Convergence, you'll find yourself facing much worse than Logan."

She snapped her fingers, and the dark fairies began to slip back into the shadows, their forms flickering like flames extinguished. Sable lingered for a moment, her eyes boring into mine, as if she was reading every thought, every fear, every doubt. "You're out of your depth, girl," she said, her voice softening, almost pitying. "Walk away. While you still can."

With that, she turned, and the last remaining fairies followed, disappearing into the mist like they were never there, leaving me standing alone under the moonlight, my heart pounding. Sable's warning echoed in my ears, chilling me to the bone. Whatever Logan was planning, it wasn't just a threat to me—it was a threat to something far bigger, something I was only beginning to understand.

But I had no intention of walking away. Not now. Not ever.

The night was thick with mist, swirling around the dilapidated farmhouse in patches of moonlight. I narrowed my eyes as I scanned the scene ahead. Rick was beside me, his muscular frame tense, ready for action. Aamon lounged against a tree with unnerving calmness, his pale skin almost glowing, gaze flickering, as if seeing things we couldn't.

Ahead of us, ancient standing stones loomed, towering like silent sentinels, their presence pulsing with a quiet, thrumming energy. A faint shimmer flickered between the stones, a magical barrier that tasted the essence of anything that dared approach. I could feel the spell's touch, like a cold tongue on my skin, sampling the magical energies around it. I grimaced, pushing back against the intrusion.

"Whatever's guarding my mother in there, it knows we're coming," I muttered, my voice low and determined. "But we have to spring the trap if we're going to get her out."

Rick cracked his knuckles, a feral grin stretching across his lips. "Sounds simple enough. I say we go in and tear it apart."

Aamon's voice was a silky murmur, cool and detached. "It's never that simple, wolf. Logan used the fairies. This isn't brute strength—it's cunning magic."

I ignored their bickering, already stepping forward, my boots sinking slightly into the damp earth as I approached the barrier we needed to cross before we would reach the standing stones. "Stay close and be ready. Once we're in, it won't let us go easily."

As we crossed the threshold, the air crackled, and the shimmering veil snapped shut behind us. My heart pounded, but I kept my gaze steady. The mist grew thicker, coiling around our ankles, and then it began— the spell activated. From the mist, ethereal figures began to form, their bodies lithe and graceful, but unnaturally transparent. They had the sharp, angular features of fairies, their eyes hollow and glowing a faint, eerie blue. Each carried a long, ethereal sword that flickered with a dangerous light, like moonlight on the edge of a blade.

"Just what we needed," Rick grumbled.

Then a low, guttural snarl escaped him and echoed through the night. I saw his body contort, bones snapping and reforming in a blur of motion. He wasn't just a wolf—this was something ancient, primal, a hybrid of man and beast. His eyes burned with a wild light, and his form towered, muscles rippling under bristling fur. For a moment, I was breathless, caught between terror and awe at the transformation.

Focus, Roxy. What's in front of you? I told myself. "Ghost fairies with swords."

"They're not ghosts. They're projections," Aamon said, his lips curling in a faint smile. "But they can still kill you."

My hands tingled as I summoned my magic, a faint glow wrapping around my fingers. "Then we take them out fast, before they overwhelm us. Rick, you enjoy a frontal assault, so go for it. Aamon, you're sneaky, so slip around the side. I'll aim for the heart and deal with whatever spell is keeping them active."

Rick lunged forward, meeting the first of the ethereal fairies head-on. His claws raked through their misty forms, but they recoiled, reforming swiftly, their swords lashing out. One sliced across Rick's arm, leaving a deep gash that oozed dark blood. He snarled in pain but pressed on, tearing into another of the apparitions, his movements wild and furious.

Aamon darted around the side, a blur of motion. He struck with deadly elegance, using his speed to his advantage. Each time one of the fairies came at him, he slipped behind them, striking at their backs, disrupting their forms, if only momentarily. Yet, no matter how many times they scattered, the apparitions kept reforming, circling closer, as if driven by a single, relentless will.

My heart sunk at seeing how ineffective they were—what had we gotten ourselves into—but I couldn't let myself falter. I raised my hands, whispering an incantation, trying to unweave the spell that held the fairies together. The air around me shimmered, my magic fighting to push back against the ancient energies entwined in the spell, but it was slow work, too slow.

"Roxy!" Rick's shout made my head snap up. One of the apparitions had slashed deep into his side with a sword that was much more real than it seemed, and he was staggering, blood staining the ground beneath him. The sight of him, barely able to stand, sent a jolt of rage through me.

"No," I breathed, my voice shaking with fury. "You don't get to take him."

With a fierce cry, I thrust my hands forward, lightning-like energy blasting from my fingertips, striking the nearest apparition. The energy crackled around it, searing through its form, and it dissipated into nothing. I could feel the spell pushing back, resisting my efforts, but I didn't care. I pushed harder, my magic flaring brighter, hotter.

The air grew thicker, strangling, as the spell fed off my energy, trying to consume me. But I gritted my teeth and pressed on, my power surging. "You want magic? Take it," I snarled, my voice resonating with authority. I poured everything I had into the spell, letting my magic lash out, not just at the apparitions but at the threads of the enchantment holding them together.

The fairies began to flicker, their forms growing unstable, their movements jerky and disconnected. My vision blurred, but I didn't let up, channeling all my strength into unraveling the spell. Finally, with a deafening crack, like glass shattering, the enchantment snapped, and the apparitions dissolved into mist, fading back into the night.

I stumbled, catching myself before I fell. The air lightened, a breeze stirring the mist, the standing stones silent, as if the battle had never happened. But my heart ached as I turned to see Rick slumped against one of the stones, blood dripping from his wounds, his breathing ragged. He had transformed back to his human visage.

I rushed to his side, kneeling beside him, my hands glowing softly as I tried to staunch the bleeding. "Rick, hold on. We're not done yet," I whispered, my voice trembling. He managed a weak smile, his eyes barely open.

"Always knew ... you'd be the death of me, witch," he muttered, and I let out a shaky laugh, tears prickling at my eyes.

"Not today, you stubborn wolf," I said, my hands steady as I tried to heal him. "Not today." But I couldn't repair the wound, the ethereal fairies had done something. All I could do was stop the bleeding.

Silence fell, broken only by the sound of our ragged breaths. My knees wobbled, but I stood, trying to steady myself as I wiped Rick's blood on my jeans. Aamon watched me, his obsidian eyes hungry, no teasing smile, just raw, unguarded emotion. The moonlight cast shadows across his face, highlighting the sharp angles, the dark intensity, and I could see a lingering fear.

Tension filled the night again as Logan's clapping echoed through the eerie silence of the standing stones. My heart raced, the soft whispers of the wind around us turning into a deafening roar. I could hardly believe my eyes as the remaining mist dissolved, revealing Logan, a smirk dancing across his lips, as though he reveled in the chaos he had orchestrated.

"Roxy," he drawled, his voice dripping with mockery. "Things would have been so much simpler if you had just joined me, helped me break the curse. But if this is how it needs to be, so be it." His confidence was paralyzing, and before I could react, he shoved me into the circle of standing stones.

As I crossed the threshold, a surge of energy engulfed me. The air crackled with power, and I felt an invisible barrier rising around me like a cage. It was as if I had stepped into another realm, a dimension fraught with danger and despair. Spinning sensations clouded my mind, yet through the blur, I caught sight of Logan facing off against Rick, who stood defiantly, returned to wolf form and bristling with fury even in his bloodied and injured state.

"You won't stop this, wolf," Logan sneered, his eyes gleaming with malice. "I only need to keep you occupied for a short time."

At that moment, Aamon emerged from the shadows, a dark figure amidst the chaos. "What about me, little vampire?" he taunted.

But Logan was not alone.

A spectral form began to rise from the earth—a swirling mass of darkness that solidified into a hauntingly beautiful woman, her features both familiar and terrifying. Victoria. This was the vampire who had tormented my friend, Emily. The monster who had broken her.

"I've missed you, Aamon," she cooed, her voice an alluring whisper laced with malice. "It's been a long time ... or at least as far as you know. Clouding your mind has always been easy for me."

"Tar," Aamon said, as though some nightmare had come to life. "I thought you were dead."

"You hoped I was dead. I have been working unseen through my more reliable offspring. Logan has served me far better than you ever did."

"Wait a minute," I said, trying to take a step forward, but I couldn't. I was now trapped by some invisible force emitted by the standing stones. "I thought your name was Vicky. It's really Tar? And you're, like, Aamon's and Logan's ... what?"

Her gaze shifted to me, sharp and predatory, but she ignored my question and said, "Aamon, you must obey me. You will not help this red haired witch escape the trap. You will help Logan and I remove the curse. I am your master, and I demand you serve only me."

My mind raced as I watched Aamon struggle against her control, frozen in place, fists clenched, as he fought for control of his own actions. Tar, Vicky, whoever she was—she was his creator. I knew it was impossible for a vampire to resist their maker's orders. Just like that, he and Logan would be on the same side, no matter what Aamon wanted, it was outside his control.

The battle within him was palpable, and I felt a fierce determination surge through me. Whatever was to unfold hinged on my choices. I couldn't rely on him or anyone else.

Then, I caught sight of a figure lying on the ground— my mother. Pale, limp ... but as alive as a fledgling vampire could be. She was unconscious, bound by chains that glimmered ominously in the dim light, radiating a dark energy that seeped into the very air around us.

"Roxy," Harper's ghostly voice broke through the chaos of my thoughts, rasping and strained, pulling me from the depths of my worry to a new level of terror. "I am becoming the wraith ... I can't control myself. You should not have come here." Her words hung heavy, filled with sorrow and desperation as she materialized before me. First a misty white shape, then taking on a deep black shroud of fury. Before I could respond, she lunged at me, her smoky claws raking my skin, sending sharp pain coursing through me as blood trickled down my arm.

I fought back, summoning magic to contain her wraith form, for I couldn't touch her without it hurting me, draining me. Her enraged eyes flamed, her gaze bored into me, and it felt as if time stretched infinitely, the struggle dragging on like a cruel torment.

The only way to stop her from killing me was to break the anchor as I had before. But Tar and Logan wanted me to destroy this last anchor, to severe Harper's bond to the wraith that she had become. What would happen if I gave them what they wanted? I would be alive, but what then?

My intuition allowed me to know things my mind couldn't, and I knew that the anchor wasn't an object; it was this very place, the site of Harper's past, where she had once loved and lost. This was her last tie to the world of the living and the thing that bound her to her wraith form. I had the power to sever that connection easily. I hesitated.

Harper's ghostly fingers tightened around my throat, and I gasped for air, darkness creeping in at the edges of my vision. Desperation clawed at my heart, and my survival instinct betrayed me—I summoned all my strength, reaching deep within myself to sever the anchor.

The moment I did, Harper's form erupted in a tempest of sorrow and rage, her shriek piercing the air like a banshee's wail.

"No, Roxy! Now I have no free will. Logan can command me."

Logan approached with a cold smile, stepping over Rick's unconscious body, his power intense as he walked through the barrier of stones. "Harper, at last. This time, you'll do as I command. Enter the witch's body. Take her soul."

"No," I protested. I had given them what they wanted, but it still wouldn't save me. "Don't do this," I begged Harper.

I watched the struggle play out in Harper's ethereal eyes—anguish battled with a flicker of defiance.

"I'm sorry, Roxy. I must do what Logan says, but only to the letter," she whispered the last, suddenly turning away from me and toward my mother, whose form lay helpless at the center of the stones.

Magic surged, swirling around us like a tempest, knocking me to the ground as Harper entered her body.

I felt my mother's soul die: A shriek, then a sense of relief, a brush of her invisible lips on my cheek as she told me, "It's alright, child. You should be the one to live." Then the sense of her faded entirely. She was gone.

Tears welled, and a sob choked me.

"Always defiant, Harper," Logan mocked. "Why must I be plagued with women who think they are clever? But this doesn't stop my plans. Mother or daughter, whoever you take, I still command you. Take Roxy's power too, Harper. Drain her magic—we need all we can to break the curse."

A weight of despair crushed me as I stood there, my will to fight fading. I didn't move as Harper sadly reached out with my mother's hand. But it was not a comforting touch—it was more like the wraith's, cold and painful. I could feel my magic being siphoned away, like a candle snuffed out by the wind.

I turned my gaze toward Aamon, who was locked in a battle of his own. Tar, his master, had bitten into his throat. He could not even struggle as she drained him, feeding deeply, taking his blood and his life, leaving him pale and gasping.

"Roxy, I'm sorry," he croaked, his voice a whisper in the wind. "I can't help you."

Thinking of me, when he needed help as much as I did.

Tar released him, and his body crumpled. Her attention turned to me, cold and calculating as she said to Logan, "Stop. This is neither the time nor the place to break the curse. I've told you before, we can't do anything until the Convergence."

"Yes, Master," Logan replied, his voice dripping with disappointment even as he complied and told Harper to stop.

I gasped. I should be grateful to be alive, but despair filled me. It was a dark well I could not climb out of. I felt I might never feel warmth or joy again.

"Your power will return," Harper whispered to me. "Give it time."

"What of Roxy?" Logan asked.

Tar sneered, her disdain evident. "You wish to have her as a plaything? Fool. Witches are dangerous to keep as pets. They need to run wild, like wolves."

"You're letting her go?" Logan asked, surprised.

"I've lived a very long time. Never destroy all your options." Tar kicked my knee, knocking me to the ground, and dragged her claws toward my face. I raised my hand and felt a horrible pain as she cut deep gashes into my palm. More pain jarred through my skull as she kicked me again, and darkness blurred my vision. I teetered on the brink of unconsciousness, hearing their voices grow distant, until darkness overwhelmed me.

When I finally came to, the world was a hazy blur of shadows and dim light. I crawled over to Rick first, heart pounding as I checked for signs of life. He was breathing, but his wounds were grave. Panic surged through me, and I struggled my way towards Aamon, who lay still and silent. The dawn was creeping closer, and I couldn't let him perish in the sun, not after everything we had faced together.

With trembling hands, I pressed my bleeding palm to his lips, whispering, "Drink, damn it."

Time slowed as I felt his body respond, tightening around me as he began to feed. I felt something shift within me, a connection unlike anything I had experienced with Logan—a deep, consuming bond that surged through my veins, igniting every nerve ending in my body.

Darkness blanketed my mind again.

"Roxy, wake up. Damn it, you need my blood," Aamon urged, his voice a shaky whisper, laced with desperation. "Drink."

I smelled the tang of blood, but I saw that the bleeding from my palm had stopped. The wound was licked clean, and my skin was deathly pale. Aamon had fed on me, and my heartbeat felt sluggish. I felt paper thin. First drained of magic then of life's blood. There was nothing of me left.

"I don't think you'll make it if you don't drink," Aamon insisted. "But I won't force you. It has to be your choice."

As the sun spread red on the horizon, and pale blue light began to wash out the starlit sky, I knew I wouldn't surrender, not to Logan or the darkness that threatened to consume us.

I had fought too hard, endured too much. With renewed determination, I made my decision. I wouldn't give up. I bit down on Aamon's neck, over the wound Tar had left, feeling the rush of his blood flood my senses, intertwining our fates in a way I could never have anticipated. I was ready to embrace whatever came next, no matter how difficult the path ahead might be.

12 Whirlwind

"I'll put Rick in the van, but I need to go," Aamon said, his voice calm but with an edge of urgency. "The sun's coming up. I'll head back to your place. You've had my blood, so you'll probably need to sleep during the day, at least for today. Things will balance out. Just be quick getting home."

As his body began to fade, shadows curling around his form, smoke rose from the ground like tendrils reaching up to claim him. And then—no joke—he turned into a bat. An actual bat, wings snapping out wide before he soared up into the dawn sky. I watched, jaw slightly slack, until he was just a dark smudge against the lightening horizon.

"Well, that just happened," I muttered to myself, still half-expecting to wake up and find this was all some bizarre fever dream.

But no. Everything was sharp, clear, like I'd stepped into a world that was more real than real. My senses were on overdrive; I could smell the faint scent of rain that hadn't even touched the ground yet, the musk of the leather seats, and the metallic tang of Rick's blood. And the colors... wow. They were more vivid than I'd ever seen. The oranges and blues of the sky looked like an oil painting come to life, swirling and blending. I'd never done drugs, but this had to be what it was like, that euphoria, that rush. Everything was so vibrant, so intense, and I felt ridiculously strong. Guess that's what happens when you drink vampire blood.

I slid into the driver's seat, my muscles taut, like they could bend steel if I really wanted to, and started the engine. The rumble felt like a heartbeat under my fingertips. Reaching into the glove box, I found Rick's phone and dialed 'Home', half expecting one of his goons to give me attitude.

"This is Roxy. You need to come pick up Rick. He'll be at my place. He's been hurt, so you'll need to get him to a hospital or something just to be safe. But he should be fine; I've healed him," I said, my voice sounding steadier than I felt. There was a pause on the other end, then a grunt of acknowledgment. I hung up before they could ask questions.

As I drove, the sky shifted to a paler blue, and the yellow sun started to peek over the horizon. With it came a wave of exhaustion, like someone had flipped a switch inside me, and all the strength I'd felt a moment ago was slowly draining away.

"Keep it together, Roxy. You're almost home," I muttered, gripping the wheel tighter, my knuckles turning white. Every blink felt heavier, my vision blurring at the edges.

I pulled up to my place, the engine ticking softly as it cooled. I glanced over at Rick, still slumped in the passenger seat, his breathing shallow but steady. With a sigh, I forced my legs to move, stumbling out of the van and making my way to the door.

Aamon was already there, leaning against the frame, his dark eyes watching me. "Roxy," he said, his voice low and smooth, "when you share blood with a vampire, sometimes you pick up certain things they deal with—like needing to sleep during the day. It should only last a little while. I've never fed on a witch before, and now I'm starting to see and feel things differently than I ever have. So, the bond goes both ways. Let me help you to your room."

He slid his arm around my hips, and I almost melted into his touch. My skin was hypersensitive, every brush of his fingers against my side sending sparks skittering across my nerves. We made our way down the stairs, the world around me a blur of light and color, everything so vivid it was almost too much. The exhaustion clawed at me, and when I collapsed onto my bed, it was like sinking into a cloud, soft and cool against my skin. Aamon's presence lingered beside me, a steady warmth in the swirling haze.

"I'll keep an eye on you," he murmured, his voice distant, yet close enough to feel like it was echoing in my head. "Everything will be fine by nightfall."

I was lost somewhere between sleep and waking, the world around me shifting and shimmering. It was like I was floating, drifting in a sea of warmth. My bed felt like silk beneath me, cool and slick against my bare skin, and I was alone ... but not really. I could feel him. Aamon.

His presence was electric, crackling along my nerves. I knew it was a dream, but this one felt more vivid, more consuming, than anything I'd experienced before. I tried to fight it, to pull myself out, but I was drawn to him—like a moth to a flame, like the tide to the moon.

He appeared at the foot of my bed, his dark hair falling in soft waves over his alabaster skin. His eyes, almost black in the shadows, pierced through the fog of my mind, holding me captive. He was unbearably beautiful, and the way he looked at me took my breath away, as if he could see through me, to every secret, every desire I tried to bury deep inside.

"Roxanne," he whispered, and my name sounded like a promise on his lips, dark and sweet. He moved closer, and I could feel the heat of his body, even through the thin veil of the dream. My breath hitched, and I tried to speak, but the words died in my throat as he slid his hand up my leg, leaving a trail of fire in its wake.

"This isn't real," I murmured, trying to convince myself, but the way he touched me made it hard to believe anything but the heat between us.

"Does it matter?" he asked, his voice low, seductive, as he leaned down, his lips ghosting over mine. "I can feel how much you want this. How much you want me."

I wanted to deny it, but my body betrayed me, arching up to meet him, seeking out his touch. His lips brushed against mine, teasing, tasting, and when I opened my mouth to protest, he deepened the kiss, slow and possessive. I melted into him, my hands tangling in his hair, pulling him closer, until there was no space left between us.

The world around us disappeared, leaving only the sensation of his skin against mine, his hands exploring every inch of me. It was like he knew exactly where to touch, how to make my body sing, and I was powerless to stop him. I didn't want to stop him. And I knew it was just a dream, so I embraced it.

When he pulled away, I whimpered at the loss, but he only smiled, a wicked glint in his eyes. He murmured, trailing kisses down my neck, my collarbone, lower still. "It was just a matter of time."

I moaned softly, my fingers gripping the sheets as he kissed his way down my body, his hands cupping my hips, holding me steady as he worshipped me with his mouth. It felt so real, every touch, every kiss, and I gave myself over to the pleasure, drowning in it, losing myself in him.

When I woke, I was panting, my skin flushed, my heart pounding in my chest. For a moment, I thought it had been real, but then I saw him—Aamon, sitting casually in the chair by my bed, watching me with that same intense gaze.

"I'm sorry, Roxy," he said, and there was a hint of regret in his voice. "The dreams come with sharing blood. I didn't mean to ... influence them. It's just a natural thing between a vampire and its... lover."

I felt a flash of anger, mixed with embarrassment. "I'm not your lover," I snapped, my cheeks burning. "That didn't really happen, you know."

He didn't look away. "Of course not, Roxy." But there was something in the way he said it, a glint of amusement, like he knew something I didn't.

I realized then, with a sinking feeling, that he had been there with me. He had experienced the dream, every touch, every kiss, right alongside me. My face turned scarlet, and I turned away, hiding my blush behind a curtain of red hair.

I vowed to myself, right then and there, that I wouldn't let this happen again. No matter how intoxicating it was, no matter how he made me feel.

But as I glanced back at him, at the way he was still looking at me, like he was hungry for more, I wasn't sure if it was a promise I could keep.

Aamon said, his voice soft, "The sun's setting, Roxy."

I blinked, trying to shake off the grogginess.

I frowned. "How long is this going to last?

The air was thick with tension, a mixture of dread and anticipation that tingled beneath my skin. Aamon's presence was as commanding as the storm brewing outside. He shrugged, his dark hair falling across his forehead, and I couldn't help but notice the way his eyes—ancient and unreadable—held mine captive.

"It's different for everyone," he began, his voice low and steady, like the rumble of distant thunder. "Usually, you'll have trouble staying awake during the day. And you'll share experiences through the small connection that we share now. The most disturbing part for you will probably be feeling a hunger for others—not just sexual, but a need to feed on them. Don't worry. I'll be here to make sure you don't harm anyone. It'll pass. You're not truly a vampire, you're just feeling what I feel. I have never experienced it go beyond a few weeks, but with you it seems to burn hot, and it probably won't last as long as that. A few days perhaps."

I frowned and crossed my arms in defiance. Then I snorted, incredulous. "A mere few weeks? Let's get one thing straight—we're not actually going to sleep together. You can invade my dreams, but not my real life."

His expression shifted, becoming serious, and I felt the weight of his gaze. "I have no intention of forcing you to do anything you don't want to, but I need to know—are you going to try to stop Logan? If you are, I'll help. If not, I must leave. I need to stop him and Tar from using Harper to break the ritual."

My heart raced at the mention of Logan. "Of course, I'll try to stop them. I just have no idea how."

He nodded, a hint of approval in his eyes. "The ritual won't happen here in the U.S. It'll be somewhere in Europe, where the original curse was created. I've narrowed it down to a location near my castle in Ireland."

I gaped at him, my mind racing. "Wait, you have a castle in Ireland? Are you rich or something?"

A small smile tugged at his lips, softening the sharp angles of his face. "When you've been around as long as I have, you accumulate wealth. It means little to me, except that it allows me to isolate myself. I was hoping you'd assist me with Logan. My ... servant should be arriving soon. Although, I guess you might call her my personal assistant. Terminology changes so quickly."

"Fine," I said, my voice edged with urgency as I grabbed a few essentials. "Go upstairs. I need a minute alone."

As I rummaged through my drawers, my mind raced with possibilities. Ireland? What was I doing? A passport? I didn't even have one! "Aamon, I don't have a passport! How is this even going to work?" I yelled, my voice echoing off the walls.

"I've already informed Brianna about you," he called back, his tone casual as if he seemed to float through the chaos. "She had me take a photo of you while you slept. It's for documentation, I'm sure."

I stomped up the stairs, indignation bubbling within me. "You know, it's kind of creepy to take photos of a woman while she's sleeping." But as I paused, laughter bubbled up. "What am I talking about? We just had a sex dream together, and I'm worried about a photo?"

Before he could respond, a loud noise filled the air, shaking the very foundation of the shop. I raced to the front, heart pounding, just in time to see a sleek helicopter descending into the parking lot, its blades slicing through the air with a ferocity that matched my growing anxiety.

"You have a helicopter?" I shouted over the cacophony, my voice tinged with disbelief.

"It's not mine," Aamon replied, completely unfazed by the spectacle. "I'm renting it. Well, Brianna is. And technically, you're not supposed to land them just any-where."

"By the time the authorities get here, we'll be gone," he added, almost as an afterthought. "Also, Rick's okay. One of the pack came by and said he's fine. The ethereal blades are especially painful for werewolves. He'll heal, eventually. Wolves are tough."

As the helicopter door slid open, a woman emerged, her business suit contrasting sharply with the chaotic scene. She looked like a sun-drenched surfer chick who'd just wandered into a boardroom, exuding an air of confidence that was both disarming and intimidating.

"Hello, I'm Brianna," she introduced herself, her voice laced with a beautiful Irish accent. "And I think we should leave before the authorities show up."

I grabbed my bag, still processing the whirlwind of events, and followed Aamon toward the chopper. "So, we're taking this thing all the way to Ireland?"

"There's no airport near where you live, but there is one a few hours from here. We'll fly there, then take Aamon's jet," Brianna explained, her tone brisk and effi-cient.

I raised an eyebrow, trying to mask my disbelief. "You've got a jet too? Did you rent that as well?"

"No," Aamon interjected, a smirk playing on his lips. "I own that one."

As I climbed into the helicopter, the reality of what lay ahead settled around me like a heavy cloak. I was about to embark on a dangerous journey alongside a man whose very essence was shrouded in mystery. Beneath it all, I felt the flicker of something daring and intoxicating—a thrill that made my heart race faster than the helicopter blades overhead.

The trip was beautiful. Loud, even with the noise-canceling headphones I had on, but still, there was something almost peaceful about it. The drone, the rhythmic sway—it was like a lullaby, coaxing me into a rare moment of calm. Guess I'm not afraid of heights after all. Or maybe it was the thought of leaving everything behind, even just for a while, that made everything seem less daunting? The sense of adventure I'd always craved but never had the guts or the money to chase.

When we landed at the airport, there was a delivery service waiting for Brianna. She moved with confident grace, striding over to a uniformed courier who handed her a package. She signed for it without hesitation, a mysterious little smile playing on her lips as she headed my way.

"This is for you, Roxy," she said, handing the box over.

I took it, eyeing the sleek, black shape suspiciously. "What is it?"

"It's your passport and some other things."

I blinked, feeling the weight of it in my hands. "How did you get something like that so quickly? It's been, what, half a day? Is this a forgery or something?"

"No, Roxy," she said with a knowing smirk, clearly amused by my naivety. "A lot of things can get done quickly if you have a great deal of money. Normally, applying for a passport takes weeks, sometimes months. But I work with a man who handles these things. He has contacts. I pay him well, and it gets done fast. All above board. It's a real passport. You've even got visas to a few places in Europe for a vacation trip. Plus, I got the full package. You've got a new driver's license and a credit card with a couple thousand on it. And before you look at me like that, no, this isn't about buying you off. When you travel, you need a little money to get by, and ... well, I took a look at your bank account, and 'dismal' doesn't even begin to describe it. My fixer was able to access your social accounts to get photos of you. The photo that Aamon took was kind of funny. Your eyes were closed, and you were sleeping."

I sighed because she wasn't wrong. If I didn't have a place to crash below the video shop, I'd probably be homeless. Money had never really been my thing. Even now, the thought of being handed this kind of luxury felt heavy, like I didn't quite deserve it. But Brianna's eyes didn't waver. She wasn't backing down.

"Don't we have to go through immigration or something to leave the country? Isn't that how this works?" I asked, still feeling a little lost.

"Yes and no," she said, shrugging like it was no big deal. "Where money can't buy you something, a touch of glamour can. We rented a hangar for the jet. It should be ready to leave shortly."

Jet. The word alone was enough to snap me out of my daze. I'd seen them in movies, but to actually be flying on one? It was surreal. When we finally reached it, the sight of the sleek, black craft waiting under the lights made my heart skip. It was beautiful in a way that felt almost forbidden, like touching something you shouldn't.

A man, who I assumed was the captain, greeted me at the bottom of the ladder wearing a crisp uniform and an easy smile. "Welcome aboard. Get comfortable, and we'll be taking off soon. My co-pilot, Susan, will also be attending to you. Still heading toward Ireland, I suppose? The weather's looking rough, but we'll try to get there before things get shut down."

"Do flights usually get canceled for that?" I asked, trying to keep the nervousness out of my voice. "Can't you just fly through rain?"

"Major airlines, sure. They can usually land through just about anything. But with a smaller craft like ours, sometimes we'll get waved away and have to wait until it clears up. Hopefully, that won't be a problem, but it's a long flight. We'll see. I'll keep you informed."

When I finally boarded, the interior was nothing like I expected. There was a softness to the space, a mix of warm leathers and polished wood that made it feel like stepping into a penthouse rather than a plane. The faint smell of leather and freshly cut flowers in vases attached to the tables added to the air of luxury. There weren't a lot of seats, but what was there was ridiculously plush, like they were designed to sink into and never leave.

"It seems smaller than I expected," I commented to Brianna, trying to sound nonchalant even as my eyes widened at the sleek surroundings.

She just grinned. "Oh, there's a room in the back. This plane was made for Aamon. Take a look around before we take off."

I wandered down the aisle, letting my fingers brush against the smooth surfaces, feeling like a child in a candy store. I found a bathroom that was way nicer than the one I had at home, with dark tiles and a mirror that didn't make me cringe when I looked at it. At the end of the seating area was a door leading to a room in the back of the plane with an actual bed, dressed in silk sheets that gleamed under the soft lighting. And at the foot of it? A coffin.

I was never going to get used to this. The sight of it was enough to make my skin prickle as I tried to process the incongruity of it all. Just as I was trying to wrap my head around it, Aamon appeared behind me, too close for comfort. His presence was like a shadow, dark and compelling, the air around him seeming to hum with energy.

"If you need to sleep, please, take the room," he said softly, his voice low and smooth, like honey poured over ice. I could practically feel the tension between us, a taut string pulled tight, ready to snap.

"I shouldn't be so angry at you," I admitted, almost to myself. The words slipped out before I could stop them, my voice barely more than a whisper. "You're not Logan. You didn't hurt me the way he did. I'm sorry I've been so mad at you. You've only ever tried to help me, as far as I can tell."

Aamon's eyes darkened, the storm in them seeming to swirl with something I couldn't quite place. He stepped closer, and I could feel the warmth radiating from him, his lips curving into a sad, almost bitter smile. "You don't have to apologize, Roxy. I'm not here to replace him, or to make you forget. I just ... want you to be safe. To be free. If that means stepping back, I'll do it."

I felt a pang in my chest, an ache I hadn't expected. The words were so simple, yet they carried a weight that made it hard to breathe. He reached out, his fingers brushing a strand of hair behind my ear, lingering just a moment too long, and I caught the faint scent of cinnamon and something else that I could not place, but it was intoxicating.

He stepped back, his eyes never leaving mine, and for a moment, the world seemed to narrow down to just the two of us, suspended in that strange, charged silence. And then, as if realizing he was so close to me and intimately touching me, he said, "Get some rest, Roxy. It's going to be a long flight."

I nodded, but even as I turned to head back, I could still feel his eyes on me, and I couldn't help but wonder if there was more to his words than I'd realized.

13 City of Lights

The hum of the jet engines was a low, soothing murmur, but it couldn't drown out the remnants of my dream. I blinked awake, groggy and disoriented, the slick leather seat crinkling beneath me as I shifted. I glanced around, taking in the luxurious cabin—the polished mahogany, the soft lighting, and the glass of half-empty wine on the table beside me. Who was I kidding? Half empty glass of wine? It probably would have been two or three glasses. I lost count. I hadn't drunk in days, but apparently, I was still a bit of an alcoholic. My pulse thrummed in my ears, and I knew it wasn't just because we were thirty thousand feet in the air. No, this was thanks to the vivid, all-too-real fantasy that had dragged me under just moments ago.

Aamon. Those dark, predatory eyes, that smile—wicked and knowing. Heat flushed through me just thinking about him, about the way his hands had felt on my skin in that dream. Damn it, not again. I pressed my lips together, trying to stifle the tingling sensation that still lingered in my body. Part of me wanted these dreams to stop; another part ... well, that part wasn't willing to admit anything just yet. Not that I'd ever let Aamon know, of course.

I was jolted from my thoughts by the sound of footsteps, and the pilot appeared at the front of the cabin, a nervous smile on his lips. "Miss Roxy, Mister Aamon," he addressed us, glancing at both of us briefly. "I'm afraid we've encountered a storm over Ireland. We need to re-route—either to London or Paris."

I sat up straighter, my heart leaping at the unexpected opportunity. "Paris. We have to go to Paris!" The words burst out before I could think twice. I could feel Aamon's gaze on me, his lips quirking into an amused grin.

"Paris would be fine," he said, chuckling softly. "How long will we be delayed there?"

"At least a few hours," the pilot responded. "We could circle, but we'd eventually need to refuel. It's best to head to Paris now."

Aamon's assistant, who was sitting a few rows ahead, turned and added, "We should be landing just after sunset. Roxy, you could check out Paris for a bit."

I caught Aamon's gaze, and he raised an eyebrow, as if daring me to say no. "Looks like I'll be your tour guide then," he said, leaning back with a lazy smile. "I haven't been to Paris in a long time. What I found most intriguing when I was there before was walking beside the River Seine and letting the City of Lights unfold before me. That's how you truly experience the beauty of the place."

The way he said it, low and smooth, made my breath catch. For a moment, I forgot where I was, the dream of Aamon still fogging my senses, now mingling with the allure of this dark, mysterious vampire beside me. Aamon was right—Paris had to be experienced, and I had the sudden, thrilling feeling that this night might test my resolve against being with another vampire.

After we landed, Aamon took the lead, guiding me off the plane and toward a sleek, black limousine waiting just beyond the tarmac. The darkened windows gleamed under the airport lights, a promise of shadows and secrets within. "Shall we?" he said, opening the door with a flourish.

I hesitated for a second, staring out at the glittering metropolis in the distance, before slipping inside. Whatever Paris had in store for me tonight, I was ready to let it unfold. The limousine glided through the streets, the city lights flickering like stars just for us. Everything felt surreal, as if the entire city had conspired to set this perfect scene. Aamon sat across from me, his dark, ancient eyes shimmering with that familiar, timeless charm. The way he carried himself, with an air of elegance that didn't quite belong to this era, always fascinated me. He was from another time—one that still lingered in his every word, every look.

When the car finally came to a gentle stop near the Seine, Aamon was out before I could even adjust my dress. He moved with a grace that was almost unnatural, a smoothness that belied his strength. There he was at my door, his hand extended, a small smile playing on his lips.

"Accompany me, my lady, on this beautiful evening," he said, his voice dripping with that old-world charm. It was like he had stepped out of a forgotten novel, the kind you'd curl up with on a rainy afternoon. Silly or not, it worked on me. I took his hand, feeling that electric spark shoot up my arm, a jolt of something familiar yet thrillingly new.

I let him lead me, and we strolled along the river. Paris at night was a different world—soft, romantic, and full of secrets. Aamon started talking, his voice low and smooth, sharing stories from the distant past. He spoke of the Paris he knew, centuries ago, when cobblestone streets were lit by gas lamps and the air was thick with poetry and revolution. Even though I knew these stories were well-worn memories for him, there was a wistfulness in his tone, like he was savoring each lost moment.

As we walked, he pointed out spots he once frequented, now a little rough around the edges but still with that undeniable charm. A small café here, a bridge there, a hidden alley, where he claimed to have seen the start of dawn after a long night of debauchery. I could almost see it, this version of Paris he was painting for me—a Paris of velvet cloaks, secret rendezvous, and whispered confessions.

We talked, and it felt easy, natural, as if the night was carrying us along with it. But there was also something underneath, a tension that buzzed between us. I couldn't ignore it forever, even though part of me wanted to.

"Oh, quit trying to put on the charm," I teased, nudging him with my shoulder. "I see right through you."

His lips curled into a smirk. "Do you, now?" he asked, his tone playful. But there was a flicker in his eyes, something dark and unreadable, that made my heart skip a beat.

We continued our stroll, but then something shifted inside me, deep and intense. I tried to brush it off, but the feeling grew stronger, until I couldn't ignore it any longer.

"Aamon, I'm feeling ... this weird craving. Predatory, almost." The words tasted strange on my tongue, foreign and frightening.

He stopped, and the playful mask he had been wearing fell away, replaced by something far more serious. "I warned you about this, Roxy," he said softly, his voice like a caress. "With our bond, you're feeling my hunger. I haven't fed in a while, and when I gave you my blood, it drained me. I need to feed soon. It's not something I wanted you to see, but it's a part of who I am, and you'll have to accept it."

I swallowed hard, trying to process his words. We kept walking, but there was a tension now, like the air was charged with electricity. Aamon's tone grew more strained, as if he was fighting to keep control. "The reason you're feeling that predatory urge is because, for a while now, we've been followed—by a few men who mean no good."

I felt my pulse quicken, and before I could ask him to explain, two figures emerged from the shadows, trying to corner us. My heart leaped into my throat, but Aamon was already moving, faster than I could track. In a blur, he had them both subdued, his hands gripping one of them, his eyes glowing with a dark, predatory light. I watched, frozen, as he fed, his lips brushing against the man's neck, the other man held firm in his grip. The sight was both terrifying and strangely hypnotic. And I felt it too—the same urge to take, to feed. It was like a hunger gnawing at me from the inside, a dark, insistent craving that I didn't want to understand—just indulge.

I crept forward, but then Aamon released the men and pulled me back, holding me tight against him.

"You're not a vampire, Roxy; you're just feeling what I feel," he whispered, his voice almost gentle despite the situation. "This is my life, how I choose to feed. Unlike many others, I seek out those who prey on others and make them my prey. My conscience is clearer that way. These men... they've done horrible things. Feel it, Roxy. Use your mind and sense what they've done—they are monsters."

Tentatively, I reached out with my mind, like he said, and it was like stepping into a dark, cold place. I could feel the shadows clinging to them, the awful things they had done, and it made me shiver.

Aamon's voice brought me back, grounding me. "When I feed, I try to give something back. In this case, I'm going to implant something in their minds: if they ever harm anyone again, they'll feel the pain and suffering they inflict on others, magnified many times over. It won't change who they are, but it might stop them."

I felt a strange mix of emotions—fear, confusion, and a bizarre kind of admiration. "If you don't usually feed on people like this, then how do you feed?" I asked, my voice barely a whisper.

Aamon's eyes softened, and for a moment, he looked almost vulnerable. "I find people seeking connection," he said, his gaze distant, as if he was seeing something far away. "Those looking for companionship, or simply someone to listen. I feed on them, then clear their memories of the event, but I try to leave something positive behind. I might make them feel worthy, as if they can do more with their lives. Sometimes, I leave them money or give them the courage to walk away from a harmful relationship. In rare cases, I might step in and remove the real monster in their life."

He paused, and there was a weight in his eyes that I hadn't seen before, a somberness that made my heart ache. "Don't misunderstand, Roxy. I've done dark, evil things that weigh on my conscience. But every day, we choose to walk in the light or embrace the darkness. Living in the dark, I try to bring a little light to others."

I didn't know what to say to that. I could feel the truth in his words, the conflict that raged within him. So I just squeezed his hand, letting him know I understood. Even if I didn't fully, I wanted to. And for now, maybe that was enough.

We left the muggers, implanted with new memories and compulsions to do better, behind us like memories of a past life, as Aamon and I continued our romantic walk by the river in Paris, hand in hand.

"We'll take a bit of a sidetrack," he said, his voice smooth as velvet, wrapping around me like a warm embrace. The sound of the Seine lapping against the stones whispered secrets of the city, and I felt a flutter in my chest, a wild mix of anticipation and trepidation. "There's a place that I want you to see, a place that meant a great deal to me for a long time when I was here in the past."

I realized I was still holding his hand, and despite the hurt Logan had caused me, this felt right. The feel of Aamon's cool fingers intertwined with mine ignited something I thought had been extinguished. I searched my mind, wondering if Aamon was clouding it, manipulating my emotions. But I could tell he wasn't. Now that I knew what to look for, I was sure. This was my truth—crisp and vibrant, like the cool night air that tinged my cheeks.

After a shortcut through an alley of cobblestones, we arrived at a breathtaking view of Notre Dame church. The gothic architecture loomed before us, a magnificent silhouette against the star-studded sky.

"Come with me, Roxy; let me show you the wonders inside," he urged, his dark eyes alight with something more than just desire—something deeper.

I hesitated, a thought creeping in. "Isn't it strange that you can go into a church? You're a vampire." The words slipped out, fueled by a lingering caution.

Aamon smiled, his eyes gleaming with warmth that dispelled the chill of doubt. "Many things that people believe about us are true, but others are misunderstood. A church is a public place. Everyone who needs to be there is invited. Why would I be any different?" His words resonated with me, weaving a tapestry of understanding that calmed the storm within.

As we walked toward Notre Dame, the lights cast a warm, golden glow over the river, illuminating the path beneath our feet. I marveled at the intricate architecture, the towers rising majestically against the starry sky, each stone whispering stories of love and loss. Inside, the air was cool and hushed, filled with a sense of reverence. The stained-glass windows glowed like jewels, each one telling a story of love, sacrifice, and faith.

One window depicted a couple I imagined were in a tender embrace, their faces illuminated by the soft colors of the glass, echoing the warmth I felt in Aamon's presence. Another window showed an angel, wings spread wide, bathed in brilliant blues and greens, as if guarding the space with pure love. I could almost feel their ethereal touch brushing against my heart.

As Aamon recounted his memories in this sacred place, I was deeply moved. The connection we shared felt profound, electric, crackling between us like the first spark of a flame. In that moment, lost in the beauty of our surroundings and the intimacy of our shared silence, I decided to kiss him.

Our lips met softly at first, an exploration, a question. But as the kiss lingered, it deepened. I felt a rush of desire as our tongues intertwined—more erotic than I had expected, igniting the embers of a passion I had buried deep within. But I had decided long ago to start living, to let go of the chains that bound me to my past. Aamon was not going to shut me off; this was what I wanted, what I needed—what we both needed.

We kissed for a while, lost in each other, until the distant sound of music broke our moment. "Let us go see," Aamon said, his voice low and inviting, pulling me back from the depths of our shared bliss. "Some of the sweetest music I've ever heard comes from Paris."

We walked a short distance and found a small pond near the river, adorned with lily pads and illuminated by the soft glow of the moon. A violinist played a romantic tune for a nearby couple, the melody floating through the air like a soft caress.

As Aamon took my hand and led me to the edge of the water, he said, "Lady, may I have this dance?"

"You may."

Under the starry sky and the beautiful moonlight, we danced together. I felt his hand on my hip and mine on his shoulder as we swayed, holding each other close, the world around us fading into a distant hum.

The moon cast a silvery glow on the surface of the pond, making the water shimmer like a blanket of stars ... far below. To my amazement, we hovered over the water, thanks to Aamon's vampiric magic, as if defying gravity. It was exhilarating and terrifying all at once, as if we were not just dancing but soaring. He kissed me again, and I kissed him back, breathless, the night wrapping us in its tender embrace.

"You make me feel amazing," I murmured, my voice a soft whisper against his lips. "Even if you're not clouding my mind, this might be a little too fast for me. I know it seems hypocritical since I was with Logan so quickly after I met him." The words tasted bitter, a reminder of the pain that still clung to my heart.

Aamon looked deep into my eyes, his gaze unwavering, filled with sincerity. "He clouded your mind. It was a form of rape—not something anyone should have to live through. With me, it will be your choice. I will never cloud your mind, and I will never rush you." His promise settled between us, a weight of truth that anchored my fluttering heart.

I sensed the honesty in his words, and in that moonlit dance, I began to believe. Under the soft glow of the stars, we swayed and held each other, floating above the water, wrapped in the warmth of newfound trust. It felt like we were part of something timeless, a moment crafted by the very hands of fate, where the past melted away and the promise of the future shone brightly ahead.

As much as I wished the night would never end, I could sense the sun creeping closer, maybe an hour away. The cool air that wrapped around us warmed slightly, a gentle reminder that dawn was coming. It was hard to believe the whole night had passed; it felt like just a moment, but it was ours.

Aamon's voice pulled me back to reality as he said, "I'll call Brianna and have the car come to get us."

The idea of returning to the real world felt too soon. I hoped the weather had cleared over Ireland. But if not, I guessed we could always stay on his plane. Just the two of us trapped in that confined space? The thrill sent a rush through my veins.

While we waited, I sat down next to him on the edge of the pond, our hands intertwined, fingers delicately woven together as if they were meant to be there. His warmth sent a rush of heat through me, chasing away the chill of the night air. We talked about the most nonsensical things—what our favorite flavors of ice cream would be if they were enchanted, or what it would be like to dance under a thousand fireflies. Those topics wouldn't matter to anyone else, but in that moment, they felt like the only things that existed, the only reality I wanted to cling to. It's as if we were in our own world, insulated from the chaos that lay beyond this moment.

The car's arrival felt like the toll of midnight, ending the ball, but enchantment still clung to us. The trip back to his jet was a blur, the stars twinkling above us as we walked from the limousine, lost in each other's presence. The sound of crickets filled the air, a serenade just for us. I couldn't help but wonder if this was the first real date I'd ever been on. As pathetic as that sounded, it truly was. Every other encounter in my life had been overshadowed by expectations or complications. But with Aamon, everything felt simple and honest.

Looking at him, I mustered the courage to say, "I'm not going to sleep with you, at least not now." My admission hung in the air between us, heavy yet freeing. I braced myself for his reaction, hoping he didn't pull away or dismiss my words.

He took both my hands in his, his grip firm yet gentle, and gazed deeply into my eyes. The intensity of his stare made my heart race, as if he could see right through me, peeling back the layers I'd carefully constructed. "I've told you many times, Roxy," he replied, his voice low and steady, "I won't touch you unless you ask me to and want me to."

His words wrapped around me like a soft embrace, soothing the fluttering nerves in my stomach. There was something reassuring about his respect, something that made me want to trust him even more. The weight of my past relationships, filled with unwanted pressure and expectation, lifted slightly, replaced by an air of anticipation. I couldn't help but feel that whatever this was between us, it was something extraordinary.

As the darkness began to lighten, I wondered if this is where the story truly started for us. The thought brought a smile to my lips, and Aamon mirrored it, his eyes glinting with mischief. "So, what do you say we create our own adventure, one that doesn't end with dawn?"

His playful tone drew a laugh from me, light and free, and I nodded, excitement bubbling within me. "I'd like that. I'd like that very much."

14 Veiled in Mystery 

A thrill pulsed through me as Aamon and I re-boarded his private jet. The vampire, pale and beautiful like some haunting masterpiece, brushed my hand as he guided me up the narrow stair into the plush cabin. His presence was magnetic, and even here, surrounded by the quiet hum of luxury, his allure was unmistakable. There was something thrilling in the intimacy of sharing this sky-bound sanctuary practically alone with him.

"Are you ready for Ireland, Roxy?" His voice was silk, drawing my gaze up to his midnight eyes.

"As ready as I'll ever be," I murmured, settling back into the smooth leather seat opposite.

The plane began to rumble, rising over the lights of Paris and pushing us further into the night. Somewhere over the Channel, he reached out, brushing a strand of my hair back with cool fingers.

"You fascinate me," he whispered, his lips hovering close enough that I felt his words on my skin. If I had been weaker, I would have gone back to the bedroom with him to explore our bodies together. But I remembered what Madge had said to me, not to give my heart so quickly. I told myself, Roxy, think before you leap.

A little over an hour later, the green hills of Ireland came into view. I looked out, expecting to see another city approaching, but instead, the vast countryside stretched out beneath us. "Weren't we going to Dublin?" I asked, slightly puzzled.

Aamon's mouth quirked in that enigmatic smile he wore so well. "I have a private airstrip near my home," he said simply.

Soon, the jet descended toward what looked like a quiet, unremarkable field. But something beneath the surface felt ... off, like a vibration just below the edges of reality. I looked at Aamon with a raised brow, sensing the magic like an electric current beneath the land.

"You feel it, don't you?" he said, satisfaction glimmering in his eyes. "It's an illusion, a glamour cast by a league of Fae I persuaded ages ago, using more favors than I care to remember."

With a whispered spell and a wave of his hand, he allowed me to see beyond the veil. The simple field below transformed before my eyes into an ancient forest, stretching as far as I could see, thick with towering oaks, shivering ferns, and green that seemed to breathe magic. I'd thought Ireland's forests were long gone, but here, preserved in secret, was a lush wilderness that defied time itself.

He grinned at my astonishment. "The glamour prevents any unwelcome visitors from entering, and while satellites might see it, I have enough resources to make sure no one bothers."

"A bit over the top, aren't you?" I teased, grinning.

He just raised an eyebrow. "I like my privacy."

Once we landed, I caught my first glimpse of his castle—a towering marvel of glass and stone nestled at the top of the hill. The castle was old and grand but with touches of the modern: sleek panes of glass framing stone turrets and twisted gargoyles, reflecting the pale light of dawn.

"Won't all that glass fry you in sunlight?" I asked, suppressing a grin.

Aamon laughed, a low, rich sound. "There are ways, Roxy. It's all about UV filtering. In my home, I can watch the sun rise without a burn. Come, let me show you."

We walked through a lush garden, and I found myself enchanted by rows of roses and strange flowers that seemed otherworldly.

"What are these flowers?" I asked, curious.

"Remnants of my youth," he replied, his tone softening. "I collected plants, rare ones. I've saved species that might no longer exist outside my lands."

Inside, the castle was a gothic dream, every inch immaculate, yet charged with a dark, seductive edge. Brianna, Aamon's assistant, appeared like a shadow and offered to show me to my room. She led me through winding halls to a bedroom fit for royalty, with a massive bed framed by carved wood and etched with images of angels and gargoyles in poses that left me laughing out loud.

"That's a rather ... enthusiastic choice for bedpost décor," I mused, raising a brow at Brianna.

She chuckled. "A bit tame, actually. Vampires have a penchant for dramatics."

"Clearly," I murmured. Then, curiosity took hold of me again. "How do you know all this? About the supernatural?"

Brianna's eyes twinkled. "You'd be surprised how many know. Governments, certain families, those with power and influence. And it's best kept that way; otherwise, those like Aamon and you, Roxy, would be swamped by the curious or the greedy, those who want what you could do for them without understanding the cost."

I nodded, sensing the truth of her words. Even in my sleepy little town, more people knew than didn't know. And those who didn't know, didn't want to know. They just ignored everything that was obvious in front of them.

"Sunrise approaches," Brianna said, noting my yawn. "Sleep will come soon."

As I sank into the decadent bed, I felt the secrets of the castle around me, like shadows waiting to reveal themselves. In the glow of dawn, Aamon's world felt limitless, and as I drifted off, I knew I was falling deeper into his mystery.

When I woke, the bed felt far too empty, too cold. The dawn light hadn't even broken over the mountains, and yet, somehow, my eyes were wide open, heart racing, breath shallow. Aamon had warned me the bond might weaken quickly. Witches could resist better than others, he'd said, although he hadn't been thrilled about it.

Still groggy, I glanced around the grand room. Massive stone walls, tapestries older than I could date, and the faint hum of hidden modern tech gave the castle a strange, layered atmosphere. And now, curious and restless, I slipped out of bed, wrapped myself in one of

Aamon's absurdly long robes, and padded barefoot into the hall, determined to explore.

The castle felt like a world caught between times. Ancient artifacts and polished, glinting weaponry lay in cases beside the warm glow of modern fixtures, like someone had casually threaded the past with the present. I wandered through corridors lined with portraits, some with unsettlingly lifelike eyes that seemed to follow me, down stone steps that spiraled into torch-lit alcoves, and into a high-ceilinged hall where Brianna was already waiting, as if expecting me.

"Brianna," I said, my voice a little raspier than usual, "what can you tell me about the Convergence? Aamon mentioned he was going to research it while I slept. What did he find out while I was out?" I could tell from her expression that she knew exactly what I was talking about.

Brianna's gaze flickered, a glint of worry in her eyes. "The Convergence? Let's see what you already know first."

I nodded, clearing my throat. "There are three worlds—ours, the fairy world, and the demon realm. They overlay each other, but the Convergence ... it's when they align, right?" I paused, catching her reaction. "I'm not certain, but I think that's when the realms come closest, touching in ways they normally don't."

Her face softened with a hint of a smile. "More than I knew when I first started researching it. A Convergence is significant because it's at such times that powerful magics can be cast. The binding ritual was created during a Convergence millennia ago. It took immense power, drawn from all three worlds. The spell wove laws that bound supernatural creatures to certain ... limitations." She looked away, as if choosing her words carefully. "To undo it, you'd have to go to where the ritual was first cast—and it must be during the Convergence."

"Where is it?" I asked, suddenly a little breathless.

"The Fae may know. The castle's grounds rest on a ley line. There's a nearby rift to the fairy world, guarded by ... something." She paused, looking uncomfortable. "A creature. Aamon plans to take you there tonight to confront it."

"What exactly do you mean by 'creature'? You're not exactly putting me at ease, Brianna."

She swallowed, lowering her voice. "Aamon calls it the Banshee. Beyond that, I don't know, and I'm not sure I want to."

Before I could respond, I felt his presence as surely as if he'd whispered in my ear. I turned, and there he was, moving toward me with his quiet, graceful steps, his hand extended.

"Roxy," Aamon murmured, his voice smooth as silk. "Will you accompany me on a little journey this afternoon?"

I took his hand, feeling his cool fingers close around mine as we walked out into the early night. Towering trees formed a shadowed canopy overhead, broken only by the glimmer of a high, pale moon. I couldn't help but look up, thinking of someone far away.

"Have you heard from Rick?" I asked.

"Yes," he replied, his face unreadable. "He insisted on being brought here, so I arranged it. He should be arriving shortly. I would have told you earlier, if you hadn't been asleep."

"And what's this about the Banshee?" I asked,

"It's what the locals called her, long ago. She's said to be a young woman, lost and wailing in the marshlands nearby." He hesitated. "The Fae who I dealt with to create the glamour on this place, they came from that marsh, so there must be a rift somewhere in it. The Banshee protects it, but her ability to be reasoned with I cannot predict."

I gave a sardonic chuckle. "So ... just the usual stroll, facing dangerous supernatural creatures, huh?"

His smile was faint, but I could see a hint of amusement flicker deep in his eyes. "With me, Roxy, there's no such thing as 'usual.'"

We walked deeper into the forest, his silent presence beside me both comforting and unnerving. Our bond, that unnamable pull between us, flared as we moved together. His fingers brushed the back of my hand, sending a thrill through me.

"And when we find the Banshee?" I asked, my voice almost a whisper.

He turned, his gaze sharp, intense. "When we find her, Roxy, you'll look into her mind with that power of yours and learn why she guards the rift. She'll test you as much as she tests me. And if we fail..." He trailed off, the rest left unsaid, hanging heavy in the air.

I tightened my grip on his hand. Whatever awaited us in the marshlands, I was ready. Aamon walked beside me, his silhouette framed against the moon's glow, his skin paler than the stars casting light upon the marsh. I could feel his presence, an alluring, dangerous pulse in the otherwise silent night. Fireflies drifted lazily around us, little lanterns illuminating the dark places between twisted trees and hanging moss. Every now and then, I'd catch Aamon glancing at me, his crimson eyes lingering just a bit too long, lips curled into that smile of his. With Aamon at my side, I felt as though I could face any-thing—even the unknown.

As we stepped deeper into the bog, the damp air grew thick with the weight of old, restless spirits.

He chuckled, and I hated how his laughter slid un-der my skin. "This marsh has a history," he said, his voice darkening as his gaze drifted over the water's glis-tening surface. "Long before any Roman set foot here, it was the site of a brutal battle. Two Celtic princes, once brothers in arms, torn apart by their desire for the same woman. They fought until only death could end their ri-valry." He stopped, his tone softening. "They say her heartbreak, her despair at losing them both, turned her into a Banshee."

A heaviness settled over me, a sadness that wasn't my own. The echoes of lost lives filled the air, like whispers too faint to understand, yet unmistakably present. I tried to shake the feeling, but Aamon was right. This place felt like a bruise on the world—painful and beautiful in equal measure.

"Tragic, isn't it?" he murmured, his gaze fixed on me as if searching for something I didn't want to give. "To be bound to a place by sorrow alone."

I looked away, suddenly unnerved, my pulse racing. "Not all bonds are so easily broken," I replied, though the words felt hollow in the face of that ancient sadness pressing down on us.

As we walked further, a wailing sound echoed from the depths of the marsh, a chilling, mournful sound that seeped into my bones. There she was, hovering just above the ground, an ethereal figure with hollow eyes and hair floating like mist around her gaunt face. The Banshee.

"What do you seek here?" she demanded, her voice sharp with an agony centuries old. "What right have you to tread upon these lands where lives were lost?"

I could feel her pain, an open wound that refused to close. I took a step forward, ignoring the way Aamon's hand tensed at my elbow. "I'm here to set you free. This sorrow—it's kept you bound for too long. Your pain isn't your own anymore; it's been woven into this place, caging you here."

The Banshee's hollow eyes bore into mine, and for a moment, I could see the depth of her grief, the weight of lifetimes spent in mourning. "They died because of me," she rasped. "The curse ... the bloodshed. They couldn't pass on, nor could I. I am their keeper."

"Only because you chose to be," I said softly. "The curse doesn't own you; it never did. Their deaths were their own doing, their choice, not yours."

Her expression shifted, a flicker of hope breaking through centuries of torment. "But if I leave ... who will protect the gate?"

I held her gaze, channeling the warmth of my magic, feeling it curl around the threads that bound her. "You're not meant to protect it anymore. Let yourself be free. Let go."

With a soft exhale, the Banshee's form began to dissipate, her hollow eyes softening into something almost grateful. "Thank you," she whispered as she faded. "Thank you...."

And just like that, she was gone, leaving a strange stillness in her wake. But there, where she had vanished, a faint tear in the air pulsed, as if reality itself was fraying.

Aamon's fingers laced through mine, his cold hand reassuring, his gaze intent on the rift ahead. "That, my dear Roxy, is the gateway to the fairylands."

I felt an almost electric charge when our eyes met—he captivated me in a way I'd never experienced before. Aamon's presence was like a flame, drawing me in with an irresistible warmth that wrapped around me like a silk scarf in a chilly breeze.

"You make it sound so tempting," I teased, a playful smile dancing on my lips. My voice came out as a sultry whisper, holding a challenge. "Are you sure you want me for a sidekick in your dangerous escapades?"

His laughter rolled through the stillness like thunder, making my pulse quicken. "Oh, I'm definitely seeking a partner in crime like you," he replied, his eyes sparkling with mischief. "But it's not just for my sake. You have a fire in you, Roxy. I see it flickering every time you dare to challenge me."

Then his gaze turned serious, piercing through my playful facade as if trying to uncover the hidden depths of my soul. "I don't want you to hold back. I want you to embrace everything you are."

With those words, the last thread of hesitation unraveled within me, like an ancient spell breaking under the weight of truth. The air shimmered with unspoken promises, and I felt the power of his conviction resonate deep inside me.

"Then what are we waiting for?" I declared, my voice brimming with newfound determination. "Let's find out what the Faelands have in store for us."

Aamon's smile widened, a flash of triumph igniting the depths of his gaze. "That's the spirit!" he said, leaning closer. His breath tickled my ear, as he whispered, "Together, we'll face whatever awaits us."

With our hands intertwined, we stepped toward the rift, the pulsing energy enveloping us like a lover's embrace as we crossed the threshold. I could feel the world around us shift, the familiar fading into a kaleidoscope of vibrant colors and intoxicating sensations. Aamon's presence was a steadying force beside me, grounding me amidst the chaos. As we plunged into the unknown, a thrilling sense of purpose surged through my veins. There was no turning back, and I wouldn't have it any other way.

15 Dark Desires

The world spun around me as Aamon and I stepped out of the swirling portal. My vision blurred, and a wave of disorientation washed over me. The aftereffects of crossing dimensions. But there was also something deeper. The metallic tang in the air seeped into my bones, the kind of taste that lingers longer than it should. I blinked rapidly, trying to regain my bearings. When the haze finally lifted, I was met with a scene that shattered every fairy tale I had ever known.

Before us sprawled a vast city, stark against a murky sky. Flying vehicles zipped overhead, leaving trails of iridescence in their wake, but the colors were faded and grim. The buildings, tall and angular, stretched towards the clouds like fingers grasping for something lost. The landscape was a concrete jungle, devoid of greenery—nature smothered by the relentless advance of industry. I turned to Aamon, his pale beauty a stark contrast to the harsh reality surrounding us.

"Not what you were expecting?" he asked, his voice tinged with a hint of melancholy.

I shook my head slowly, still absorbing the sight before me. "Not at all. I thought it would be magical—lush and vibrant. But this ... it's all wrong."

Aamon sighed, a heavy sound. "When I first saw the Fairy Lands, I was disappointed too. I'd heard tales of beauty and enchantment, but what I've learned from others tells a different story. This place is advanced, yes, but at a cost. They destroyed their environment, enslaved each other..." He paused, scanning the horizon. "And what you're seeing now, Roxy, is what some call the 'good' fairies, the Seelie—not the dark ones, the Unseelie, who we encountered earlier. They live side by side, much like we do. It's a complex web of nations—"

"How do you know this isn't a dark fairy place?" I interrupted, squinting at the banners fluttering in the distance.

"The banners are Seelie, not the dark court," Aamon explained, his gaze steady. "They represent the light fairies. There are also wild fairies, those who aren't under the thumb of either court. They're numerous but lack ambition and power."

I crossed my arms, feeling a chill despite the oppressive warmth of the air. "So, what can we find here that we couldn't learn in our own world?"

"The fairies possess knowledge beyond our comprehension," he replied, a distant look in his eyes. "Their magic is ... profound. And their lifespans are incredibly long. They've had centuries to unravel the mysteries of existence, far beyond our imaginations."

As I pondered his words, a rumble of engines filled the air, drawing my attention to a fleet of airships approaching from the horizon. Panic surged through me. "Should we go back?" I asked, anxiety creeping into my voice.

"We came here for answers," Aamon reminded me, but before I could respond, a familiar voice slithered through the air—sultry and seductive.

"Roxanne."

I turned, and there stood Sable, her dark beauty instantly captivating.

"Have you been following us?" I demanded, crossing my arms defensively.

"Yes and no," she replied, her lips curving into a sly smile. "When you crossed over, I sensed your presence.

A little tether I set on you to see what you were up to. I didn't think you would actually come here. Your kind usually avoids the Fairy Lands if they want to dodge bureaucracy, questions, and, well ... probable imprisonment. Oh yes, and then there was the good old days. Slavery. We need to bring that one back."

My heart raced. "What do you want from us?"

"Come with me," she urged, gesturing toward the outskirts of the metropolis. "You might not want to be caught by those airships. It's your choice, of course."

I glanced at Aamon, who gave me a slight nod, urging me to trust my instincts. With a deep breath, I followed Sable, weaving through the shadows to avoid the looming threat above us. The airships buzzed like angry hornets, scanning the area with ominous precision.

We followed Sable without looking at our feet, scanning the sky for danger, and I stumbled into the shadowy depths of a tower. It was built in a medieval style at odds with the advanced technology all around. An electric awareness pulsed in the air, an instinctive warning that something malevolent lingered just out of sight. The stone walls loomed around us, slick with moisture and shrouded in a darkness that swallowed sound itself. My hair hung dull and limp in the oppressive gloom, like a red flame stifled under a heavy weight. The atmosphere thickened with dark magic, a taint that made the hairs on my arms stand on end, the very air was charged with threat. Something here was corrupted, and my instincts screamed that I was in deep trouble.

Sable turned, her eyes glinting like shards of ice as she spoke, her voice smooth. "Now that you've crossed the threshold into the Unseelie Embassy, little witch," she purred, a cruel smile twisting her lips, "I have control over you. None of your spells or magic will work here."

Aamon, by my side, stood tall and immovable, his pale beauty almost ethereal in the dim light. His eyes went crimson and narrowed as Sable continued her gloat, her gaze shifting to him. "And you, vampire, we've dealt with your kind before. If you do anything, I'll destroy Roxy. So, you will obey me if you want her to live."

A chill settled in my chest, and I could feel Aamon's tension, the way his body coiled, ready to strike. Before I could protest, guards swarmed in.

"Seize them!" Sable ordered. "Take them to separate holding rooms. I'll deal with them soon."

They dragged us apart, my heart racing as I was thrust into a dark cell in the depths of Sable's tower, the door slamming shut with a finality that echoed in my mind. Hours wore on, each second filled with gnawing anxiety. I could sense Aamon nearby, yet he felt so far away, separated by thick walls and magic. I could almost feel the heat of his anger radiating through the stone, a stark contrast to the cold that enveloped me.

Finally, my cell door creaked open, and I braced myself as Sable entered. Her presence filled the space, a predatory grace as she stepped closer.

"Ah, Roxy. My little toy," she said, her voice sultry and teasing, as if we were lovers in a twisted game. "Now that you're mine, I'll do as I please."

I felt a shiver run through me, not of fear but of defiance. "You think I'll let you use me?" I shot back, my voice stronger than I felt. "I'm here to find out where the curse was made in my world and to stop Logan from breaking it. I don't care about your twisted games."

"Ah, but how am I to believe you?" she replied, tilting her head, eyes gleaming with dark interest. "If you want to stop Logan, that's something I want also. But you could be lying to me."

"Why don't you just stop him yourself?" I asked, frustration boiling over. "You have resources, magic. Is it because the portals are small and random most of the time? Is that why your people haven't come over to take Earth's resources? I can sense that's what you truly want."

Sable stepped closer, invading my space, her breath warm against my skin. "Yes, we do need what your world has to offer," she said, her voice low and conspiratorial. "You have a talent, Roxy, for getting information. I sensed you pull it from me just now. It's powerful."

"Would you listen if I told you to release me? What do you have to lose?"

"I have plenty to lose if I release you," she replied, her voice cold. "We Unseelie have our own plans for the Convergence. I can't risk you helping Logan."

"I'm not helping him!"

"Perhaps. Traditionally," Sable continued, her eyes narrowing in thought, "I'd just kill you to be safe—after I torture you to discover the truth. But I can sense your power, the depth of it. The most remarkable thing I've seen you do is break a bond between two supernaturals. Bonds are unbreakable. That shouldn't even be possible."

I could feel the weight of her words, that mixture of intrigue and desire flickering between us again. She stepped closer still, her fingers brushing against my cheek, her touch both soft and possessive.

"Maybe I'll just keep you as a pet, something to toy with. Maybe I'll learn how you perform that little trick of yours. And perhaps, just perhaps, I can use you for other things."

As she caressed my face, I felt a jolt of conflicting emotions—rage, fear, and an unexpected thrill. "In time," she whispered, leaning in so close I could feel her breath against my lips, "you'll enjoy my caress."

I fought to suppress a shudder, forcing my voice to steady. "You can't break me, Sable. I won't be your plaything."

Her laughter echoed in the dark chamber, a haunting sound that both aroused and disgusted me. "Oh, we'll see about that."

After Sable left, I couldn't shake the feeling she hadn't been entirely honest about my magic being suppressed in the tower. Sure, she'd blocked some of it, but I could still read people, so not everything was off-limits. I even had a faint sense of where Aamon was—though maybe that was just desperation talking.

I realized that if I wanted to get out of here without becoming some disturbed fairy's plaything, I'd have to rely on myself. So, what could I do?

I started by focusing on my ability to read the people around me. I could pick up surface thoughts; they weren't fully blocked. There was a guard, Cosmo, standing in front of my cell door, thinking about how his feet ached from standing too long and wondering why he even needed to guard a woman already locked up, how he was from one of the greater families and this was beneath him to do. Nothing helpful there.

"Push a little harder, Roxy," I muttered to myself. A few cells down, I sensed someone else's thoughts— someone saying hello to me in my mind. That was new.

"Hello," I replied cautiously. "Who are you?"

"Well, who are you?" she shot back, like we could go in circles forever.

So, I broke the loop. "I'm Roxy. How can you even hear me?" I asked. "I've never met anyone who could connect like this. Are you human?"

"Please don't insult me. I'm Fae—a wild fairy, if you must know. And you, obviously, are human... with a bit more going on. A witch, perhaps?"

A scary thought crossed my mind. "Wait—what if Sable planted you here to get information from me? I've seen that trick in movies."

"It's easy enough to check," she said calmly. "I'll open up. Look in my mind, see what I've got, and you'll know if I'm telling the truth. I've already looked in yours. You don't seem to have any mental barriers; you might want to work on that."

"I'm not even sure how."

"You've been doing it naturally for a long time," she reassured me. "But it fails you when you are off balance. You need to be more intentional. Enough about you. Come say hello to me. Welcome in...."

Slowly, I reached into Ida's thoughts. I knew her name immediately. I continued gently probing, as I'd instinctively done with everyone's thoughts since I was a child. I sensed she was afraid. She'd been locked up here for quite some time, so I asked, "What do you think of Sable?"

The answer came instantly, a mess of complex emotions. I gathered that Ida and Sable had once been lovers, and Sable had convinced her to work for her, infiltrating groups to read people's thoughts and memories to gather information for Sable and her companion, Naida, who served Tristan. There was real fear of this Tristan person, but Ida had never set eyes on him.

"So, what did you do for Sable? What did she want to know?" I asked.

She hesitated, thoughts spilling out in a jumble. She'd embedded herself among Sable's enemies, trying to learn their plans and find ways to gain an edge. Knowledge was her currency, and she'd spent years researching the Convergence, piecing together information from fragments she gathered, all for Sable. She believed that if she proved herself, maybe they could become more than just lovers. Ida had fallen for her, even feeling embarrassed for letting herself be drawn in by a dark fairy. She'd deceived herself, convincing herself that Sable's cruelty could be softened. But in the end, she'd only lied to herself, winding up in this cell, feeling used. And yet, a part of her still wished for what they could have had.

I could relate. I'd realized most of what I'd felt for Logan had been his manipulation. In such a short time, he'd made me believe I felt something profound, planting thoughts and feelings in me, making it seem like I'd loved him forever. Ida and I had both thought we were in love, but we'd been used.

Suddenly, a wave of panic hit me. "The Convergence? Is it soon? Am I going to miss it?"

Ida paused and reassured me, "Time doesn't flow the same way here as in your world. There's still time—if we can ever get out of here."

I sensed a hint of resentment from Ida directed at me. "Why are you angry with me?" I asked.

"Sable put me here, close to you, so I could feel everything you're feeling. She's trying to seduce you. It's another form of torture. For her, it's a win-win. She tortures me by making me sense what she's doing to you, and she tortures you by forcing you to fall for her. You think it's not possible, but most Fae have an innate ability in this realm, and seduction is Sable's. She's so skilled at it that you don't even realize you're being seduced; you think you're falling in love. You believe you can change her, but that couldn't be further from the truth."

"That's ridiculous," I scoffed.

But as I sat there, waiting, hours passing with nothing but my thoughts and the occasional exchange with Ida, I felt my focus shifting from Logan and Aamon to Sable. I couldn't help remembering the perfect shape of her lips, their color like ripe plums. I smelled her, recalling the soft brush of her hair against my face, sable like her name, when she'd been close to me....

Days of confinement blurred together, Ida's presence the only thing keeping me grounded. Even in separate cells, our telepathic connection was a lifeline in this dark place.

Then, one moment I blinked, eyes well-adjusted to the dim, damp cell, feeling the rough stone press against my back—and she appeared.

Sable, the dark fairy with curves and an aura as intoxicating as it was sinister. Her gothic beauty was a sharp, elegant contrast to the dungeon walls, and her steps echoed with confidence. She stopped just outside my cell, eyes smoldering as if her gaze alone could bend my will. Her voice wrapped around me like a spell, daring me to succumb.

I wasn't going to give her the satisfaction. With Ida's help I had been inoculating myself against her manipulation. I steadied myself and met her gaze. "Your powers won't work on me, Sable."

She smirked, but there was a flicker of irritation in her eyes. "In time, you'll be mine," she hissed, storming off with a flair.

As her presence faded, Ida's voice reached me, soft but steady in my mind. "It's okay, Roxy. We're in this together. We'll get through this." Her warmth bolstered me, helping me find strength in the quiet after Sable's departure. I ached for her and wanted more than anything for the feeling to go away ... to have her come back and smile at me again. Have her open my cell and touch my cheek, kiss my lips....

I drifted in and out of fitful sleep, until a loud crash broke the silence. There were sounds of shouting, metal tearing apart. Suddenly, my cell door burst open, and there stood Rick, fully transformed into his hulking werewolf form, all fur and muscle. In an instant, he shifted back to human, his massive frame barely contained in torn clothes, almost entirely naked save for a grin full of wicked promise.

"Roxy," he said, voice laced with amusement, "don't swoon, but yeah, I'm here to rescue you. Okay, maybe you can swoon a little."

Thank God. I was in dire need of a rescue, but I wasn't going to admit it to him.

I shot him a smirk. "Save the hero speech. We've got to find Aamon and Ida—the fairy next door. But how in the world did you track me down?"

He gave a playful eye roll. "Followed your scent. Tracked you through Aamon's castle, waded through a swamp, and walked right into a shimmering portal. Next thing I know, I'm in fairyland, of all places, and I just followed my nose here."

Despite the tension, he chuckled, but then his face grew serious. "I'm late ... or maybe early? Time's strange here. Either way, we need to hurry. Timmy's outside causing a ruckus and is soon to be swarmed by Fae."

As he helped me up, he paused, annoyance flickering in his eyes. "So, about Aamon. Do we really have to save that insufferable—?"

"Yes, Rick," I interrupted with a grin. "We're saving Aamon."

He groaned, rolling his eyes. "The guy makes me fly Economy Class to Ireland, then sends me on a bus to his castle, when he's got a private jet just parked outside! Vindictive as hell, Roxy."

Together, we hurried to Ida's cell. She stood, small but fierce, barely reaching five feet, her pink eyes flecked with green. With her half-shaved pink hair and fierce gaze, she looked like she could take on the world.

"This way," she said, indicating the best path to Aamon's cell.

Inside, Aamon lay chained in a coffin, gaunt from hunger. Rick paused, taken aback by the vampire's sorry state, but then tore the chain apart to free him.

Aamon barely managed a nod as I helped him up. I wanted to give him blood, restore his strength, but it would weaken me too much. I needed to keep my head if we were to escape Sable.

We hurried, silent and tense, Rick taking the lead with surprising stealth as we navigated the winding corridors of the tower. There were no guards to stop us, everything eerily silent.

"This seems too easy," I said. "I thought getting out would be harder."

Rick looked at me. "It was hell of a lot harder getting in here. Timmy and me made it easier getting out, that is, if we're quick."

Once we made it outside, Ida halted, catching her breath. "The portal's out—they'll be watching it. But I know a place where we can hide, at least for now."

Following her, we moved through a futuristic cityscape alive with neon lights and towering skyscrapers, a contrast to the Unseelie Tower. It was difficult to breathe, the air was so polluted. Flying cars whizzed overhead as we threaded through gritty alleyways, finally arriving at a dingy, abandoned bar. Inside, the air was thick with the stale scent of old beer, but for the first time, it felt like we could catch our breath.

Rick draped his arm over my shoulders, his warmth grounding me. Aamon's intense gaze lingered instinctively on my neck, and Ida stood by the window, watching the city lights flicker. In this moment, I felt the weight of it all, but also the fragile hope of safety.

"Alright," I murmured, voice low but resolute. "We've made it this far. Now, let's figure out how to keep from losing everything."

16 The Underground

"Won't Sable be able to find us?" I asked Ida. "She said she'd been tracking me."

Ida shook her head. "This place is magically shielded. It used to have rooms upstairs, back before it was a pub, and it was a safe haven for people who didn't want to be found. The spell is still in place; no one's removed it." She paused, then added, "We probably won't be able to use the portal you came through from Earth, though, as Sable will look for you there. There are, however, a few other portals around. Wild fairies know about them, but we don't usually share that info. It gives us a way to slip out when we need to."

"We need to get out of here as soon as we can," I said. "But first, we need to help Timmy. He's still out there somewhere, werewolf or no, he'll get overwhelmed and caught. Can you call him to you or something?" I asked Rick. "Can alphas do that?"

Rick growled, glancing at Ida with suspicion. "Who's this pink-haired fairy, and why are we even listening to her? I don't trust the fair folk."

"She's all we've got, and I trust her," I said.

"If you say Ida's on our side, then I'll take you at your word," Aamon said, weakly.

I noticed the weariness etched across his face. "Aamon, will you be alright? What did they do to you?"

He managed a fragile smile. "It wasn't just the coffin and chains and lack of food .... They used some sort of draining magic on me, weakening me slowly. They've held vampires before, it seems. I'm ... not at my best, and I'd be lying if I said I wasn't tempted to feed on Rick over there."

Rick clenched his fists. "Bring it on, vampire."

"Both of you, enough!" I said, exasperated. "We're in this together, remember?" I turned to Aamon, softening my tone. "You should show Rick a little gratitude. He did save us, you know."

Aamon looked down, a hint of regret in his eyes. "You're right, Roxy. I apologize. And thank you, Rick.

What you did was ... impressive. I owe you. Don't worry, I've gone without feeding for longer than this. And now that I'm out of that coffin, I can feel my strength slowly returning."

A loud banging suddenly shook the door. I cursed under my breath. Have they found us? But then I thought, If they'd found us, would they really be knocking?

"It's Timmy," Rick reassured us. He sniffed, double checking the scent.

My tension eased as I sensed Timmy's thoughts. He wasn't radiating fear or panic—just exhaustion.

"It's doesn't seem like Timmy's being chased, his mind seems calm," I pointed out.

Rick shot me a look. "Getting into people's heads like that screams 'no secrets allowed.' Some might not take it so well."

I bristled, even though Rick had a point. "I know, but it's a reflex—one that's keeping us alive."

I opened the door, and Timmy stumbled in, catching himself against the frame, looking every bit as worn as I'd sensed.

"Thought I lost you guys," he panted, casting a wary glance over his shoulder. "Led them on a merry chase. Eventually I got a whiff of Rick's scent and tracked it here. There's some kind of barrier around this place, like a glamour. It messes with my senses a bit, but pack magic cut right through it. They didn't count on that."

Relief washed over me, and I reached out to clasp his shoulder. "It's good to see you, Timmy. Thank you for coming for me. You didn't have to do that. Thank you…"

"Roxy, you're practically a member of the pack now," he said, grinning. "And the pack always sticks together."

Ida caught my attention, her eyes sharp with urgency. "A portal's close, but we shouldn't travel topside. It'll have to be the sewers. I hate going that way."

"Why's that?" I asked, immediately thinking it a stupid question. Hello, the smell.

"You never know what's down there—magic leaks from the upper city, warping the creatures that live in the shadows. It's dangerous, but it's our best chance."

She looked at Aamon, her brow arched. "Can the vampire handle the daylight?"

I nodded. "He can be awake but not in direct sunlight. That rule still holds."

Ida's shoulders relaxed, her relief visible. "Good. Dawn's almost here, and there's an entrance to the sewers in the basement. Let's get moving."

The basement door creaked as we stepped down, and soon we were trudging through damp, ancient tunnels. The stench was worse than I expected, like nothing I'd ever encountered—decay, rot, and magic so thick I could feel it clinging to my skin. Each footfall echoed against stone walls, amplified in the silence, until a skittering sound grew around us. Eyes glistened in the dark, and massive, twisted rats emerged from the shadows, their fur matted, eyes an unnatural red.

"On it," Ida muttered, extending her hand. A shimmer rippled through the air, forming a protective shield around us. Rick lunged forward, claws out, while Aamon's fangs gleamed as he used a quick surge of strength to bring down a rat. I focused, weaving my magic to ensnare the rest, grateful for the return of my power now that we were out of the tower.

Rick let out a low chuckle as he crushed the final rat beneath his boot. "Rats the size of dogs—never thought I'd see the day. Why didn't we just take the surface route again?"

Ida rolled her eyes. "Trust me," she explained. "I could probably make it topside alone, but not with you four. Not a chance I could glamour enough to keep two werewolves, a witch, and a vampire hidden. The sewers might be unpredictable, but I'd take mutated rats over a face-off with Sable and her Unseelie friends any day."

As we pressed deeper into the tunnels, I couldn't shake the feeling we were being watched. I hoped Sable hadn't found us already.

After we emerged from the sewers, the humid weight of an underground labyrinth gave way to something altogether new—a sweeping sense of vitality and an ethereal glow that seemed to spill from every corner of a hidden, underground world.

My breath caught as we stepped into what could only be described as a fairytale brought to life, or at least the version I'd always dreamed of: sprawling, moss-covered stalls filled with shimmering potions, enchanted crystals, and colorful flowers that smelled sweet enough to eat. Fairies of every kind floated, flitted, or glided through the air with vibrant wings. Some resembled the Fae I'd imagined, with their delicate wings and light-filled eyes, while others were far stranger, marked by horns, twisted branches, and eyes that glowed with unnatural hues. Everywhere we looked, the marketplace thrummed with life—far more alive and lush than anything on the city streets above.

Ida informed me that she needed to go and get permission to enter the portal. "Take some time, check things out. I'll be back shortly."

Aamon held out a hand to me. "May I escort you and show you the beauties of this land?"

"You may." I smiled, ignoring the eyeroll Rick gave me.

I felt Aamon's cool hand slide into mine, and a thrill ran through me at his touch, as if I could feel the promise of something deeper. In the subterranean glow, his face looked even paler, his dark eyes filled with an unreadable intensity that pulled me in. We strolled among the stalls, pausing to admire some trinkets and unusual charms. At one point, I picked up a small, glowing vial filled with a sparkling liquid.

"What is it?" I wondered.

"Something to drink. You'll like it."

The vendor held out his hand, and I asked Aamon, "How do I pay for this?"

A small smirk played across his lips. "The fairy lands have their own currency," he explained, "but you can always pay with a vial of your own magic." He took my hand and guided it over an empty phial. "Just put a bit of your essence in here. Others can use it in spells. In my case, a drop of my blood is quite desirable."

Before I could figure out how to deposit 'my essence', he paid for the drink with a bit of his blood. Considering how low on it he was, I appreciated the gesture even more.

Aamon watched me put the drink to my lips, curious to see my reaction. It didn't smell much, perhaps a bit like melon.

"Hopefully this isn't poisonous," I murmured, downing it in one swift, reckless gulp.

The drink burned like whisky, just enough to remind me that I was alive. I didn't feel the same effect as alcohol though, no fuzziness, but there was a jolt of confidence. Maybe even a little bit of wildness ... Bring it on Sable, Logan, and whoever else dared to cross me! I smiled. It felt good. After the days I'd had, I was due a bit of fun.

While boldly exploring the street market, I noticed Aamon looking at me with a new kind of seriousness. His gaze was fixed on me with an intensity that made my skin prickle.

"Roxy," he began, voice a low murmur, "I can sense that the bond between us is fading. Don't take this the wrong way—I think it's a good thing. Now you'll know I'm not influencing you, that I'm truly interested in you for who you are."

His words lingered in the air between us, and my heart stuttered. The bond—the strange, magical link that had tied us together since that first shared taste of blood—was weakening, and yet, the tug I felt toward him felt deeper than ever. I wasn't falling for him just because of some vampiric hold. It was him. It was the way he looked at me, saw me, as if nothing in the world could pull his attention away. I let out a shaky breath and met his gaze.

"I am sorry I had my doubts," I whispered. He pulled me closer, his eyes softening as he brushed his lips over mine in a kiss that was both searing and delicate, a promise just beneath the surface.

We walked deeper into the marketplace, and the strange city seemed to grow around us—roots and ivy clung to the stone walls, and overhead, a massive tree's branches stretched into the cavern, its leaves glittering with soft fairy light. Every glance I cast over at Aamon only seemed to pull him closer, to make my heart race faster. His hand stayed in mine, but as we neared a secluded alley lined with ivy and blooming flowers, he leaned in close, his lips grazing my ear.

"There's something I need, Roxy," he murmured, voice almost a growl. "I'm still weak—I need blood. I need you. I don't know what we will face soon, and in this weakened state I won't be able to defend you."

My pulse quickened, and I leaned back against the wall, the ivy cool against my back. "You can take what you need," I whispered, my voice daring, "but I won't drink your blood again—not until I know that what we have is ours, real, unclouded by a magical Bond."

He stared at me, the hunger clear in his eyes, but there was something more—respect, restraint. It made my heart beat even faster.

In one fluid motion, he closed the space between us, pressing me gently but firmly against the wall. His lips were on mine, and I lost myself in the kiss, in the taste of him, cool and dark and utterly intoxicating. His hands rested at my waist, pulling me closer as he deepened the kiss, his body pressing against mine as his fangs grazed my lips, a wicked promise of what was to come.

"Yes," I whispered, and with that permission his mouth moved to my neck. I felt the sharp prick as his fangs broke skin, the pain giving way to an exquisite pleasure that coursed through me, leaving me trembling as he drank. The sensation was overwhelming—pure, electric, a heat that unfurled from where his mouth met my skin and spread, spiraling down until it was all I could feel. I gasped, my hands gripping his shoulders as he held me, the world narrowing down to the two of us. I felt a tightening ... and then a massive release. A shudder of ecstasy coursed through my body, and I wished this connection, this moment, would never stop.

When he finally pulled back, he brushed his thumb over my bite mark, and I watched as he took a tiny drop of his own blood and gently rubbed it against my neck. The skin tingled, and I felt the wound begin to close, the warmth of his touch lingering. He leaned down and pressed a soft kiss to my neck, as if sealing something between us.

Our gazes locked, and I saw that same longing mirrored in his dark eyes. But beneath the hunger, there was patience, restraint. I could see how much he wanted me—how much I wanted him.

And I felt myself smiling, breathless, reaching for a calm I knew was long gone. "I think..." I managed, still caught in his gaze, "it might be time we find the others and ... temper this, don't you?"

He chuckled, pulling back but only slightly, his voice a low, wicked promise. "For now," he murmured. But I could still see that heat in his eyes, that longing that was anything but finished.

When we finally caught up with Rick and Timmy, Rick had a knowing look in his eye. He tilted his head as I joined them, then asked with a suspicious glint, "What did you two get up to?". He smiled slyly and then sniffed the air dramatically. "What do I smell?"

I felt the blush creep across my cheeks, my body betraying me. "Nothing," I replied quickly, trying to keep my voice even. "Well, none of your business, anyway."

"Roxy," he said, that smirk of his widening. "You could do much better." He gestured toward himself in exaggerated fashion. "There's still time, you know. You could get on the Rick train."

He didn't seem to care that Aamon was standing right there, expression deliberately blank.

"You're shameless." Despite myself, a smile tugged at the corners of my mouth. He had this ridiculous way of making light of everything.

"So, have you seen Ida?" I asked, hoping to shift the conversation back to the task at hand.

"Yeah, she came by looking for you," Rick replied, his grin fading. "She told us to meet her on the other side of that huge tree. Mentioned something about stairs." He hesitated, a flicker of doubt crossing his face. "I don't fully trust her, Roxy, but without her, I don't know how we'd get out of this place."

I nodded, recalling the time Ida and I had spent imprisoned together. "When we were in that cell, we built a bit of an understanding. I know she has her own intentions, but none of them aim to harm us."

With each step, we delved deeper into the underground city, marveling at the architectural wonders surrounding us. Towering structures of stone and shimmering crystal filled the city, vines curling around arches and bridges, with glowing orbs floating along the streets like phantom lanterns. A strange beauty enveloped everything, mystical and alluring, making me almost forget the danger we faced. It was surreal compared to the bleak metropolis above.

Spotting Ida ahead, I called out to her. She waved.

When we were close enough, I asked, "Why is this place so different from the surface? It's beautiful, magical. Nothing like the city above."

"Because it's still Wild. The Seelie and the Unseelie—the Light and Dark Royal Courts—rule the lands above. Though divided into their various nations, one or the other always controls the balance of power. This place is one of the few free regions, where the Wild Fae dwell, like me."

She paused, her eyes dimming. "Once, our world was lush, beautiful everywhere. But over time, we turned to technology, and slowly we began to destroy the natural balance. Now, most of those above ground live off the scraps left behind. The Unseelie think they can restore what was lost—and are willing to achieve it by any means necessary." Her eyes met mine, deadly serious.

"If it were up to them, they'd invade your world, enslave humanity, and drain every last resource to rebuild their empire."

I felt a chill as her words sank in. "What's stopping them? Even without magic, your technology is more advanced."

Ida's eyes gleamed knowingly. "You don't understand how the portals work, do you? There are natural ones that appear and vanish, but the more stable ones require both magic and technology. Each use weakens it. So, if they were to try to invade en masse, it would seal the portal behind them." She sighed. "But during a Convergence, when our three worlds align, it becomes easier to open portals. It's rare, and this is their moment."

Her voice softened, and guilt flashed across her face. "Sable had me gather intel on the Convergence. In my eagerness to please her, I told her things I shouldn't have. She'll use that knowledge to help the Unseelie." Ida shook her head. "I've spoken to the council here. They're letting us use a wild portal to get close to the main one, but the fools won't intervene with the Dark Fae."

"Why not?"

"They want our lands restored too—and they are willing to look the other way. They don't understand that undoing the supernatural curse in your world would shift the balance in all realms. When the witches in your world got together and cast the spell to balance the supernaturals, they used energy from all three realms, which affected us all," she explained. "It restricts the power of supernatural beings in your world and keeps beings like us from crossing over freely. Breaking it would complicate things for everyone. No matter what they say, I'll help you stop Logan. I can't help much, but we all need to do our small part."

She extended a hand toward a towering, spiral staircase that descended deeper into the cavern. Ivy and luminescent vines framed it, and delicate, glowing jellyfish-like creatures floated around us, illuminating the path with their soft blue light. We began our descent, shadows dancing around us as we moved down the winding steps. A chill hung in the air, the silence punctuated only by the faint sounds of wings flapping from shadowy bat-like creatures above.

At the base of the staircase lay a small dock on an underground lake, the shore shrouded in mist. A small boat awaited us, floating as if by magic on the glassy, black water. Ida gestured. "The portal's on an island, so we must take the boat. But don't fall in. There are creatures in these waters, and they won't be so kind if we enter their domain."

"I can't swim, so I definitely don't want to fall in," I said.

We boarded the boat, which glided forward on its own, crossing the lake toward a small, mist-shrouded island. Three ancient stones stood in a circle, surrounding a shimmering, flickering portal. It pulsed with vibrant colors, as though alive.

"Is it safe?" I asked, although I already knew the answer.

Ida chuckled darkly. "No, Roxy. It's wild, unpredictable. The council's magic guides it, but without their influence, the portal could lead anywhere—maybe even to the demon realm. And trust me, you don't want to end up there. If you think we're dark, the demons are far worse. Make sure that you have contact with each other, hold hands. We all must be touching, or we'll end up in different places."

Rick slid up to me, wrapping his fingers through mine, and then Aamon did the same on my other side. My skin buzzed with the contact, a spark jumping between us that had nothing to do with the portal and everything to do with the magic pulsing from Rick on one side and Aamon on the other. How had I, in such a short time, turned into such a ... well, let's just say it, a horny mess? Standing here between the two of them, feeling their touch, sent a wave of heat through me that I hadn't even realized was possible.

Aamon's eyes caught mine, and I knew he could feel my unexpected hunger. His thumb traced over my hand, sending another jolt of something raw and electric through the three of us.

Rick grinned, breaking the silence. "Hey, Roxy, you feeling something funny?" His words made me giggle.

Leave it to Rick to break the tension, although I could tell he was feeling it, too—whatever strange, thrilling thing was passing between us.

In that moment, I thought things might just take a turn into uncharted territory, somewhere I never thought I'd go. But then, Ida's hand landed on my shoulder. Timmy's on the other. Instantly, my intense passions shattered as reality snapped back into place. As we were all pulled through the portal, I prayed to anything listening that we make it to the other side alive.

17 Crossing

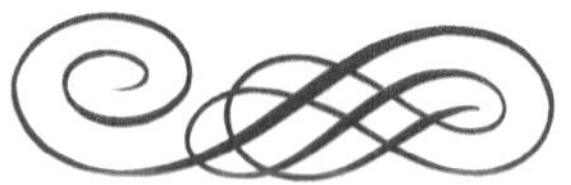

As we passed through the portal, a surge of electric energy rippled up my arm, pulsing between my fingers, which were tightly intertwined with Rick's and Aamon's. The magic of the crossing hummed in my bones, each sensation heightened—as if every nerve in my body had been rejuvenated, washing away the weariness I'd been feeling. This portal felt wildly different from the one Aamon and I had used before, and I wasn't sure if the others experienced the same, but for me, it was invigorating.

In front of us stretched a sprawling green glade, dotted with bright shamrocks that gleamed with magic in the light of the moon. The stream that snaked through the glade caught the silvery luminescence, scattering the light like shards of glass or crystal. The stars glistened in the night sky, each one a tiny beacon beckoning to us with a soft, enchanted glow.

Reluctantly, I let go of Rick's and Aamon's hands, the connection between us breaking but leaving a lingering warmth that I felt deep in my palms.

"How far do you think we are from the castle?" I asked, my gaze lingering on the unfamiliar landscape, heart pounding with the anticipation of the journey ahead.

Rick grinned, pulling out his phone with a flourish. "I've got a magical way to find out. It's called GPS." His face was lit by the faint glow of the screen, making his features look sharper, yet somehow more playful in the moonlight.

I rolled my eyes, unable to hide my smile. "Rick, you're such a pain. Though I have to ask, since you turned into a werewolf and ended up wearing basically just your shorts—where exactly are you keeping that phone?"

He chuckled, tucking his phone back into the waistband of his shorts, which, quite frankly, were hanging on by a miracle.

Aamon raised an eyebrow, his dark gaze moving from Rick's phone to his almost nonexistent outfit. "Rick, I'm starting to see some of your ... more interesting qualities." He crossed his arms, amusement glinting in his eyes as he looked at Rick with a slight, teasing smirk.

Rick's grin faltered for a split second, his cheeks tinging pink under Aamon's playful stare. "You're both impossible," he said, clearly flustered.

"You're so easy to wind up, wolf," Aamon added, his smirk widening.

Rick mumbled something under his breath, which I could only guess was a curse, and then led the way as we all laughed, the banter lifting the tension. Step by step, we moved forward together, the sound of the stream trickling nearby, our voices mingling with the quiet rustling of the leaves in the gentle night breeze.

Eventually, we crested a small hill, and there it was in the distance—the castle. My breath hitched as I took it in, struck by its beauty and grandeur. Gothic towers rose high into the sky, their pointed spires slicing through the night. The castle was immense, its towering glass windows reflecting the moonlight in ethereal shades of blue and silver. It had a timeless quality, like it had always been there. Only someone who loved the past and held a vision for the future could have created something so awe-inspiring.

As we descended toward the castle, I caught sight of a figure waiting for us at the entrance. Brianna stepped forward, a relieved smile lighting up her face as she spotted us. She looked tired, but the relief in her eyes was unmistakable.

"How did things go?" she asked, her voice warm as she came to meet us.

"The Fae were a bust," I said.

I quickly filled her in, giving her a rundown of what we'd faced on the other side of the portal, and then turned to introduce her to Ida, our newest ally. As their hands met, something shifted in the air. Their handshake lingered a beat too long, and I noticed a slight blush creeping over Brianna's cheeks. Ida, too, seemed captivated, her gaze fixed on her as if she couldn't look away. There was a softness in her eyes I hadn't seen before. Watching them, I couldn't help but smile. It was like something out of a fairy tale. Had I just witnessed love at first sight? No matter what it was, it was beautiful to see.

Aamon's voice cut through the stillness, snapping me back to the present. "We should freshen up and rest before we talk about the next step to take."

I frowned, folding my arms across my chest. "I don't need rest. Just tell me now, Aamon. Things have been rough enough—I can handle more bad news."

Aamon looked at me with a mixture of exasperation and sympathy, running a hand through his dark hair. He exhaled slowly, as if bracing himself.

"There's a witch," he said, his voice low and measured. "Her name is Hazel. She may know where the ritual took place, but there's one problem: she's ancient, powerful, and she lives on an island off the coast. No one who's gone to see her has ever come back. She's our last resort—or your last resort. No vampires allowed."

"You can't come?" I asked. His answer was already forming in my mind, plucked from his thoughts as dread curled around my heart.

Aamon shook his head. "No. Only witches can enter her domain. She lives in complete isolation, far removed from everyone. But if anyone holds the knowledge we need, it's her."

I took a deep breath, trying to steady myself. My hands clenched at my sides. This was going to be dangerous. Hazel's very name felt like a weight on my soul, but I refused to back down. I'd come too far to let fear stop me now. Meeting Aamon's gaze, I nodded, my voice steady with resolve. "Then Hazel it is. So how do I get to this island?"

Rick spoke up and said, "Well, if I had to get there, that damn vampire would probably send me on a bus and then make me hike for about three days." I could tell he was still slightly angry about how he had been brought to Ireland.

Aamon said, "It was petty of me, but I still take a little joy in picturing you with your knees up to your chin on that plane, and stuck on the bus in that narrow seat, despite your large frame."

Aamon was having too much fun messing with him, still glancing at his torn clothing from time to time—or more like what was revealed by it.

"I'll just shut up now," Rick said, blushing and wanting to get away badly. "Timmy and I probably should get something on."

"I don't know," I remarked, catching Aamon's playful emotion, "I like it."

"I'd appreciate the sentiment more if we were alone," Rick said, uncomfortable. "I'm not into menage a trois ... or menage a sees."

"Six?" Brianna squeaked, realizing there were six of us, and a lot of sexual tension all around. She cleared her throat, changing the subject. "Many years ago," she said, "while doing some research for Aamon, we found there was no way to reach the island ourselves. But I did, at his instruction, invest in the fishing village near the closest point to the island. Well, it's just another sign of how bloody rich he is—he bought most of that village.

"I suggest that we all rest for a while and refresh. Then I will prepare the helicopter, and I'll fly you to the village, Roxy. From there, you'll have to take a fishing boat, and you'll have to handle that yourself. I don't know what you'll find there, but I have faith in you."

Ida looked at Brianna and said, "You're a pilot too? Sexy."

Brianna blushed and smiled. "Just one of my many talents"

"Maybe you could show me around?" Ida asked.

Rick jumped in with that goofy grin of his and said, "Hey, you know, you could show me around too." Subtle as a sledgehammer, as usual. I could tell he had a thing for her—of course he did. Rick always had a thing for some girl, like it was his full-time job or something. This one, though, she barely batted an eye at him. I almost felt bad for the guy. Almost.

I went to my room, which had a magnificent bed with velvet sheets, the headboard covered in carvings of angels and gargoyles having sex. "Wow, that's over the top," I mumbled to myself, but then I shrugged. I was getting comfortable with what used to make me uncomfortable.

When I awoke, I saw that the others were already downstairs, nearly finished with their breakfast. I must have needed more sleep than I had imagined. Brianna had provided an amazing spread of bacon, eggs, fruit, pancakes ... everything.

The bond between Aamon and I must have weakened. I had no sexual dreams about him ... and I kind of missed it. I smiled at him shyly, and thrilled when he smiled back with a heat that made me want to experience some of those dreams for real.

Focus, I told myself.

After a quick breakfast, Brianna and Aamon led us all down a long hallway beneath the castle, which connected to a hangar outside. There, a sleek black helicopter with darkened windows awaited us.

"So, this is how a vampire gets around when he can't go out in the light," I remarked.

"Money can buy many things," Brianna said, "but Mister Aamon still can't fly it."

I noticed that Ida and Brianna were standing closer to each other than they had the night before. I also noticed that Rick looked jealous. Rick? Jealous? I'd never seen that expression on his face before, and it threw me off for a second. What did he have to be jealous of? Was he having serious thoughts about Brianna? The way he avoided looking directly at me, how his hand lingered just a little too long on hers, earlier—it wasn't just in my head. Was it? I chewed on that thought. Rick and Brianna ... or it could just be more of Rick's games. Although ... he looked serious.

"I would love to accompany you," Ida said, eyes fixed on Brianna who now seemed to be at the center of a love triangle. "But I should stay and do research about the Convergence."

"Let's go," I said, trying to hurry Brianna up. As fun as all this was to watch from afar, we had to stop Logan and Tar.

Rick sat beside Brianna during the helicopter trip, while Timmy tried to ignore Aamon and I curled up together as we watched the world through darkened windows. After nearly an hour of beautiful landscapes below—mostly green fields and rocky terrain—we came to the coastline of a small, charming fishing village. We landed at a small airport just outside of it.

When the chopper was wheeled into the hangar, and we stepped out, headsets off, Rick said to me, "I don't like that you're going alone."

"I'll be fine," I reassured him.

"Please be safe. You are important to me," Aamon said, as his hand gently touched my shoulder. I impulsively got on my tiptoes and kissed him. I think my impulsiveness surprised him as much as it did me, but it was a good kiss. A really good kiss.

Brianna drove me through the small fishing village, showing me how they had been fixing it up the best they could so it wouldn't just fade away like so many other small villages around the area. The fishing had been dying out, so they brought in a bit of tourism to give the villagers a way to make money.

"Aamon can be a bit much, but his kindness can be surprising," she said. "I think it's a way to hold back the darkness inside him or atone for the dark things that he did before he got control of himself. I don't really know. In any case, he gives me the opportunity to do things for others that I would not be able to do on my own. And I'm very grateful for that."

We pulled up to a dock where an old, craggy fisherman was waiting for us. He said to us in a very deep Irish accent, "You're the one that wants to go to the island? I wouldn't recommend it, but since no one listens to me, I'm told I need to give you some lessons on how to run the ship."

After a short time of him explaining what I needed to do and how to do it, I waved goodbye and set off across the water toward the island. Looking at the GPS on the boat, I knew it wasn't far, but I could sense a cloud of magic around the island that made it hazy and hard to see in the distance.

Once I got closer, I saw that the island was stony and overgrown with foliage, mosses, and ferns that grew well in the damp air. When I arrived at the ancient stone dock, I noticed a winding pathway going up to a higher point on the island.

I sensed that if I wasn't a witch, I would never have been allowed to step foot on the shore. But something was here, bidding me enter. Was it Hazel? Whoever it was, I accepted the invitation, and I climbed up the winding, stone path.

18 Island of the Dead

As I crested a hill, I gasped, both from the climb and the view that opened before me. It was vast, stretching beyond anything I'd imagined. Standing at the edge of a high plateau, I took in the sprawling, desolate landscape of what could only be a necropolis—a city of the dead, ancient and sacred. Stones marked the graveyard in endless rows, their carvings faded with age, weathered and softened by centuries of wind and rain. A strange cocktail of awe and dread settled over my senses. I was excited to be here but knew also that something dangerous awaited me.

The climb up had been surreal enough, and now I saw lazy cats lounging on sun-drenched rocks as if the world beyond this place didn't matter. They blinked at me with slow indifference, purring and stretching as I passed. Their shadows stretched long and languid, and I couldn't help but smile at the absurdity of it all. I stopped, surveying the massive graveyard before me, and I felt the subtle pulse of something alive—or rather, something undead.

With every step deeper into the necropolis, my witch's senses buzzed with the energy of beings buried here, their presence lingering just beneath the surface. Ghouls, I thought. Spirits, surely. They hovered at the edge of my awareness, neither alive nor dead, tethered to this place by something unseen. Their energy felt ancient, feral. Not dangerous but deeply powerful.

And then, through the mist that drifted between the headstones, I sensed her—a presence like mine but older, definitely wiser. Hazel. The witch I'd come here to find.

She was waiting, as I'd suspected, but her energy was not as I'd imagined. It was ... layered, like she wore a mask within a mask. Her presence tugged me forward through the endless graveyard, each step taking me deeper into the heart of this strange island.

The graveyard was a blend of beauty and decay. Vines twisted over the stones in intricate patterns, a living testament to the centuries of life that had come and gone. Wildflowers bloomed in small clusters, defiantly vibrant in this place of death, and I marveled at their bravery, their tenacity. The air was thick with the scent of damp earth and ancient magic, the kind that clings to old places where spirits don't always rest.

Finally, after what felt like hours, I reached the end of the graveyard. There, nestled against a dense thicket of trees, stood a small, crooked house. It was everything I'd expected from a witch's dwelling—quaint yet strange, with plants trailing down from every window and an air of mystery that made me pause. More cats of every shape, size, and color sprawled across the front steps. Many more than I could possibly count. They flicked their tails in unison, almost as if they'd been expecting me too.

A girl appeared in the doorway, or at least she looked like one. Maybe fourteen or fifteen, with hair so pale it was nearly white. She raised an eyebrow, her eyes glinting with a challenge.

"So," she said, crossing her arms, "are you going to stand there all day, or are you coming in? I've been waiting."

Taken slightly aback, I stepped forward, her words echoing in my mind as I crossed the threshold. Inside, the house was small and cluttered, every surface covered with vials, dried herbs, and strange artifacts. A crystal ball sat in the center of a small table, glowing with a dim light. It felt like I'd stepped into another world entirely.

"Yes, that's how I knew you were coming," Hazel said, following my gaze to the crystal. "An old relic. Most witches can't get their hands on real ones nowadays. What they sell now," she added with a dismissive wave, "are toys. Nothing like this."

She nudged a few cats aside, gesturing for me to sit, and with a smirk asked, "So, are you here to kill me?"

Her question threw me. "Kill you? Why would I...? Why would I want to kill you?"

She chuckled, a sound both young and ancient. "The crystal doesn't show me your intentions. Just a hint of what you've done, what you might do. At least that's what it does for me. For others, sometimes it's different. And given that you're the first witch to make it to this is-land in ages, well... it raises some questions."

Hazel's gaze softened as she read me, as if she saw more in me than I could see in myself. "You're here to break the curse, or to stop it from being broken. I'm not sure of your true intentions. I'm not even sure if you are."

"Yes, I'm confused," I replied, the weight of it sud-denly feeling heavy. "But I know I want to stop Logan and his master, Tar, from undoing the curse."

Hazel tilted her head, studying me with a piercing in-tensity. "To break or create anything, you must under-stand it first. And you, Roxy, you're more powerful than you realize. The magic you wield—the power to affect supernatural creatures and their prey, to either break or forge their connections—is very rare."

Her words sank deep, unsettling something within me, yet her tone held a strange kind of reverence. I opened my mouth to question her, but she continued, "It's remarkable that you even made it to my home. This island is ... well, let's just say it's not easy to find, even for a witch. This is a graveyard for creatures that can never truly die, ones who linger in spirit when their bodies have long since turned to dust. They've been my only company for a very long time."

"But you look so young," I said, unable to hide my surprise. "I thought you'd be ancient."

"I am ancient." She gave me a knowing smile and said, "There's more than one way to extend life. Watch."

With a subtle gesture, she released the illusion, and her appearance shifted. Her skin grew paler, more skeletal, her eyes shadowed with unnatural darkness. She became something ... undead, yet more alive than any spirit I'd known.

"I'm a lich," she said simply. "And it takes great magic to live beyond life, to become what I am."

I stared at her, horrified but captivated. "How long have you been like this?"

She shrugged. "Time is different for someone like me. But long enough to cast the curse on the supernaturals, and long enough to regret what that curse has taken from all of us. But don't get me wrong, I would do it again. Creatures like Tar, the vampire you've met—they don't live the same after the curse. None of us do."

"Why are you telling me all this?" I asked, my voice softer than I intended.

"Because you need to know everything, Roxy, if you're going to stop Logan and the true power behind him—his master, Tar. I haven't seen her for a very long time. She can't bear being diminished by the curse. If she could have come to this island and ended me, she would have done so long ago. She had to wait for someone like you or Harper to be born. You need to understand that power like yours, without knowledge, is like wildfire—uncontained, destructive." Her voice grew distant as her gaze lingered on the ancient crystal ball. "You're here to make a choice, one that will ripple through our world and beyond."

Her words hung in the air like a spell, capturing me in that moment. In the dim glow of Hazel's home, walls lined with faded tapestries and scrolls, I stood across from the ancient witch. Hazel's beauty was unsettling, ethereal—her youthful face betraying none of the centuries she had roamed this world and beyond. Her face was just a mask, and she was tethered to life by dark magic. Her silver eyes glimmered as they fixed on me, a sly smirk tracing her lips.

"So, you want to know where the ritual took place," Hazel murmured, "but knowledge has its price, young witch. You must prove your worth first, and then you must retrieve something that I cannot retrieve."

My red hair fell in loose waves over my shoulders, my hands clenched to hide my impatience. I nodded. "Tell me what I have to do."

"This crystal ball will question you, test you. Answer correctly, and you may seek its guidance. Fail, and your ambition ends here." Her tone held a note of warning. "But know this—it is dangerous. The spirits here grow restless, drawn to any who dare to pry into their secrets. They may lash out to keep the truth buried."

I swallowed, my heart pounding. I had faced enough challenges already, but the weight of Hazel's words lingered. I met her gaze and nodded.

Hazel leaned closer. "Then, let us begin with a riddle."

Her voice grew soft, almost whispering, as she wove the words of the riddle:

"I am something you seek, although I can't be found;
The more you chase me, the further I'm bound.
When you stand still, I draw near.
Not seen in your youth, yet cherished when clear.
Some say I am woven, others say I grow.
For I come to those who nurture, not sow.
I bend but don't break, and heal as I tear.
I am heavy and light, but hold none with despair.
"What am I?"

"Wisdom," I said confidently. Why did I need to answer a riddle? I already knew the answer in her thoughts. Hazel had been alone for so long that she sought any opportunity to talk to someone. Words were a small price to pay.

Hazel's smile deepened, her eyes glinting with a dark satisfaction. "Very good, Roxy. You may approach the crystal."

I took a slow, steadying breath, feeling the weight of the moment pressing down on me. I moved closer to the orb, reaching out and letting my fingers brush its cool surface. The second I made contact, my vision blurred, and my surroundings melted away. It felt like slipping into a dark, endless void as my consciousness merged with the shadowy ether within the crystal.

A voice echoed hollowly in my mind, ancient and distant. "What is it that you wish to truly know, Roxy?"

The question cut through me, making me pause. What do I truly want? The intensity of my emotions clouded my thoughts, leaving me momentarily dazed. Finally, I forced myself to focus, and a tight ache rose in my chest as I whispered the words I'd been afraid to ask. I sensed that asking for the location of the ritual was out of my reach. But I had another question, something that had been haunting me. "I need to know ... about my mother. Is she really gone since Harper took over her body? Is there any way to get her back?"

The voice seemed to sigh, its tone heavy and know-ing. "You already know the answer, don't you, Roxy? She's gone. Only fragments remain—echoes, hollowed out by hunger and time. She doesn't remember, nor can she answer why she left. But a trace of her spirit still lingers, trapped ... yearning to be freed. She remains bound to her master, Harper. You can free her, but you will never truly get to know her...."

The message twisted something deep inside me, a toxic mix of fury and sorrow. I wanted to scream, to curse the crystal and everything in it, but instead, I pressed my palms harder against its surface, anchoring myself to the painful truth.

Then it hit me—a frigid, clawing sensation burrowed into my mind. Shadows crawled at the edges of my consciousness, like wisps of smoke seeping from the graveyard beyond these walls. Cold tendrils wrapped around my thoughts, tugging me into a bleak, spectral realm where formless spirits drifted. Their energy was sharp, biting, as if they were here to guard something—and they weren't here to help me.

The phantoms closed in, their whispers as sharp as knives, slicing into my defenses. They didn't want me to find the ritual's location or to even think about breaking the curse. Why is it that everyone thinks I'm going to break the curse? I thought, bitterly amused even as I struggled.

"She's ours," one spirit hissed, its voice scraping across my mind, cold and possessive.

Grinding my teeth, I pushed back, summoning the strength I knew lay buried within me. My magic stirred, bright and fierce, a hot surge of defiance resisting the icy assault. I focused, channeling everything I had, forcing my energy to counter the shadows' grasp. My mind became a battlefield, my essence colliding with the spectral forms that clawed and bit at the edges of my soul.

It was brutal. For a moment, I feared I wouldn't make it—the spirits of the necropolis were relentless, their numbers overwhelming, their strength crushing. Their laughter was a chorus of hollow mockery, pressing harder, pushing me to the edge.

But I wasn't going to back down.

With one final, desperate surge of magic, I threw them from my mind, sending the phantoms reeling. They screeched in fury, dissipating into shadows that scattered and faded, leaving me trembling but victorious.

Panting, I released the crystal and staggered back, feeling the world return around me. The dim room sharpened into focus, and Hazel stood there, her eyes gleaming with something close to admiration.

My voice came out a hoarse whisper, raw and filled with a hard-won resolve. "Now, Hazel," I said, locking my gaze onto hers, fierce and unyielding. "Tell me where the ritual was cast. I've earned it."

Hazel looked at me, her eyes intense. "If only it were that easy, Roxy," she said with a sigh. "You survived the crystal. Most witches go mad or never come back at all. There's something I must tell you—something I've kept to myself for a long time." She paused, the weight of her words sinking heavily into the air.

"My sisters and I ... we created the curse. It took thirteen of us, and we drew magic not just from this world, but from others as well. It wasn't a simple spell; it demanded a price. Nearly all the witches alive in that day paid with their lives. We sacrificed our own kin to restore balance. We lost so much of ourselves in the process. Once, we were powerful—almost beyond mortal comprehension, like the Fae. There was no three-fold law binding us, no governing force to restrain our will. But the cost was greater than we anticipated. We severed the deeper connection we once had with nature and the spirit realm. We could still access the magic, yes, but it was like looking through frosted glass; we could never truly connect as we once did."

I watched her face, seeing the shadow of sorrow etched into her features. "To cast the curse, we did something unheard of. We intertwined our souls, each of us offering a piece of ourselves, like creating a new life. Together, we forged something unique, something that had never existed before—a soul with a spark from each of us. That soul gave us the power to create the curse."

She exhaled heavily, "But we knew ... we knew we couldn't leave it within our reach. So, we took the last, painful step as sisters. We cast a spell to hide that soul from all of us. None of us could find it, so we couldn't reverse what we did. It's hidden, even from me. I can't say where the ritual was first cast, or where Logan would go to try and end it. Without that lost piece of me, I cannot know."

She looked down, her voice a whisper. "Without that fragment of my soul, I won't be able to help you. And I know you're capable, Roxy. You can sense bonds, the connections between people and things. I'll open myself to you, let you sense the tether to my lost fragment. It's risky, but it's our only hope."

I hesitated, staring at her outstretched hands. A voice in my head whispered, Can I trust her? What if she's only using me to retrieve this piece? But deep down, I knew it didn't matter. If I didn't help her, I'd never stand a chance against Logan. Someone else might walk away, but not me. Not when I'd come this far. I'm impulsive, for better or worse, and right now, I was betting on "for better."

I took her hands, feeling a faint warmth pulse through my palms, something deep and ancient. The moment I opened myself to the bond, I felt a jolt—a tether forged between us. The lost fragment of her soul felt close, but at the same time, impossibly distant. I tried to make sense of the sensation, glancing at Hazel.

She nodded, her face grim. "This place is a nexus. There are portals here, gateways to other realms, accessible only under dire need. I cannot go with you, but I can show you to the portal that hides my soul. However, you're not going to like this." Her gaze shifted, a flicker of dread in her eyes. "You've shown me that it isn't on

Earth. It isn't in the Fae lands, either. It's ... in the realm of demons."

I blinked, then swallowed hard. "Oh, hell no. You're telling me to go there? Alone?"

Hazel shook her head. "The portal will only allow one to pass, yes. But you're still tethered to that vampire, aren't you? If you go with him, you'll count as one— like you're a single entity. He would be with you, not leaving you completely alone. But it's your choice. I've never been to the demon realm. I don't know what you'll find. All I know is that without that fragment, I can't help you."

I took a deep breath, weighing her words. "What good would it do to bring a vampire? The limitations of day and night are hard to deal with."

"Roxy, you're so powerful, but sometimes I forget how young you are and the things you don't know. Do you know about the Demon Realm? Of course not. Let me enlighten you. Their star is different from ours. Creatures of the night here, who can't go out during the day, can move freely day or night there. It's a different world altogether.

"The only real challenge is that the undead can't cross into the Demon Realm on their own. But since that vampire is tethered to you, he can come along, riding on your coattails. His strength and power could be useful to you."

"Fine, I'll do it. Where's this portal?" I replied.

Her eyes softened, relief flickering in them. "It's near where you first arrived on the island—a cave, just beyond my reach. Close enough that your vampire could accompany you if I lower some of my wards, letting him step onto the island, at least along the fringe. Even though the tether between you two is weak, it's enough for you both to pass through the portal together."

"Hard to believe a few days ago, I'd never left my hometown. Now I've flown everywhere and crossed to another world—what's one more?"

19 Threshold

I stood at the beach, just by the mouth of a cave that only opened at low tide. If the tide had been high, I wouldn't have been able to reach it. Around me, the cats from Hazel's house had followed, curious as ever, dancing with shadows and crabs that scuttled near the water. Their carefree play brought a lightness to my heart. Amid all the chaos I'd been tangled in lately, this small moment felt like a gift, a reminder that life had beauty, even in unexpected places. I could feel it filling me up, rejuvenating me. But I knew that wouldn't last.

My focus drifted back to my objective. I had to get Aamon here, and fast, before dawn broke. A recent memory flickered, of the time I connected mind to mind with others in Faerie. Could I do the same with Aamon? I searched deep within myself, reaching for the thin thread of our connection. It was ragged, almost lost, but still there. When I grasped it, a surge of heat poured through, clenching deep in my core. Aamon always affected me this way; we had so much tension between us, unspoken and unspent. Pressing that feeling down, I called out to him.

Aamon, I need you. Can you reach me? Can you hear me?

There was a beat of silence, and then his voice echoed in my mind, as surprised as I was. Roxy? I didn't know you could do this. It's ... amazing. You're in my mind, and I'm in yours. Are you in danger?

No, I'm okay, I replied. But I need you with me. I'm about to enter a portal to the demon world. Will you come with me?

His hesitation was brief. I don't know how that's possible, he said, voice rough with emotion. But I would follow you anywhere. Stay where you are. I'll be there shortly.

I perched on a rock by the water, watching the cats playing, as the first birds stirred, their early calls weaving into the calm sound of waves. I couldn't help wondering if it was just the bond that drew me to Aamon, or was it more? With my new senses, I could tell he wasn't manipulating me. But could I be fooling myself? After all, it wasn't the first time I'd felt this pull. Part of me questioned if I was losing myself in him, and if I'd ever truly found my own power, my own worth, outside of others.

And then, through the stillness, a fog rolled over the water. It moved faster than any fog should, thickening until, impossibly, it solidified. A figure took shape within, a stunning man standing waist-deep in the surf. My heart jolted as he strode toward me. The morning light caught his outline, and for a moment, I felt fully alive. Denying that would be denying everything I was trying to embrace—to truly live, to seize life instead of watching it drift by. Whatever was coming, I knew I had to take this chance.

Aamon stopped before me, his gaze warm as he took me in. "Roxy," he murmured, "you look more beautiful each time I see you. In this early light ... you're angelic."

"You're ...." I didn't know what to say. "... here. Thank you," was all I managed. He took my breath away, so even those words were no small feat.

I led us toward the cave, feeling his eyes roam over me, lingering. Inside the dim entrance, I paused, allowing my vision time to adjust to see the path ahead, though not as keenly as Aamon's. I knew he could see every detail in the darkness, could feel him still looking at me. The tension between us pulsed, drawing us closer, until just his presence stirred a deep arousal.

I kept walking. There was no time to analyze what I was feeling ... although. I enjoyed it.

The narrow tunnel led us to a small cavern, where I noticed a pentagram etched into the stone floor—a reminder of the dark magic we were about to face. I didn't know much about demonology, but I knew enough to understand that demons couldn't cross into our world without being summoned and bound. Without those constraints, they could wreak havoc. Our world's supernatural beings couldn't cross into theirs either. But as a witch, I was neither fully human nor fully supernatural. I could cross over. I could feel it in my bones.

I stepped toward the portal, Aamon's warm hand settling on my hip, sparking that familiar tightness in me. Just his touch could affect me so much. But I knew that the tenuous bond between us wouldn't be enough for what lay ahead.

"I need to strengthen our bond," I told him.

"Can you? Only vampires can do that," he replied, surprised.

"I'm finding I can do more than I realized." Gazing into his eyes, I reached for our bond, holding it in my mind's grip. Pouring my magic into it, I tried to weave it stronger, despite its frayed edges.

Is this what a vampire does? I wondered. This felt wrong, as if I could control him. So instead, I tore down the walls, leaving nothing between us—no control, just a raw, deeper connection. Our souls meshed, and I could feel his shock and wonder as keenly as I felt my own.

He looked at me, his voice barely a whisper. "Roxy, I've never felt anything like this."

I held his gaze, feeling the same, but I knew we had no time to savor it. Hazel had warned me the portal would be strongest at dawn. "Aamon, we need to go now if we're doing this. Are you still with me?"

"Even more so," he said, his eyes fierce with resolve. "Whatever awaits, I want to face it with you."

He took my hand, his warmth seeping through, his calloused fingers enveloping mine, grounding me but also giving me a sense of soaring. How could he affect me so much by just his touch? I truly didn't know how much longer I could go on before this had to become much more between us.

Then, the portal came alive—a swirling mass of black, red, and gold veins, pulsing like a heartbeat. There was a dark beauty to it, magnetic and menacing. Small crabs scurried toward it, as if drawn by an unseen force. The portal felt vast, distant, as if stretching farther than Faerie yet closer than ever, thanks to the Convergence.

Hand in hand, we stepped through, crossing the threshold into the unknown.

A thick air washed over us, heady and foreign. I tightened my grip on Aamon's hand, trying to steady the bubbling anticipation inside me as we stepped into the demon realm. I wasn't sure what I expected. Maybe crimson skies, fire spilling over rocky cliffs, and the stench of sulfur. But this ... this wasn't what I imagined.

The landscape before me was breathtaking. Glowing plants in hues I'd never seen seemed to shimmer, their veins pulsing as though they drank from a well of magic rather than sunlight. Tendrils of misty pink clouds drifted lazily across the sky, framing the scene with an almost surreal beauty. And in the distance, jellyfish-like creatures, colossal and elegant, floated across the horizon, trailing tendrils that waved like banners. Further out, creatures stood—towering figures with spindly, delicate limbs that bent gracefully as they fed on the high branches of ethereal trees. They looked like giraffes reimagined by some artist who'd dabbled in dreams and nightmares.

The scent in the air was almost intoxicating. Flowers bloomed all around us, releasing a fragrance that was part floral, part wild, and entirely fascinating. Every breath pulled me deeper into this place, my senses overwhelmed.

"Beautiful," I murmured, caught up in the splendor around us. It was only when Aamon squeezed my hand that I realized he wasn't watching the realm's landscape at all. His dark, intense gaze was on me, his lips quirked in that familiar, mysterious way.

"It's not as enchanting as you," he said, voice deep and smooth, stirring something in me that went beyond the magic in the air. "But I'll admit … it's unexpected."

A rush of heat rose to my cheeks, my heart beating wildly in my chest. A boldness I hadn't felt before took over as I looked at him, his face shadowed with the allure of something dangerous, something inevitable. What am I waiting for? I thought. This was what I wanted, wasn't it?

I took his other hand, and my pulse quickened as I gazed up at him, my voice soft but steady. "Kiss me, Aamon. Now. Don't say anything … just kiss me."

Without a word, he pulled me close, his arms wrapping around me as his lips met mine. The world faded; there was only the feel of his mouth, warm and consuming, every inch of me drawn to him as though we'd been pulled together by invisible strings all along. I felt his hands cradle my face, his fingers brushing along my skin, rough and possessive. His scent—dark, warm, and dangerously sweet—filled my senses, dizzying and irresistible. His lips trailed down my neck, lingering just long enough to make my breath catch.

His hand trailed down my back, pulling me flush against him, and I felt his heart pounding just as wildly as mine. And in that moment, I knew. Whatever was waiting for us out there, however strange or dangerous this place was, none of it mattered. I wanted him, and I wasn't going to wait another second to have him.

I could almost hear his heartbeat, just beneath my own, which was pounding in my chest—pulsing, relentless. It still surprised me that a vampire could have a heartbeat. What else didn't I know? I could feel how much he desired me, how much he wanted me. In that moment, nothing else mattered to him, and I felt the same way.

Breathless, we pressed against each other. I got on my tiptoes and kissed him again.

I pushed him away and slowly started to undo my blouse, teasing him with the curve of my breasts in the soft light. As he unbuttoned his shirt, I touched his chest—strong, masculine. His scent was driving me wild. I took his hand and placed it against my chest, then kissed him again. Our tongues mingled, and I could feel his fangs, sending a shiver of fear and desire down my spine. For a second, I thought I was opening myself for more heartache.

Damn it, Roxy, live for once. Whatever happens, will happen. Be here. Be in the moment.

I started kissing down his chest, gently sucking on his nipple and giving it a soft bite. I kissed and licked my way down to the curve of his hip as I squeezed his firm, tight ass. I began to pull his pants down, until he was naked and exposed. I soaked in the sight of him.

Mine.

I took his cock into my fist, and he shuddered with surprise. I slowly stroked him, watching him sway, entranced by the rhythm of my touch. I kissed the tip of him, moving my lips down his shaft before putting all of him in my mouth, letting his cock slip deep into my throat. I felt him stiffen instantly. I had all the power now.

I pulled him down to the soft, glowing grass, and he reached under my skirt and removed my panties, lightly touching me between my legs with his thick fingers. I moaned in response and shifted my body, so we were stretched out on the beautiful, warm grass.

He looked into my eyes and kissed me, gently nibbling and pulling on my lip with his teeth. I could feel his hands cupping my breasts, squeezing them, and then he slightly tugged at my nipples. All the while, he kissed down my neck, squeezing me, and breathed hot, warm breaths on my body.

I was slightly afraid he would bite me, but part of me wanted him to. His weight on me was making my muscles pulse and tighten. His fingers caressed the outside of my pussy, then slowly slid inside me, while he ran his thumb across my clitoris. I was wet, dripping and wanting him inside me.

"More," I breathed. I wanted him deeper, so deep, kissing me and filling me forever. Then he maddeningly stopped, raised himself up, and looked into my eyes.

"Roxy, do you want this?"

"I never wanted anything more in my life. I need this. I need you," I told him. "Yes, Aamon," I said, looking into his eyes, "fuck me."

I was stroking his massive cock in my hand. I looked into his eyes and told him, "I want you inside me. I want you. Now."

There was a slight bit of pain until I stretched enough to take all of him. I never thought anything could feel like this. His hips grinding against mine, I could feel the buildup of massive pressure. His nibbling on my neck was becoming frantic. Then I felt a sharp bite. The pain made the pleasure more intense. It was incredible.

When I thought I couldn't take any more, he pulled my hips up and thrust deeply into me again and again. What felt like an eternity built up to an unbearable crescendo. I pushed myself against him and felt his warmth empty into me. The release was like nothing I had ever felt before. I could barely breathe, let alone scream, as I felt a matching, pulsing release within myself.

The both of us spent, he put all his comforting weight on top of me and whispered against my neck: "We're just getting started."

I turned and kissed him deeply, our tongues mingling, as I grabbed the back of his head and pushed him down between my legs. "I know. I'm not done with you. Don't stop—" I commanded, not letting him pause as he built me up to another massive release.

We pleasured each other until we were beyond exhausted. I dozed, the sun high when my eyes fluttered open again. Slowly awakening, I luxuriated in warm sunlight all over my naked body as I lay there. I felt satiated yet knew I would be wanting more. I raised up slightly and looked down at his naked form lying in the glowing grass. I lightly touched him and watched him get harder again while he slept.

That was the most amazing experience I'd ever had. Why had I fought against this for so long? Fear of losing myself in someone else? I needed to lose myself. Abandon myself to sexual desire. Coming out on the other side, everything was so much clearer. It didn't take anything from me; it just let me feel something I never imagined I could.

Where are our clothes? I wondered briefly, before I realized I didn't care.

As I lay naked against him, looking up at that alien sky, I thought that as beautiful as it was, it was nothing compared to what we had shared together.

20 Dark World

The faint rustle of something nearby broke the silence of my contentment. And a gravelly voice sliced through the dimness.: "Hey, lady. Are these your clothes? Finally ready to put them on? I wasn't sure you and he were ever goanna stop. More stamina than a succubus, that's for sure."

I jumped and instinctively covered myself with my hands. The creature speaking was about three feet tall, with wide, kaleidoscope eyes, mottled green-gray skin, and leathery wings that, despite flapping furiously, barely enabled him to hover above the ground. He held my clothes in one gnarled hand. His expression was amused and a little too knowing.

"Don't tell me you were watching the whole time?" I managed, voice sharper than I intended, my cheeks hot with embarrassment.

"Okay, I won't tell you," the creature replied, smirking. "But I was. Quite the show. My master sent me to fetch you."

Aamon stirred beside me, instantly alert, his dark blue eyes coldly fixed on the creature, all traces of warmth gone. I felt the shift in him as if a current passed through the air.

"And who's your master?" he asked, his tone smooth but edged with a warning.

The creature gave a careless shrug, his wings fluttering a bit faster as though unconsciously revealing his nerves. "Oh, my people don't give out true names freely. Master is master. You can call me Hugo. It's a human name, right?"

"Hugo." The name rolled off my tongue with an odd familiarity, and he seemed to puff up slightly, relishing it. Still covering myself, I chuckled. "Fine, Hugo, but could you maybe turn around so I can get dressed?"

The creature's gaze remained on me, mischievous and unblinking. "I mean, I've already seen it all. But sure, lady. Not like I've got anything better to do." He didn't move.

Rolling my eyes, I snatched my clothes out of his grip and slipped on my pants. I felt the coolness of the early dawn air against my skin as I buttoned my blouse. Aamon sat up slowly, nonchalant and shameless. He remained suspicious as he carefully dressed, one brow slightly raised as he kept an eye on our peculiar guest. Hugo's wings flapped a bit more urgently, betraying a restlessness.

"So, Hugo," I asked, lacing up my shoes, "can you tell me anything about your master? A hint?"

He tilted his head, a mocking glint in his kaleidoscopic eyes. "Master's the ruler of all you can see. But a name, now ... that's personal. You'll have to earn that privilege."

I crossed my arms. "Then how about we strike a bargain, to make things clear? I won't harm you, and you won't harm us."

A gleam of childlike delight lit up Hugo's face. "A bargain, you say?" He cast a quick, wary look at Aamon before bowing slightly. "Such agreements are indeed the way of my people. Very well. If you agree to come along without a fight, I agree not to harm you—today." He grinned as if he'd achieved some grand victory.

Aamon muttered under his breath, shooting me a cautious look. "Good enough, for now," he said, though I knew he wished we could know more about the creature's master before we walked into their trap.

"Now, if you two are finished," Hugo said, "we'd best get moving. The land may look peaceful, but it doesn't take kindly to strangers. Especially tasty, human ones. So don't fall behind."

We set off, Hugo leading the way through a surreal landscape that stretched out like an eerie painting. Pink and crimson clouds tinged with gold blazed across the sky, and the black sun cast a deep red hue from its corona, as though it was coal dipped in blood. The air was thick, charged with an otherworldly energy that made my skin prickle. Beauty clashed with danger here, like a trap disguised in allure.

I couldn't help watching Hugo, curiosity sparking. "Don't take this the wrong way, but I imagined the demon realm would look ... different."

Hugo's head swiveled back toward me. "Oh? How so?"

"More fire, brimstone, shadows lurking everywhere," I replied, gesturing to the bright, vibrant landscape. "This is more like some twisted fairyland."

He laughed, a crackling sound that echoed. "Those places exist, but my master likes to stand out, show strength. This land mocks the other lords, flaunting the power to create beauty out of chaos."

The ground seemed to shimmer, rippling like it was alive, the black sun looming like an omen. We walked in silence for a time, Hugo flitting ahead, occasionally looking back to check if we were still following. As we walked, I noticed pairs of eyes gleaming at us from the shadows of twisted trees, their gazes hungry.

"Hugo?" I asked again, like a child full of questions, glancing at the shadows. "Are those ... creatures dangerous?"

Hugo flicked his gaze towards the trees before looking back at me. "Oh, them? They're terrified of me. You have nothing to worry about." He gave an exaggerated wink.

I stifled a smile, exchanging a glance with Aamon, who was suppressing his own smirk. There was something endearing, if not slightly absurd, about our tiny imp guide leading us through a land of dark creatures. But his confidence hinted at something more, a strength beyond his size.

As we continued, the sky brightened with dawn, but eerily the shadows were stretching out like dark fingers. It was a strange sunlight—one that Aamon did not have to hide from.

A distant howl split the silence, the sound echoing across the strange land.

"Not much further," Hugo called, his voice barely audible over the eerie growls. "But keep up! I won't be responsible if you lag behind."

I moved closer to Aamon, murmuring, "Seems our little guide is not as all powerful here as he claims."

Aamon's lips curved into a slight grin. "Noted. But somehow, I think we will be fine if we stay close to him—at least for now."

Shadows grew longer, reaching like tendrils. The ground beneath was soft and luminous, each knee-high blade of grass glowing faintly, casting a warm, spectral light on my skin. Aamon walked beside me, his gaze sharp, assessing every detail of the alien landscape with wariness.

Hugo flitted ahead, cackling occasionally, his small green-gray form an odd sight against the vivid backdrop. He led us onward, winding through giant, pulsing flowers that released glowing pollen in our path. Each plant and tree seemed alive, subtly shifting as if watching us, responding to our every move.

A sudden prickle at the base of my neck made me glance at Aamon. His gaze flickered, the only sign he sensed it too. The tall grass parted, revealing a creature that defied explanation—a sinewy mass of muscle, its eyes black and hungry. Its face was a snarl of fangs and ridges, a nightmare incarnate.

Before I could react, Hugo zipped in front of us, his eyes blazing with mischievous glee as he hissed in a guttural language. The creature paused, narrowed its gaze at Hugo, and, after a tense moment, slunk back into the shadows.

Hugo grinned. "Just a curious little critter. Not used to many guests here."

"Let's hope the other inhabitants aren't as curious," I muttered, my hairs still standing on end from the sight of that thing. Aamon, on the other hand, had a glint of exhilaration in his eyes. An ancient vampire like him must have seen it all, and this newfound danger was exciting.

With a triumphant pose, Hugo rose higher, his wings buzzing with excitement. "Look ahead, travelers! Soon, my master's city will greet you in all its splendor."

We crested a ridge, looking down at a winding path that led to a dock on the edge of shimmering black water. Across the water loomed an island, crowned by the Demon City. Though distant, I could see shadowy figures moving within, more strange and terrifying with every glance.

Hugo led us down to the dock and onto a rickety boat, each lurch of the creaking wood as we cut across the water heightening my pulse. Aamon's calm presence was a steady anchor beside me, and I found comfort in his solidity as the boat neared the island.

The city pulsed with life—demons and creatures of all forms, from angelic faces with unsettling eyes to monstrous figures cloaked in shadow. Some wore garbed in elaborate robes, while others seemed part of the shadows they wore.

"Quite the welcoming committee," Aamon murmured, his eyes gleaming with curiosity.

Hugo grinned. "Welcome to my world. Hope you're ready to meet the master."

He led us along a winding path, a route thick with shadows that twisted and curled like ink in water, moving with a life of their own. The path was silent except for our steps, muffled by the fog that clung to the ground like something alive. I felt the weight of unseen eyes pressing on my shoulders, a darkness that seemed to hum with intent, heightening my senses to every creak and whisper around us. I cast a glance at Aamon, who moved beside me, and despite the oppressive atmosphere, there was something in his presence that felt reassuring. His calm was uncanny, his every step deliberate, as if the darkness slid off him, barely daring to touch.

As we neared our destination, the fog began to thin, slowly revealing more of the city that lay ahead, pulsing with life—or perhaps an imitation of it. My breath caught at the sight. Narrow, twisted streets and open squares sprawled out, filled with an array of demons and creatures I'd only ever read about in dusty old books and heard whispers of in darkened rooms. Some figures wore the faces of angels, ethereal and almost holy, yet their sharp, predatory eyes glinted with a hunger that betrayed any semblance of innocence. Others were monstrous and grotesque, their twisted limbs bending at angles that defied nature, faces warped into leering grins filled with too many teeth. The deeper we went into this city, the more unsettling it became.

One demon with sleek black feathers, shimmering ominously in the light, had unblinking eyes that stretched unnaturally across its skull, a cold and focused stare fixed solely on us. Another being, whose form seemed to flicker and shift, had a face that changed continuously—a sneer one moment, a glare the next, as if searching for the perfect expression to unsettle me. The beings that moved around us wore elaborate robes embroidered with symbols I couldn't recognize, alien glyphs that seemed to shift and shimmer, drawing the eye with a hypnotic pull.

Hugo's chuckle broke the spell, harsh and mirthless. "They're nothing compared to the master. Stay close—unless you're eager to become a snack." His tone held a thinly veiled hint of amusement, the kind that seemed all too familiar with the creatures' appetites, remembering the fate of all those who'd strayed too far from the safety of his lead. The hairs on the back of my neck prickled, but I forced myself to keep my head high and my steps steady, following close behind him.

As we moved through the crowd, every step felt like wading through layers of dark magic, thick and clinging, an oppressive energy that sapped the air from my lungs. I could feel the demons' eyes follow our every move, the weight of their gazes scraping against my skin like claws. Aamon's hand brushed mine briefly, an accidental touch that sent a jolt of warmth through me, grounding me, and I glanced up at him, remembering just recently what we had shared, and I wondered if I was reading too much into it. Was it truly more than just physical? I felt that it was. But I've been wrong before.

We finally came to a towering black spire at the city's heart, a structure that loomed above us like a dark warning sign, twisting up into the sky in a defiance of natural form. It drew in every sliver of light, a vacuum that seemed to absorb all hope, casting the area around it into an abyssal darkness that pooled at its base, merging with the ground in an inky emptiness that made it difficult to see where the earth ended and the building began.

Hugo halted just before the spire's threshold; his usual smirk replaced by a look of solemnity. "This is it. The master is expecting you and has known about your arrival since you first set foot here." His eyes held an intensity, a warning that flickered behind his usual bravado. With a final nod, he disappeared into the shadows, leaving us alone before the massive stone doors.

I looked at Aamon, my heart pounding as he turned to me, his dark eyes holding a rare glint of something ... almost tender, hidden beneath his anticipation. There was something both calming and electrifying in his gaze, and for a brief moment, the danger around us felt insignificant, like a distant hum in the background of his silent, steady presence.

The doors began to groan open with a slow, ominous creak, unveiling a darkness so deep it seemed to devour the little light spilling in from the outside. The shadows pooled within the doorway, thick and impenetrable, swallowing all detail beyond the threshold. I glanced at Aamon one last time, drawing in a breath that was thick with apprehension, and together we stepped forward, crossing into the unknown, blanketed in an all-encompassing shadow.

The air felt thick as I entered the chamber, and I froze, disorientated, until the oppressing darkness withdrew. There was something solid beneath my feet, some space to move, so I walked. Every step I took sent a hollow echo across the black marble floor. It was a vast hall— and at the end was a throne.

A figure rose gracefully from the throne, her presence demanding every bit of my attention. She was breathtaking, unlike anything I'd ever seen. Her golden blonde hair spilled over her shoulders, framing a face with fiery red eyes that shimmered with an ancient, dangerous allure. Petite, dark horns curved elegantly from her temples, and her wings—glinting with a metallic shimmer—added an eerie grace. Her body was flawless, a figure that seemed crafted to seduce. With each measured step, her tail coiled playfully around her thighs, adding a hypnotic sway. A smile—knowing, almost predatory—played on her lips as she glided toward us, her voice a haunting melody as she spoke.

"I've been expecting you, Roxy," she purred, her words like silk wrapping around me. With a graceful gesture, she beckoned us toward a long banquet table nearby.

It was laden with dishes I couldn't even begin to imagine—fruits glowing with impossible colors, meats that steamed with wild, exotic spices, and goblets brimming with dark, mysterious liquid. The intoxicating aroma made my stomach tighten with an unexpected hunger, but I kept my guard up as I followed her and took a seat.

"How did you know I'd be coming?" I said, suspicion threading my voice. "I didn't even know I'd end up here."

"Like a spider, I sense every fly that lands in my web." Her haughty expression made me want to shrink, but I fought the feeling.

My eyes met hers, unblinking. "What should I call you?"

A glimmer of something old and amused danced in her gaze. "Dev will do. A name I've used before, one I gift to you. Worry not, Roxy. I mean no harm to you or your lover." Her eyes flicked to Aamon, a smirk dancing on her lips. "Ah, young love. Embrace it while it's sweet."

Despite her easy words, a strange feeling settled over me—a tension between thrill and unease. Under the table, Aamon's hand moved to my thigh, supporting me with his touch, even as it stirred a warmth that sent a blush creeping up my cheeks. I forced myself to stay focused on Dev, which was not difficult, as her presence wove around me like an intoxicating spell.

"If you knew I'd come here, do you know why?" I managed to ask, the heat of Aamon's touch a constant distraction.

"You need a soul, one tethered to your world," Dev replied, her gaze sharpening as the words left her lips. "Long ago, I found the soul you seek and struck a bargain, as my people do. That soul has been a source of immense power for me—one I've drawn on for ages, giving a lowly succubus like me far more influence than I ever dreamed. And yet, it has its price. I am bound to this place, unable to leave the demon realm and go to yours where all true delights await."

There was a hint of bitterness in her voice when she said the next: "By the pact I made, I must release the soul when the time comes. And now that time has arrived. I am bound to serve you ... once and only once."

I narrowed my eyes, suspicion clawing its way back. "Why would you help me? Doesn't the curse on supernaturals affect you as a demon. Isn't it what binds you here and keeps you from entering our realm? Wouldn't you wish it broken?"

A flicker of amusement crossed Dev's face, her fiery eyes gleaming with a dangerous playfulness. "It only binds me when I cross into your world. I am free in mine. But yes, without the curse, we demons would raze your world to ash. A mercy, I do say in my twisted way. But your curse is not my only concern." She paused, a sly smile dancing on her lips. "My people, and the Fae you're familiar with, each have their own designs for this Convergence. For that reason, and because of the bargain I mentioned—I must help you."

Her coyness was maddening, her words like riddles, leaving truths just out of my grasp. The heat between us grew, a nearly tangible pull. I fought to remain wary, but her allure was powerful, magnetic. She knew it, too; her lips curled in a smile as she noted my reaction.

"Oh, darling, the attraction is mutual," she purred, her gaze darkening with a wicked glint. "But I'm not here to seduce you. As tempting as it might be, I think it would ruin the budding romance between you two. I am, after all, a romantic at heart." Her eyes lingered on me, a hint of hunger in their depths. "But should that love ever fade, know that you can call on me. I can show you pleasures no mortal could ever offer."

My breath hitched, a flush spreading across my skin, but I fought to maintain my composure. She was dangerous, and her allure was undeniable. I wasn't about to let her throw me off course. "It seems too easy," I murmured, forcing my voice steady. "You're giving me exactly what I came for without asking anything in return. Doesn't that go against your nature?"

She laughed, a sound both enchanting and unsettling. "A bargain is sacred, Roxy. The soul made a pact with me, and I will honor it to the letter. But be warned:

once you claim this soul, my rivals will consider you a threat—and they are many."

She moved closer, her voice dropping to a hushed whisper that tickled my skin. "And there is only one way to transfer the soul to you ... with a kiss."

I hesitated, her words wrapping around me with a seductive power. But after a steadying breath, I leaned in, letting our lips meet. The touch of her mouth sent a shock through my entire body, an electric charge that surged through every cell. Magic pulsed between us, swirling in a vibrant storm of color and light. I felt us lift from our chairs as energy coiled around us, spirits dancing in the air as ancient power wove through my body, binding the essence of the soul to me.

The kiss was more than a touch; it was a merging of fates, a connection more profound than any mortal vow. I felt the raw pulse of magic, the legacy of witches past, and the thread of power stretching across three worlds and a hint of a consciousness just under the surface. When we finally returned to the floor, I felt transformed, my spirit strengthened by an understanding and energy I'd never known.

Dev stepped back; her fiery eyes softened by a flicker of what might have been fondness.

"Remember, Roxy," she murmured. "In your darkest hour, you may call upon me, but only once, by the original agreement between me and that soul. But be cautious, for now, you belong to more than one world. I look forward to the future, the agreements that we can make together."

I could sense any 'agreement' that I would make with her would benefit her and not me. But I shouldn't expect anything different. She was a demon.

I took a deep breath, trying to steady myself as I slumped into the chair beside Aamon. My head still swam from absorbing that soul. But it wasn't just raw energy. There was something else, something childlike and sentient, a flicker of life and purpose tangled within it. When I reached out mentally, I could only brush the surface of its essence; it resisted, remaining fragmented and unwilling to truly connect. It was more than a part of the thirteen witches who'd created the curse. It felt ... familiar, but in a haunting way. A piece of our world was taken away and locked from itself, and it wanted to return home.

The realization struck me like cold water: this essence wasn't merely a fragment of cursed magic. It was a stolen piece of my world itself, ripped out and embedded in this soul. The witches hadn't only cursed us; they'd diminished our world by tearing away a vital, living part of it.

In that moment, every fiber of my being ached to set things right, to heal the wound they'd left behind. But I knew deep down that simply breaking the curse could mean unleashing the darkest beings in my world upon humankind. Monsters with no restraint, creatures who could destroy the little balance that we had. Not to mention the demons.

I couldn't—no, I wouldn't—let that happen.

Aamon's voice cut into my thoughts. "Roxy? Are you all right? You looked ... gone for a minute there. You took in a lot of power. Are you sure you're, okay?"

I tried to find the words to explain, struggling to wrap my mind around the strange sense of both power and burden I now carried. "It's difficult. I feel ... stronger than I've ever been, maybe stronger than I should be. But it's not something I can—or should—hold onto for long. This power ... it's like it's pressing against me, trying to mold me into something I'm not. I don't know how Dev managed to contain this kind of energy for so long. I can only imagine the toll it takes." I shuddered. "And if a demon were to control something like this back in our world? It would be a nightmare. We are so lucky that she was bound here."

Just then, a commotion broke out near the doors. They swung open, and Hugo entered flanked by two massive creatures with skin the color of molten lava and bodies rippling with muscle. They were every inch the demons I'd feared as a child—terrifying. Between them, they held a bruised, bloodied man struggling feebly against their hold.

Hugo inclined his head as he approached Dev. "Master, we caught this intruder coming through the portal. We detained him immediately."

Dev's eyes gleamed with dark amusement. "An elf. A Fae in my realm?" She stalked closer to the captured man, her voice dripping with mock delight. "My, my, it's been ages since one of your kind dared cross into my lands. This is a treat. I could feed on you for a long time, little fairy. But tell me, why are you here? This couldn't have been a simple mistake."

As I peered closer at him, I reached into his mind, and I recognized him. I had never truly seen him, but I had been in his mind before, and this was him. This was Cosmo, the guard outside the door of my prison in the Fae Lands. His face was bloodied, his body battered, but he still held himself with a surprising amount of defiance.

I leaned forward, barely able to contain my shock. "Cosmo? What are you doing here? This can't be a coincidence."

He gritted his teeth, shifting uncomfortably as the demons held him in place. "Lady Sable sent me to find you, to ensure you didn't break the curse. I was just unlucky enough to actually succeed. I found you, but not before falling right into this trap."

"Sable." I growled her name in frustration. Why did she doubt me? Had she known about this soul? The way it had made me want to undo things? Perhaps, she had been right to worry, to question my ability to resist—but I had resisted. "I wish you Fae would believe me when I say the curse is safe. Nothing will change my mind."

His relieved gaze met mine. "If you truly want to uphold the curse, then let me stand by you. That way, I can protect you, fulfill my duty, and stop skulking around in shadows. But if you try to break it ... I will stop you."

Dev was watching with a gleam in her eyes, and she slowly reached out, trailing her fingers down Cosmo's chest to his waist. "You don't have to worry about your duty anymore. You won't be leaving my web. Oh, I'm going to enjoy myself with you, little fairy. I haven't had one of your kind in a long time."

Cosmo turned his head to me, his voice low but pleading. "If it's not me, they'll send others, ones less willing to listen. Take me with you now, Roxy. Please."

I met Dev's gaze, feeling the resolve solidify in my bones. I wasn't leaving him here, not to whatever twisted games she had planned. "All right, Dev, what would it take for you to let him leave with me?"

Her smile spread wider, as if she'd been waiting for this moment. "Roxy, darling, we demons don't give favors for free. I could have so much fun with him. But if you're so eager, perhaps you could offer me something worthwhile...."

Aamon's voice broke in, "Demons cannot be trusted. They play games, and you always lose. Roxy, do not make a deal with her. It's never worth it."

Dev raised an eyebrow, feigning disappointment. "Without a bargain, the Fae won't be allowed to leave. It's your choice to make a bargain with me or not, Roxy.

You know how my kind can't enter your world without an invitation. Let me walk there, unescorted and free, for one night, and you can have him."

"Absolutely not." I crossed my arms, defiant. "I know what havoc you'd unleash. I won't give you that freedom."

Her eyes glinted with satisfaction. "Oh, come now, you know you want to. I can taste the desperation on you. So sweet. Wanting to help even this one. But I suppose I can haggle.... If you agree to summon me within a year, and let me wander free in your world for one night, I will release him."

I held her gaze, unwilling to back down. "Fine. One night, but you'll be escorted by me, and you won't harm anyone. You'll follow my lead."

"Roxy. If I was not set free, then how would I feed? What would be the pleasure for me then?"

"You feed on my world even when you're not actively feeding on anyone, just ... on the world itself," I murmured. I only grew certain of the words when I saw Dev's reaction.

"Oh, Roxy," her voice softened, the slightest smirk lifting her lips as she looked down at me with a knowing glint in her eyes. "You're starting to listen to the soul that's inside you now, aren't you? You're beginning to understand things you shouldn't."

The way she said it—amused—sent a ripple of unease down my spine. She tilted her head slightly, considering me. "But I accept your agreement. I'll release this creature to you as you've requested. And, as a gesture of goodwill, I'll even send my servant to assist you." She paused, letting the promise linger, her expression hardening just a fraction as she continued. "However, there's one extra condition."

I could feel my heartbeat thrum louder.

"In one year's, time, Roxy, you must call me. Invite me in," she said, her tone low and filled with a peculiar sweetness that sent a chill through my veins. "And then," she added, leaning closer, her eyes gleaming, "we can enjoy a lovely evening together. Do you agree?"

I swallowed, my mind racing with the implications, the potential consequences. Yet, in that moment, I couldn't see another way. I met her gaze, steady and resolute, and nodded. "Yes," I replied, my voice calm but firm.

She extended her hand, and I felt a surge of something binding between us—a pact that hummed with ominous energy, warning me of the consequences if I broke it.

Cosmo sagged with relief as the demons released him, but he looked at me with solemnity. "Thank you. I will stand beside you, guard you, and help you keep the curse intact ... so long as you don't try to break it."

I heard thoughts in my mind telling me, Get a promise from him. Before you leave. The voice echoed in my head, smooth but strange, reminding me that it would take a while to get used to something talking to me this way. It was unsettling, the one-sidedness of it. This presence could speak to me, but it wasn't like I could reply back. Just silence on the other end.

Cosmo.

I squared my shoulders, looking at him. "So be it. But you promise me here and now that you'll protect me and all my companions as long as we don't try to break the curse."

Cosmo's eyes flickered to Aamon, his expression caught somewhere between reluctance and resignation. "For how long, exactly, am I to be indentured to you?" he asked, his voice carrying an edge that hinted at his discomfort. "How long will you bind me to this service?"

"Just for the duration of the Convergence," I replied, thinking that sounded reasonable enough.

He said, "I'll agree that it starts now and ends when we've dealt with Logan and Tar, but no more than that."

"Not throughout the whole alignment?"

"The Convergence? You think it's just a one-night affair?"

My mouth went dry.

"Years," Cosmo explained, his voice heavy with unspoken meanings. "The Convergence spans many years, Roxy."

"But—" I stammered, my thoughts stumbling over themselves. "Years? I thought... well, I thought it was just one night."

"Ah, yes," he murmured with a hint of condescension. "My lady did warn me you might be a bit of a fool. It seems she was right. The Convergence is more than just a single event. When it begins, yes, there's a burst of possibility, let's call it. The first night is the most powerful. Forces can interact more freely between our worlds, and certain acts become easier to accomplish. That is when the most damage can be caused. But it is not the end of the alignment. Just the beginning. That heightened state precedes a far longer period of closeness between our worlds. Years pass before they fully separate again."

A bitter laugh escaped me. "Is this just how things are going to go?" I muttered, half to myself, half to him. "No one tells me the whole story. You all just expect me to absorb new revelations like they're no big deal."

Cosmo arched an eyebrow at me, and a smirk played on his lips as he took a step back, looking me over like I was amusingly naive. Before he could say anything, Aamon, who'd been lingering in the background, stepped forward.

"I thought you knew, Roxy," he said softly, a flicker of sympathy in his dark eyes. "It's true: the time when our worlds grow close to each other spans many, many years. But when it first begins, it's... well, the dangers are heightened. There are more risks in those early days than during the years that follow."

Aamon hesitated, the faintest sigh escaping him. "I apologize," he added. "Sometimes I forget how young you are. You seem to have such an old soul, but in so many ways, all of this is new to you."

I crossed my arms, feeling irritation. "This doesn't change anything," I said, my voice steeling with determination. "We still have to stop Logan. I'll deal with the demons, fairies, and whatever else decides to cross my path—one horrible task at a time."

Cosmo inclined his head, a barely-there glint of respect in his eyes. "Then let it be so."

"You need to go now, and my servant, Hugo, will accompany you and assist you in what you need," Dev said, smirking as she watched our strained parting. "Before my rivals realize I no longer contain the soul and a mere mortal has it. It will be too tempting for them. Tempting enough that they will come into my realm no matter how dangerous it would be for them and try to rip that soul from your body."

We left the throne room and then wove our way through the twisted, unnatural streets of the demon city. The air buzzed with secrets, and I walked with Aamon beside me, our hands brushing now and then in silent comfort.

He glanced over at me, a faint sadness in his eyes. "I'll tell you everything you want to know from now on, Roxy. I didn't mean to keep you in the dark."

I squeezed his hand. "Is this our first fight?" If so, I was not going to let it drag me down in anger. I was going to accept it was probably just a mistake. "One task at a time, Aamon. Let's just get back to the portal."

I ignored our new entourage—Cosmo and Hugo, Fae and Demon—as Aamon and I walked hand in hand. I knew I had everyone worried about the curse, and there were so many people counting on me ... but it didn't feel like it was just me anymore. I wasn't alone. And I didn't mean Cosmo and Hugo. I had Aamon. It felt like we were twin souls, two become one, and even if I was deluding myself, it didn't matter—it made me feel more confident, more certain, as we stepped back into a world poised on the brink.

21 Sundering 

On the other side of the portal from the demon realm it was dark, well past sunset. I counted heads in the gloom and noticed Hugo hadn't come through. "Oh, right. Dev forgot about that one," I said, smirking. "Demons can't come over without being summoned. Either of you know how to do that?" I asked Aamon and Cosmo. "Either of you even want to do that?"

Before I could discover their answer, my playful confidence was shattered.

It felt like the world shifted instantly—a magical surge pulsed through me, an intense wave of energy crashing into my core. Moonlight and phosphorescence danced together over the water, and the air buzzed with a strange, unsettling energy.

My fingers slid from Aamon's grip as I took in what was happening.

"Oh, damn. This can't be good," I murmured, a knot forming in my stomach as I sensed the weakened barriers around the island. They were practically gone, as if my very presence—the soul I'd absorbed from Dev, intertwined with forces I barely understood—had shattered them. Aamon's dark eyes shifted to me, his brow furrowing in concern.

"Are you talking about Rick? Out there on that boat?" he asked, nodding toward the light of a small vessel bobbing at the island's edge. Squinting, I spotted Rick waving, with Timmy beside him.

Aamon didn't feel it.

"The barrier is down," I explained. "And I feel something bad is coming ... very bad. We need Rick and Timmy here, quick."

"I'll get them." In a blink, Aamon dissolved into mist. Smoky tendrils whirled before streaking toward the boat.

I'm never goanna get over that, I thought, shivering slightly. "Spooky... but also impressive."

I turned, sensing Cosmo's prickling presence near-by, his thoughts whirring. Was he plotting something? Or truly here to help?

"What's on your mind, Cosmo?" I asked, point blank, folding my arms.

His expression shifted, from tense to resigned. "The Convergence ... it's starting."

I froze. "Now? I thought we still had time?"

He shook his head. "We were in the demon realm. Time flows differently there. More days have passed here than you realize. The Convergence is here."

"Damn," I muttered, pulse quickening. "Then we'll need to hurry. I need to find Hazel and get her to tell us where the ritual site is. We can't be late. If Logan and Tar are planning something, we need to get there in time to stop it."

Aamon reappeared, a ball of darkness carrying Rick and Timmy by their arms like kittens by the scruff. They did not look happy until Aamon set them down and assumed solid form again.

Relief softened Rick's face when he saw me. I could tell he noticed the subtle shift between Aamon and me, but he didn't mention it. "Roxy, you've been gone for nearly a week. I was really worried about you. We came back every evening and waited at the edge of the island. Something wouldn't let us in. Until now."

Urgonoy clawed at me. "It's the Convergence. We are out of time."

I rallied everyone, leading them up the narrow path toward the heart of the island. Moonlight lit our way, bright and full, glinting off leaves and casting long shadows over the rocky trail. It was beautiful, despite a sense of foreboding that I couldn't shake. I wasn't sure if I worried for myself—or for Aamon. He was starting to matter to me more than I was comfortable to admit.

As we climbed, glowing eyes blinked from the darkness—cats, dozens of them, their green and amber gazes tracking our movement as they scurried back into the underbrush. I gripped the straps of my bag tightly, sensing magic thrumming in the earth beneath my feet. The air around us stirred, awakening ancient energies that had lain dormant for centuries.

Finally, we reached the necropolis at the top of the hill. The weight of magic pressed down on us, shadows twisting and moving as creatures and spirits began to stir. Their focus shifted to us, curious and hungry. We needed to reach Hazel's house—before these things fully awoke.

"You're not gonna like this," Rick muttered, his voice tense as he glanced back down the hill. "But someone's coming up behind us. I can hear them ... smell them. It's Tar and Logan."

I narrowed my eyes, cursing under my breath. "Why the hell are they here? Shouldn't they be at the ritual site?"

Rick shrugged, his broad, beastly shoulders shifting with the motion. "I don't know. All I know is my nose doesn't lie."

"Shit," I muttered.

I turned, eyes widening as I saw them crest the hill—two figures, their outlines bathed in the now eerie glow of moonlight. Tar, the seductive and terrifying vampire, and Logan—my huge mistake. Behind them, I sensed my mother—not her, I reminded myself—Harper was in control of her body. I felt the bitter truth that my mother was truly gone. A surge of anger and helplessness rose within me.

Rick growled, his voice barely a whisper but full of fury. "They're not alone."

That's when I noticed them—like shadows emerging from the depths of the hill: Tar's creations. Vampires swarmed around us, circling with hungry, predatory grace. Their eyes gleamed with malice, their teeth sharp and glinting.

Aamon leaned close and whispered, his voice dark with warning, "Roxy, we're outnumbered. Some of these vampires ... they're old. Very powerful."

My heart thudded in my chest, adrenaline flooding my veins as the threat closed in. "Damn it. I'm not going down without a fight."

Cosmo, the fairy with the sword, pulled the weapon free from his back. It hummed with a soft, almost musical tone as he twisted it in his hand. "If this is the end, then so be it. I'll face it right here. I made a bargain with you, Roxy, and I mean to keep it."

Aamon stood beside me, his gaze steady and unflinching. The look on his face told me he was ready for whatever came.

The air crackled, charged with the tension of impending battle. Tar strode forward, her every step poised and graceful, a deadly predator disguised as a seductive woman. She stopped just short of us, her lips curling into a smile.

"Roxy," she purred, her voice like honeyed venom, "I was a bit worried you wouldn't get here in time. The Convergence was coming fast, and you hadn't returned. But you came through. I should thank you for bringing that fragment of the Thirteen Witches. It was the last piece I needed to break the curse."

I gritted my teeth, feeling anger surge through me. "Tar, you're a monster, and you won't control me."

She ignored my words, her smile only widening. "Logan has disappointed me too many times to count. I tasked him to retrieve that soul, and he failed. You've brought it to me now, but I don't need you alive to complete this. I plan to use your mother's body—with Harper in control—to break the curse.

"But I'll give you one last chance to join me. Breaking the curse would benefit you as well. Imagine it: death, a thing of the past for you; power, like the witches once held; strength, beyond anything you've known. A connection with the earth that none of your kind have felt since. Your people, Roxy, were once the strongest of us all. I can give you that again."

She paused, casting a glance at Logan. "And Logan... well, he's yours if you want him—as a lover, a servant, or a victim. He obeys me, and the bond is unbreakable. If you join me, he's yours. We are strong women in a world of weak men, Roxy. We could rule this place."

A flicker of doubt sparked within me, but I quickly snuffed it out. I couldn't let her manipulate me. I looked around at the thralls—her servants, her vampire fledglings. I could feel the cold, dead weight of their eyes on me, but I pushed it down. No time for weakness.

I reached out mentally, calling for guidance from the spirit of the Thirteen Witches. I needed something—anything—that would help me get through this. Please. Tell me what to do.

For a few seconds nothing happened, but then their answer came, faint but resolute. Flee to Hazel. That is where the curse was first made. I can help you there. The power is close.

Relief rushed through me as the ancient voice of the Witches guided me through the fear clouding my mind. Hazel. I had to get to Hazel.

I turned to my companions. "We need to move. To Hazel's house. Now."

Aamon nodded, his eyes hardening. "We'll fight our way through if we must."

Rick snarled low, his body already shifting, the beast within him rising. Timmy, the younger of the two were-wolves, followed suit, his form growing larger and more menacing by the second.

The vampires closed in, a sea of snarling, hungry faces. They were so much faster than humans, their speed almost blinding, but I knew we had to keep pushing forward. We couldn't stop now.

"Surround them!" Tar commanded, her voice smooth and cold, laced with venom. Her vampire minions fanned out, forming a deadly perimeter.

I gritted my teeth and held out my hands, calling to the elements around me. Power surged through me as I drew in the energy of the land beneath me, the earth pulsing with the heartbeat of the island. I was ready. Let's do this.

The battle erupted around us.

Aamon was a blur of motion, his speed equal to that of the vampires he once called kin. He moved like a shadow, striking with deadly precision. His fangs gleamed as he tore into one vampire after another, his strength unmatched. But even he wasn't invincible.

Cosmo danced through the battlefield, his sword flashing like lightning. His blade struck with fluidity, cutting down vampires in a flurry of precise movements. But

I saw the weariness in his eyes, the strain of facing so many enemies at once.

Rick and Timmy, now fully transformed into their beastly werewolf forms, fought with a primal ferocity. Their claws ripped through flesh; their teeth tore into any vampire that came too close. Rick moved like an unstoppable force, while Timmy was more reckless, his youthful energy propelling him into the fray. But they were outnumbered, and the vampires were quick to retaliate.

I stepped forward, raising my hands to the sky. The air thickened with power, and the ground beneath me trembled. I called to the spirits of the land, the ghosts of the necropolis, those long-dead warriors who once fought here.

Help me, I begged, my voice low, barely a whisper on the wind. But I knew I couldn't have commanded them or asked for their help without the fragment of the Thirteen Witches.

The ground cracked open, and the spirits of the dead began to rise from their graves. Ghostly figures—warriors from the ancient past—emerged. They moved with purpose, their weapons raised, ready to fight. The vampires faltered for a moment, their eyes widening in confusion.

My heart raced as I pushed forward, the dead I had raised leading the charge, the weight of the battle pressing in on all sides. I glanced at Aamon, who was locked in combat with two older vampires, his fangs sinking deep into one's throat, while the other slashed at him with a silver dagger. He tore the first vampire in half without a second thought.

But the vampires were relentless, quickly regaining their focus, pressing in from all sides. Tar stood back, watching with a cruel smile. Logan remained at her side, unmoving, a silent servant to her will.

Cosmo was surrounded by three vampires, each one faster than the last, but he danced and twirled, his sword flashing with each strike. He was holding his own—but just barely. Rick and Timmy fought with a fury that was both beautiful and terrifying.

We were getting closer to Hazel's house, but the vampires wouldn't let up. They wouldn't stop until they'd taken us all down.

I pushed forward, my magic surging through me like a wave. "We need to keep moving! Now!"

Tar's voice rang out behind me, cold and venomous. "Roxy, where do you think you're going? I will feed on you if you don't join me."

I took a deep breath, feeling the weight of her words. But I wouldn't let her win. Not now.

We fought our way through to the necropolis, the ancient stones beneath our feet slick with vampire blood. The air was thick with the scent of death, but we didn't stop. We couldn't. The house was close now.

I reached out one final time, calling to the spirits of the dead, urging them to help, and more of them rose from the ground. Hazel... Please be ready.

We burst into the green field in front of Hazel's house. And in that moment, I felt the shift. The battle was far from over, but we'd made it. Hazel's house was just ahead.

22 Convergence

The hairs on the back of my neck prickled—a warning. I knew a brood of vampires was encircling me, but I couldn't let them distract me. Tar, Logan, and Harper, wearing my mother's form, had already reached the open field in front of Hazel's house. They formed a solid line, blocking me from the one person who might offer me a sliver of hope.

Tar raised a hand, fingers curled like claws. Her voice was low, mocking, "Roxy, I told you to stay out of this little game, but you just had to keep pushing. Stupid little witch." She sneered, stepping closer. "You really have no clue who you're dealing with, do you? I was a vampire before you witches ever cursed us. I've been around a very, very long time. And as amusing as your attempts are, I am done with you."

I clenched my fists, rage simmering in my blood as I looked from her to Logan and back. Tar smirked, gesturing to Hazel's house. "I know you were planning on Hazel saving you, but strong as she is, she won't leave that house. She's trapped there. The only thing that could free her? A stupid little witch delivering her soul fragment. Logan," Tar ordered with cold indifference, "hold her."

I barely had time to process her words before Logan was on me, arms circling like steel bands around my torso, pinning my arms to my sides. I felt his hot breath on my neck, his chest pressed firmly against my back. For a split second, the memory of gentler moments flickered through me—all lies. His betrayal scorched me, an even deeper cut than his fingernails digging into my skin.

Anger replaced everything else. He and Tar had already taken my mother. They wouldn't take anything more.

"Command Harper to begin dismantling the curse," Tar told Logan, her voice sharp. "It's time to start the ritual."

I squirmed, but Logan's grip was unbreakable. My magic felt faint and unreachable, like a severed limb. Panic clawed up my throat—I could sense that my friends were too far away, just out of reach.

Logan leaned closer, his voice a cruel whisper. "Harper," he ordered my mother's sickly form, his voice dripping with control, "I command you. Reverse the spell."

I saw Harper's eyes fill with desperate resistance as she tried to fight him. Her struggle didn't last long. She dropped to her knees and put her hands on the earth, chanting in a language I didn't recognize. The ground shuddered beneath us, and I felt my own power begin to siphon away, bleeding towards her. I strained, trying to hold it back, but the flow was relentless.

"She's being difficult," Tar grunted. "Convince her, Logan."

Pain exploded in my neck as Logan bit down, his fangs sinking deep. Agony ripped through me, blood flowing over my skin in rivulets. There was no seduction, no ecstasy. He didn't let up. The world went dark around the edges, my knees weakening.

As I fought to stay conscious, Harper's tear-filled gaze met mine across the distance, her voice echoing in my mind. Roxy, you're stronger than you know. Stronger than I ever was. Remember what only you can do.

What only I could do? The words circled in my head like a mantra as Logan drained me, and the answer clicked. I thought of Aamon and the bond we shared—a connection without control or command. Bonds.

I focused, reaching out mentally, gathering what little strength I had left. "Break all bonds," I willed. "Free everyone."

Nothing happened, so I pushed harder, over and over, calling to my magic with every scrap of will I could muster. And then, suddenly, a surge like lightning jolted me. A thread of power that felt real, mine.

The connection between Logan and Harper dissolved. Harper stopped drawing power, and she stood, her gaze fierce and clear. She looked at Logan with pure hatred, her voice trembling. "Logan, betrayer of love, deceiver, tormentor."

Logan released me, and I dropped to my knees, weakened but free. Harper surged forward, glowing with a blinding light. She moved faster than he could react, clutching him in an embrace. Heat rolled off her as flames erupted, engulfing them both.

Logan screamed, his eyes wide with horror as he burned, and then it was over—both of them gone, leaving only smoke and ash.

I felt the loss of my mother anew, like a hollow wound in my chest, but I pushed the grief aside. There was still Tar to face.

Tar shielded her eyes from the flames, fury twisting her face as she turned to me. "Damn you, little witch," she spat. "I'll make you my thrall. You'll do my bidding whether you want to or not."

I laughed, hollow and fierce. "You're not only evil—you're stupid. Look around you. Everything you held is gone. They're free."

She halted, taking in the chaos of her fledgling vampires turning against her. In a rage, she destroyed two of them with swift, brutal strikes, but she knew her time was up. With one last hateful look, she lunged at me, slamming her fist into my collarbone, snapping it. I collapsed as she fled, her eyes burning with a promise of vengeance.

I looked up, finding Aamon stumbling toward me, only to be thrown back against a tree as she struck him in her retreat. A branch pierced his chest, and he went still. I felt my last ounce of strength slipping away, but I forced myself forward, crawling toward Hazel's house. In agony, I dragged myself over the threshold, collapsing onto the wooden boards inside the pentagram. Hazel would know what to do.

She appeared, her expression one of pity and quiet strength as she knelt beside me. "Roxy," she said, her voice soft but steady, "you've done what I couldn't—you returned part of me. But Tar was right; you've been foolish. Long ago, I was one of the Thirteen who cast the curse. I believed in it once, but now I know it was a mistake. I'll free myself and undo what I've done."

The spirit within me stirred, whispering to me, It goes both ways, Roxy. She is immortal only as long as her essence is divided. Return it to her, and she'll lose that.

I met Hazel's gaze, understanding the full weight of what that meant. "Take back your fragment," I whispered, releasing the spirit within me. It rushed toward her, and as Hazel absorbed it, I used my bloodied hands to trace a circle on the floor. I knew what I had to do. "Dev," I whispered, "I summon you. I offer you the soul of Hazel."

Dev appeared, her dark, beautiful form filling the room with a chilling power. "It's been ages since anyone has given me a soul like this," she said, eyeing me with both admiration and hunger. "I'll owe you, little witch. Although... giving up this part of yourself makes it even sweeter."

She meant I had given up my humanity. I'd always sworn to protect people from monsters. You could argue Hazel was a monster, but no more than I was.

I watched as Dev wrapped her demonic wings around Hazel, who stood open-mouthed, shocked, and unable to resist. The life drained from Hazel's eyes, and in seconds, she was nothing more than a skeleton in Dev's arms.

Then Dev turned to me, her eyes flashing. "Now, I'll take back what's mine—the essence of The Thirteen that I gave you."

I stood my ground, or rather sat it, as I couldn't make my legs move again. I was bloodied, shattered, but defiant. "That's not how this works, demon. I summoned you. I offered you a soul. One. You don't get them all. And you obey me."

I drew the power back into myself, using it to heal me, feeling Dev's anger and grudging respect. I reached out, my mind brushing against the soul of the Thirteen Witches as if it were alive, pulsing with energy. I grabbed hold of it, pulling it deep into myself, binding it to me. It had lost Hazel's portion but now had mine instead. The weight of it settled instantly, heavy and electric, and I knew—deep down in that place where regret likes to whisper—that this was going to be the biggest mistake of my life. But I couldn't let it slip through my fingers, couldn't risk someone else harnessing its power. No, it had to be mine. My burden now.

"So, what will you have of me now, Roxy?" she asked, a dark smile playing at her lips.

"Help me stand, help my friends, and then return to your realm. Cause no more harm here."

Dev laughed softly, her voice a purr of admiration. "You could have asked for so much more—but you were wise not to. You're better at this than I imagined. I think we'll have a very interesting friendship." She helped me to my feet, steadying me as I took a shaky breath.

"I hope not," I said, not really wanting to see her or anything but home again.

Epilogue

"Rick, you said Brianna might show up," I teased, watching him turn a shade of purple I didn't think was humanly possible.

I never thought I'd see Rick—flirtatious and ridiculous Rick—blush. But there it was, clear as day.

"Yeah," he muttered, rubbing the back of his neck awkwardly. "I haven't seen her in a week, but ... I really like her, Roxy."

My eyebrows shot up. Brianna had seemed set on Ida at first, but she'd been swayed by Rick's irresistible

... charms. She was secretly head over heels. But honestly? I couldn't blame her. He was a bit of a hunk—rugged, tall, with a quiet sweetness you'd never guess from his overly flirtatious nature. It was surreal to see Rick felt the same way about her.

"Did you tell her you're married like I told you to?"

"I was going to, but she already knew," he admitted sheepishly. "I think she did some research on me before, you know, deciding to date me."

"Is that what she's calling it? So, she's okay with you being married?" I raised a skeptical brow.

"She knows it's a pack thing," he said defensively. "And I don't think she's looking for anything too serious, anyway." He hesitated, then added softly, "Don't tell her, but ... I think I want more."

I snorted. "So, what are you gonna do about it, Rick? You can't just let things hang in the air and hope she reads your mind like I can."

"I don't know. Well, I think it might be time for me to end it with Drew. It's not good for her or me. No matter what the pack wants. ... What do you think I should do?"

"I think you should check the pizza before it burns," I shot back, smirking. "And you're really asking me for relationship advice?"

He grumbled something under his breath as he turned to the oven, and I leaned back in my chair, letting out a sigh.

"After we got back from Ireland, I told Aamon I'd call him," I said, the words tumbling out before I could stop them. "Told him not to call me. The classic 'I need time for myself' line. Truth is, I felt like all I've done lately is lose myself in someone else—never figuring out who I really am."

Rick straightened, glancing over his shoulder. "Do you really think being with someone makes you less of who you are?"

I shrugged, tracing a crack in the table with my finger. "When I'm alone, I dwell on everything I haven't done. But when I'm with someone, it feels like I disappear. Like I can't figure out who I'm supposed to be unless I'm on my own." I pointed a finger at him. "Don't give me that look, Rick. I'm not saying you have to be like me. You do you."

He huffed a laugh. "Aamon and I were fishing the other night."

"What the hell? How long has he been in town?" I sat up straighter.

"I don't know. Why don't you ask him?" he said with a mischievous glint in his eye.

"Rick."

He smirked. "I think he loves you."

The doorbell rang, and I jumped to my feet, grateful for the distraction.

"Want me to get that?"

"Yeah, sure. It's probably Brianna," Rick said, already turning his attention back to the oven.

I opened the door to find Brianna—cheerful as ever, with her perfectly styled hair and bright smile. She held out a neatly wrapped box.

"Glad you're here, Roxy," she said warmly. "This is for you."

I frowned, taking the box. "It's not my birthday. You didn't have to get me anything."

"It's from Aamon."

My heart made an uncomfortable little flip.

"What's in it?"

She grinned. "No idea. I don't go through people's stuff." Then, with a wink, she added, "Well, usually. Anyway, I'll let you open it while I ogle the chef."

As she disappeared into the kitchen, I glanced back and couldn't help but smile when I saw Brianna grab his ass while he was bent over checking the pizza. He jumped. How the tables had turned.

They both seemed happy, and I wanted that for them. Still, a part of me couldn't shake the worry gnawing at the edges of my mind. Brianna knew about him and his weird pack—at least, I hoped she did—and if she was cool with it, then it was her choice. But damn, I'd hate to see her get hurt. For now, though, the way they were grinning at each other. Yeah, maybe this could work for them.

I sat down on Rick's ratty old couch, grimacing as the springs dug into my thighs.

"Rick, you need a new couch!" I hollered.

"That couch is my family inheritance!" he yelled back indignantly.

I laughed, but the sound died in my throat as I carefully peeled back the wrapping on the box. Inside was a velvet pouch. I opened it to find an eight-inch bronze statue of the Eiffel Tower—and a handwritten note. Underneath it, a credit card.

"What the hell, Brianna? Is Aamon trying to buy me?"

"I don't know what's in the box, Roxy. Read the note," Rick called.

"How did you know there was a note if you didn't look?"

"Brianna absolutely didn't tell me. Just read it!"

I unfolded the paper, Aamon's elegant script staring back at me.

Dearest Roxy,

I don't remember much about my life before becoming a vampire, but I know this: in all these centuries, I have never met anyone like you. Yes, you are the most beautiful woman I've ever known, but it's more than that. You make me happy— something I thought I'd lost the capacity for. Just talking to you, sharing our thoughts, has been an experience I didn't believe possible.

Because there's no bond forcing us together, I know what I feel for you is real. And for that, I am grateful.

You are strong, independent, and radiant. I only want you to shine. The credit card isn't to buy you—it's to give you freedom, if you need it. Use it however you wish.

Take your time, Roxy. I'll be in Ireland.

Love,
Aamon

Two weeks later, I found myself walking out of my evening class at the community college. It still felt surreal, being back in school after so many years. The newness of it all was terrifying but exhilarating.

I was also getting to spend more time with my friend, Emily—when she wasn't with Matt. His persistence since high school had finally paid off, and one of those speed dating nights turned into some real dates for the two of them. That felt like a small victory.

Slowly but surely, Matt and I had managed to coax her out of that dark, isolating shell she'd wrapped herself in for so long after her experience with Tar/Vicky. It wasn't easy—Emily had a stubborn streak that rivaled my own—but once I convinced her to start coming to school with me, things began to shift. Her once-muted presence brightened just a little, like the first tentative rays of dawn breaking through a heavy fog.

It was good for her, I think, but if I were being honest, it was good for me too. Having someone by my side, someone to talk to when the weight of the world pressed too heavily on my shoulders, was more than I'd realized I needed. I'd been so used to carrying everything alone, hiding the cracks behind sarcastic remarks and a forced smile, that I hadn't realized how much I craved the simple connection of friendship. Emily understood that weight in a way no one else could, and sharing it, splitting the burden between us, felt like liberation from prison—an experience I knew all too well.

But even as we walked the halls together, her shy laugh bubbling up at my dumb jokes, I couldn't ignore the heavy presence lingering in the back of my mind. I could feel it—this strange connection to the Thirteen Souls, to something I didn't fully understand. It was like a shadow stitched to my insides, dark and foreboding, yet

eerily silent. The thing was there, its presence undeniable, but it refused to speak.

I couldn't shake the feeling that it was waiting. Waiting for the right moment, or the wrong one, to make itself
known. Its silence was a storm cloud, dark and oppressive, hanging just above the horizon of my thoughts. I
didn't know whether it would break into a downpour or
strike me with lightning, but I knew it was coming. The
Convergence was only just beginning.

I still worried it was a mistake to take the soul into
me, but I'd done it, and I had to own up to my decisions.
All of my worries aside, I was proud of myself. For the
first time in years, I felt like I was becoming the person I
was always meant to be. But no matter how good it felt, I
couldn't stop thinking about Aamon.

"Roxy, quit being a coward," I muttered under my
breath as I pulled out my phone. My fingers hovered over
the screen before I finally typed:

Aamon, will you accompany me on a date this Fri-
day evening? My treat.

I hit send before I could change my mind.

Beneath the light of the full moon and floodlights that
made it bright as day, the baseball stadium buzzed
around us, a cacophony of cheers, the crack of a bat
meeting a ball, and the occasional grumble of an upset

fan. I leaned back in my seat, savoring the scent of salty popcorn and warm pretzels mingling with the night air. Beside me, Aamon looked every bit the immortal anomaly he was, a stark contrast to the jovial crowd around us. His dark eyes scanned the field, a crease of confusion between his brows.

I couldn't help but laugh softly. "You've never been to a baseball game before, have you?"

His lips quirked up at one corner, the barest hint of a smile. "This ... spectacle is unfamiliar to me. But I must admit, it's oddly entertaining. The passion is palpable."

"That's what makes it fun," I said, nudging his shoulder lightly with mine. His body was solid, like marble warmed by the sun. "It's not just the game—it's the energy, the people. And, of course, the food."

As if on cue, the vendor arrived with the chili dog I'd ordered. I handed over a few crumpled bills and turned back to Aamon, holding up the messy concoction with a triumphant grin.

"What ... is that?" His nose wrinkled slightly, but his dark eyes glimmered with amusement.

"Food of the gods," I declared, taking a dramatic bite before holding it out to him. "Go on, try it. You might love it. Or hate it. But you'll never know unless you do."

He hesitated, his gaze flicking between my face and the chili dog as though it were some ancient relic he wasn't quite sure how to handle. Then, with an exaggerated air of bravery, he leaned forward and took a cautious bite.

The look of sheer astonishment on his face was priceless. He chewed thoughtfully, swallowed, and stared at the chili dog as if it had just whispered the secrets of the universe to him.

"By all that is unholy, that is ... unexpectedly delightful."

I burst out laughing, nearly doubling over as I held the half-eaten chili dog away from his sudden reach. "Careful, vampire. You might actually enjoy something mundane."

He leaned closer, his deep voice a low murmur in my ear. "You, my witch, make the mundane extraordinary."

Heat flushed my cheeks, and I quickly turned my attention back to the game, pretending to be far more interested in the score than the way his words made my pulse race. The man—or vampire—had a way of making me feel seen in a way I wasn't used to, and it was both exhilarating and terrifying.

We watched in companionable silence for a while, the crowd around us surging with excitement as the home team scored. I glanced at him out of the corner of my eye. He wasn't watching the game; his focus was entirely on me, his expression unreadable but intense.

"What?" I asked, my voice softer than I intended.

"You are ... extraordinary, Roxy." His voice was barely audible over the roar of the stadium. "I've lived lifetimes, seen wonders that defy imagination, and yet ... nothing compares to this moment with you."

I swallowed hard, my throat suddenly tight. "Aamon, you're laying it on thick tonight," I teased, though my voice wavered slightly.

He didn't smile this time, didn't look away. "I speak only the truth."

The full moon hung low in the sky, its silver light washing over me. I followed his gaze up to it, my hand slipping into his almost without thought. His fingers closed around mine, cool but strong, and in that simple gesture, I felt the weight of everything I'd been trying to avoid.

For weeks, I'd kept my distance, afraid of losing myself in him, of giving up the independence I'd fought so hard to claim. But now, sitting beside him under the glow of the moon, sharing a ridiculous chili dog and listening to the crowd cheer, I realized something I hadn't before.

He didn't diminish me.

If anything, he made me feel more like myself than I ever had.

"It's not quite like Paris," I said, breaking the silence with a wry smile.

He chuckled, a deep, rich sound that sent a shiver down my spine. "No, it's not. It's a thousand times better, Roxy." He turned to face me fully, his gaze locking onto mine with an intensity that stole my breath. "This is something I've never experienced in my entire long life. Every moment with you is new, vibrant, alive. You're ... beautiful."

The sincerity in his voice, the raw emotion in his eyes—it was too much and not enough all at once. Before I could second-guess myself, I leaned in and kissed him.

Under the garish stadium lights, surrounded by the chaos of the game and the crowd, his lips met mine, soft yet demanding. It wasn't the kind of perfect, cinematic kiss you'd see in a romance movie. It was messy, impulsive, and utterly real. And in that moment, I realized there was nowhere else in the world I'd rather be.

When we finally pulled apart, his eyes searched mine, as though trying to memorize every detail of my face.

"Roxy..." he began, but I pressed a finger to his lips.

"I know," I said, my voice steady despite the whirlwind of emotions inside me. "I know."

We turned back to the game, his arm slipping around my shoulders as I rested my head against him. The crowd roared as the home team scored again, but the sound felt distant, muted against the rhythm of his heartbeat—or maybe it was my own.

As the night wore on, I found myself thinking about all the ways my life would change if I let him in. There would be challenges, sacrifices, and unknowns. But as I glanced up at him, his face softened in the glow of the moon, I realized that some risks were worth taking.

"You know," I said, breaking the comfortable silence, "for someone who's been alive for centuries, you're surprisingly bad at baseball trivia."

He chuckled, the sound vibrating through me. "Perhaps you'll enlighten me in time."

"Perhaps I will," I said, a smile tugging at my lips. "But only if you promise to keep trying new things. Like chili dogs. And popcorn. And maybe even karaoke."

His eyebrows shot up. "Karaoke?"

I laughed, the sound light and carefree. "We'll work up to it."

As the game wound to a close, the final cheers of the crowd fading into the night, I felt a strange sense of peace settle over me. Whatever the future held, I knew one thing for certain: Aamon was a part of it. And for the first time in a long time, I wasn't afraid of what that meant.

The full moon hung high above us as we left the stadium, hand in hand. The world around us buzzed with life, but in that moment, it felt like it was just the two of us.

And for the first time, I let myself believe that maybe, just maybe, love wasn't something to fear. It was something to embrace.

THE END.

ABOUT THE AUTHORS

Lorel and Clayton were teen sweethearts, brought together by a fierce love of books (and hormones) and have been married for 35 years. As writing partners, they meld logic, creativity, and genres. Fantasy, romance, science-fiction, mystery, horror, steampunk, thrillers, the classics … they read them all, and if they can mix them, they will!

Still reading? Want to know more?

Lorel has a PhD in molecular biology and Once Upon a Time did cancer research before turning to the dark side (aka marketing), but she uses her powers for good, helping to raise funds for charity. She loves books, movies and animals, and would gladly spend all day with a cat on her lap and the wind in her hair (Conan reference there), while tapping out a story on her keyboard. Or maybe a movie script. With coffee of course. And lots of chocolate!

Clayton is a classically trained artist who learned digital painting, mostly because there's a hyperactive fourteen-year-old boy running around the house (their gorgeous son, in case you were wondering if that's normal). Clayton is severely dyslexic but loves books and storytelling. He adds vast imagination and a discerning ear for effective prose to their creative collaboration, not to mention the book cover art.

Born and raised in the western United States, they traveled to Sydney, Australia in 1997 and never left, finding the sunshine and beaches of "Oz" too irresistible. Look them up if ever you're Down Under.

Connect with Lorel Clayton

Website: www.lorelclayton.com
BookBub: bookbub.com/authors/lorel-clayton
Instagram: www.instagram.com/lorelclayton
Facebook: www.facebook.com/AuthorLorelClayton
Goodreads: www.goodreads.com/lorel_clayton

48283CB00002B/467